"You were beautiful last night in the moonlight," Scott whispered huskily in her ear. His soft, warm breath sent a sensuous shiver through her. He wanted her. It gave her a sweet thrill.

"I—I couldn't sleep," Liza explained, suddenly too shy to meet his eyes.

"I couldn't sleep either."

"You—you didn't—you didn't try...." Her voice trailed off as she wondered what she would have done if he had come to her last night. Her heart beat frighteningly fast and her breathing became strangely shallow.

"No," he explained in a voice barely above a whisper. "You drew a line. I won't cross it. Not until you decide the time is right. It's too important." And as he said the words he realized how completely he meant them. Whatever he did with Liza was getting to be more important than anything he has done with any woman before....

ABOUT THE AUTHOR

Sarah James has been married for twenty-two years and has nine children—biological, foster, and adopted—and two grandchildren. Her hobbies include sewing, needlework, reading, and traveling. She is a caseworker for a social-services agency and lives in Chicago.

Public Affair

SARAH JAMES

Harlequin Books

TORONTO • NEW YORK • LONDON
AMSTERDAM • PARIS • SYDNEY • HAMBURG
STOCKHOLM • ATHENS • TOKYO • MILAN

Nobody who is loved accomplishes a sizable feat alone.
My husband, my children, my mother and sisters,
my co-workers and friends have all played important parts
in freeing me to write.
They have also listened, read, criticized, and counseled.
In any success that I have
I am truly a community project.

Published August 1984

ISBN 0-373-16067-4

Chapter One

A chilling, prickling sensation slowly traveled up Liza Manchester's spine. She sensed she was being watched, studied.

The bold outlines of a man's trim body hovered just on the other side of her work-laden desk. Without seeing his face she sensed from his stance that he was critical, maybe even hostile. She stiffened and felt her defenses rise into place.

For a moment she kept her eyes focused on the galley proof she was reading. "Trade Routes in Pre-Columbian New Mexico." She read the words several times while she uneasily shifted position in her hard desk chair.

Liza's sixth sense told her that whatever the man's business was, it wouldn't be pleasant. She took a deep breath and steadied herself. And when she did acknowledge his presence her delicate chin was tilted proudly high.

"May I help you?" she coolly inquired, her gray eyes now confronting him.

The tall man stood in front of her desk, a strong, commanding, frowning presence.

Her assessing gaze moved slowly up from his tasteful gold belt buckle to the maroon and navy striped tie that lay against his light blue oxford cloth shirt. His chest was broad, his stomach flat. He was athletic, she quickly decided. His stance was confident, self-assured.

She took in the elegantly tailored navy suit coat and trained her eyes upward. The powerful, tanned column of his throat told her he was youthful and vital even before she saw his strongly masculine face and neat, though casually-styled, dark brown hair. Yet immediately she guessed that he was a University faculty member. For though he was sophisticated and attractive, he had the typical, vaguely distracted look of an intellectual. And he looked completely at home in the somewhat shabby, high ceilinged, oak paneled office Liza occupied in her position as secretary to the noted anthropologist, Carleton Wainright.

"Whatever you're reading must be very interesting," the man concluded a bit impatiently.

"I'm sorry," Liza apologized. Her voice quite purposefully held no warmth. "Have you been waiting long?"

Her frankly appraising look swept his form. One of his brows shot up in surprise as he realized she was returning the same boldly assessing look that he had given her.

"I've been here long enough to notice how attractive you are," he smoothly replied.

His cobalt-blue eyes scanned her face and torso. Her softly rounded feminine body was covered in proper businesslike fashion by her tailored tan linen suit and her simple ivory silk blouse. She sat primly behind an old oak secretary's desk. It had been her workplace for the past four months. Her honey-colored hair was pulled back into a neat chignon, giving a suitably severe frame to her classic features and oval face.

His remark was clearly designed to catch her off her guard. Liza's early-warning system sounded its alarm. He was too smooth, too interested, too fast. Generally the men who approached her like that were nothing but trouble.

"What can I do for you?" she crisply asked.

She straightened her back and met his gaze squarely as she assumed her most dignified air. She had developed her icy expression after years of practice. She used it whenever she wanted to discourage men at first meeting. Usually it was completely effective. This time it didn't work.

His generous mouth turned up into a teasing, seductive smile. His eyes twinkled devilishly, as little smile-lines crinkled in the corners. His cheekbones were intriguingly high. His nose was straight and his brow was uncrossed by worry or care. In short he was a handsome man, and a man fully aware of his own attractions. He had definite sex appeal and knew how to turn it on. The combination made Liza furious.

She felt a self-righteous rage rise within her. He was exactly the sort of man she hated. He was obviously eager to use his considerable charm to manipulate women.

"I've come to see Professor Wainright," he told her.

Liza immediately turned to the leather-bound appointment book on her desk. For a moment she wrinkled her brow as she studied the day's page.

"Did you have an appointment?" she asked. At the same time she checked her watch, noticing that Professor Wainright's current dictation session had lasted longer than she had expected. She was sure he had only needed to dictate a few letters to Angela, the temporary secretary. It shouldn't have taken so long.

"No, I didn't have an appointment," the man informed her. His manner told Liza that he had hardly thought one to be necessary. "I just wanted to stop by for a few minutes," he revealed, adding, "It's personal."

There was a challenge in his eyes that dared Liza to reply. But she didn't know what he expected her to say, and his smoothly flattering yet antagonistic attitude was a mystery to her. A complete mystery. Why should he be studying her, baiting her, judging her? She had never even seen him before.

She stopped speculating and retreated to the reassuring stock phrases a secretary uses over and over again. "Dr. Wainright should be free soon, if you'd care to wait. Or I can give you an appointment at four thirty," Liza suggested.

"My, you are efficient." Again his words were approving, but there was ice beneath them.

Out of the corner of her eye Liza watched her good friend Valerie slip through the doorway and into her large office. She casually leaned against the dark oak-paneled wall, patiently waiting for Liza to be free. Valerie's expressive green eyes glowed approval, and she gave Liza a knowing wink and a bright conspirator's smile as she studied the tall man standing at Liza's desk.

Liza shot her friend a brief, censuring glance, silently telling Valerie that the man was no prize. Then she returned her attention to business. Valerie blinked in surprise and disbelief.

"Would you like me to schedule you for four thirty?" Liza asked. Her voice was coolly efficient.

"That will be fine," the man agreed. He flashed her a smile that Liza was sure would melt the bones of most secretaries in the Social Sciences School. No, she amended her own thought. It was a smile that was carefully designed to melt the bones of most of the secretaries in all of Graham University. And the smiling man knew it. However, his expression had the opposite effect on Liza. She felt herself chilling to subzero temperatures.

"Your name please?" Liza inquired, pencil poised over the recently erased spot on the neatly ruled page.

"Scott Harburton," the man revealed.

There was a brief, expectant silence. It was as though

he were waiting for her to say something in response, to recognize the name and make a remark. She didn't.

"Four thirty, then," Liza confirmed. She gave him a polite, mechanical smile that did not reach her eyes.

A brief, puzzled expression crossed his face. It was quickly replaced by a nod of agreement. "Four thirty," he repeated. Then he swung his broad shoulders around, faced the door, and confidently strode out of Liza's office.

"Wow, is he ever gorgeous," Valerie pronounced as she energetically came across the big room and plopped without ceremony in Liza's office chair. Her short cap of red-blond curls bounced about her pixie face. "When he comes around on our corridor, I just can't pull my eyes away from him. Tall. Dark. Handsome. Rich. Successful. Why did you put on the ice-maiden act?"

"It was no act," Liza replied, frowning. "I can't stand his type."

"You *do* know who that is, don't you?" Valerie probed, giving her friend a sideways glance.

"I don't care if he's king of the world," Liza countered. "I don't like men like him."

Valerie frowned her disapproval. "You really *don't* know who he is, do you?"

"No," Liza quickly returned, "and I really don't care." Her usually serene features were set in an angry scowl.

"Scott Harburton is one of the fourth-generation faculty members. His great-grandfather, Albert Brill Scott, was founder and first president of Graham University, when the buildings first rose out of the Chicago prairie," Valerie related importantly, completely ignoring Liza's bad humor.

"Bully," Liza replied, unimpressed.

"He's a psychology professor and he writes best selling popular psych books, like *Think You Can*. It sold a million copies," Valerie explained, her green eyes wide with admiration. "I've heard he's coming out with a new book soon. Something about women."

"So what?" Liza countered, stubbornly refusing to be the least bit impressed.

"His family has oodles of money. They practically run the University. He has cousins on the faculty and uncles on the board of trustees. His sister is married to your boss. Whole bunches of his relatives are on the big-deal city culture scene, like the opera board and the symphony auxiliary. They give their names to all kinds of fashionable charitable causes all over the Chicago area. And if that isn't enough, Harburton himself makes speeches all over. I've even seen him on television. He has a boat and a place on the lakeshore in Michigan and cars like you wouldn't believe," Valerie continued, her face happily animated.

Instead of impressing Liza as she had intended, Valerie's arguments turned Liza's original prejudice against Scott Harburton into a strong dislike of him. "I can't stand him," Liza carefully and firmly told her friend.

"Since when have gorgeous men turned you off?" Valerie demanded, incredulous. "You are twenty-eight years old and not married! You're attractive. You've always been a healthy, normal woman, even if you are a bit of a fanatic about women's rights."

"And you know *why* I'm so concerned about women's rights, don't you?" Liza demanded, ignoring, as usual, the other comments her friend made. "And you know *why* I hate smooth, self-assured men who think I should fall into bed with them just because they smile at me?"

"Sure," Valerie answered easily, "it's because some creep of a smiley, smooth-talking boss wanted you to work after hours at a nearby motel." Valerie shrugged her shoulders. "Big deal. It happens all the time. That shouldn't turn you against all men."

"But I lost my job, a really good job, just because I wouldn't play around with my boss," Liza angrily interjected.

"That was too bad," Valerie nodded her head sympathetically.

"Too bad?" Liza parroted, incredulous. "Too bad?" She raised her voice angrily. Her eyes blazed with fury. "It was more than too bad. It was wrong. Wrong. A real injustice. He didn't even give me a good reference. If I hadn't heard about this job, and if your aunt hadn't been in the University personnel department, I might still be out of work. That sort of thing shouldn't happen to anybody, not ever," Liza furiously protested. "Nobody should lose a job because they won't pass out sexual favors."

"I don't see why you'd want to work for someone like your old boss anyway," Valerie pointed out, with her own particular brand of logic. She was vainly trying to calm Liza down. "You're better off away from him."

Valerie Bentley had never been caught up in the women's movement. She was a sweet, unsophisicated, giving person who was little and cute. Men had instinctively shielded and protected her. She'd never felt discriminated against in her whole life. She couldn't even grasp what most of the women's lib fuss was all about. However, she was passionately loyal to her friends, and Liza had been one of her best friends since grade school. So at times Valerie took Liza's side in the battle of the sexes.

"My last job had shorter hours, more fringe benefits, and a higher salary," Liza argued.

"And old hot-breath-four-hands," Valerie countered. "Besides you'll probably have a better job here soon. You're the logical one to be the new editorial assistant for Wainright. Your carefully constructed, upwardly mobile, no-nonsense, dull-and-boring business wardrobe will pay off. And instead of being a mere secretary like the rest of us peons, you'll be getting a title and an office and everything. Even more money. I mean, you've actually been doing the job for the last couple of months, as far as I can tell. And your boss isn't even *interviewing* anyone else, for heaven's sake."

Liza nodded in agreement. She had been doing most of the editorial work for the *Quarterly Journal of Ancient America*, an anthropological journal that Professor Wainright edited.

The last editorial assistant had left abruptly just after Liza had been hired. As Wainright's new secretary Liza had competently handled not only the routine secretarial work but had also taught herself the editorial work for the journal. Until the final editorial appointment would be made, Wainright had insisted that Liza get supplemental secretarial help so that she could devote most of her energy to journal-related tasks. During this time Liza was working madly to prove she could be an excellent permanent editorial assistant.

Principally because of the chance for advancement her new job seemed ideal to Liza. There had been only one brief episode that had given her pause. A week or so after Carleton Wainright had hired her, the balding, forty year old anthropologist had made a pass at her.

Liza had purposely started her new job with a basic business wardrobe of tailored suits and blouses. She did it because she had read several books about how women in business needed to look businesslike rather than attractive if they wanted to succeed. So she downplayed her generous, curving figure and tried to disguise it beneath carefully selected blouses and skirts. She wore almost no makeup. However her skin had a natural glow, and even without any cosmetics at all, Liza was strikingly attractive. She hoped, after her last experience of being regularly propositioned by her boss, that her new, unseductive wardrobe would discourage more such disasters.

So when Professor Wainright had started demanding what she saw as more than just efficiency from her, Liza had been furious. "Professor Wainright, if my job depends on any nonwork related activities, either inside or outside of the office, I might as well leave right now," she had angrily announced. "I want no part of any funny business."

Wainright had immediately declared that she had misunderstood. He wanted only a business relationship between them. After all he was a happily married man. He had never approached her again.

Liza soon decided she might have been too touchy, that Wainright probably hadn't meant anything by his casual remark. She resolutely pushed the whole incident to the back of her mind and dedicated all her energies to proving that she could handle the editorial assistant's job. And everyone in the office assured Liza that the job was as good as hers.

The heavy oak door of Professor Wainright's office swung open. Angela Adams, the temporary secretary, came out. She was small, blond, and not particularly efficient. But her very presence freed Liza for editorial work on Professor Wainright's journal. Liza nodded to Angela, who smiled shyly in return.

Valerie bounced up from her chair and waved a good-bye. "Back to my old typewriter," she ruefully told Liza, making a sour face as she slipped out into the corridor.

Liza smiled affectionately at her friend's departing form. Valerie was a warmhearted, exasperating, redheaded treasure and the best friend Liza had ever had.

Then, remembering her work, Liza picked up the phone and called her boss. "A Scott Harburton stopped by to see you."

"What did you tell him?" Wainright asked, a slight touch of unnatural anxiety in his voice.

"I told him you would be free at four thirty. He'll be back then," Liza replied.

"Good. Good," Wainright answered. "Now, back to work on the journal. We've got a deadline coming soon."

"Yes, sir," Liza immediately responded, sorely tempted to give a falsely crisp, military reply, but just barely controlling herself.

She didn't particularly like working for Wainright. He was arrogant and demanding, and neither thoughtful nor kind. But he offered Liza a chance for advancement, advancement on her own merits. She was a good editor. And he was allowing, even urging her, to fill the position, even though she didn't have the usually mandatory college degree. Liza had been able to finish only two years of college, and that mostly at night. Now, at twenty-eight, she had begun to save money so that one day she could go full time to get a degree in English.

Now that she had had a taste of something more challenging than secretarial work, Liza was throwing her whole heart and soul and mind into being exactly right for the exciting editorial job. Her current evening class was on technical writing. She was convinced that all she needed was the fair chance to prove herself capable. After that the sky was the limit.

When Scott Harburton returned for his appointment later that afternoon, he again tried to engage Liza in conversation.

"I'll announce you," was her only reply. She was relieved when he left her office and disappeared into Professor Wainright's domain.

Despite Valerie's glowing description of Harburton Liza couldn't think of one good thing to say about him, not one good thing at all.

The harsh blare of the door buzzer shattered the Saturday morning quiet at Liza's apartment. Except for the momentary worried wrinkling of her brow Liza didn't move. The buzzer sounded again.

Liza drew the smooth pink sheet over her head and groaned. The buzzer rang once more, and longer this time.

"OK. OK. I give up," she complained as she dragged herself out of the soft comfort of her bed. She blinked her eyes wildly against the insistent glare of the sunlight that streamed cheerily through her bedroom windows.

A low moan escaped her lips as she stumbled through the short hallway to her door buzzer. After pushing the button to open the downstairs door she opened the door of her apartment a crack. Then she sank back against the wall while she waited for her visitor to ride the elevator to her eighth-floor apartment.

Her heavy eyelids drooped closed again. Liza knew a blessed moment of oblivion.

"Wake up sleepyhead." Valerie's cheerful voice broke her quiet.

"Go away," Liza mumbled. "Come back later."

"Not a chance," Valerie brightly assured her. "The day is slipping away."

The tiny redhead surveyed her barely-awake friend's slumping form. It was draped in a soft blue gown of lustrous crepe de chine. Liza's full breasts were enticingly displayed by the low V neck.

"Sexy nightgown. I love it," Valerie chortled as she closed the door and breezed past Liza. "You have the nicest, most elegant lingerie of anyone I know. Too bad nobody ever sees it but me."

Liza frowned uncomfortably and opened her eyes. She blinked several times as she tried to make them focus. For several seconds Valerie was only a redheaded blur in a lemon-yellow dress.

"Why do you do this to me? Why do you wake me up like this every Saturday? You know I like to sleep," Liza complained.

"What are friends for?" Valerie impertinently inquired. "Is the coffee made? I brought almond croissants." She proudly displayed a small, white baker's bag.

"Is the coffee made? Is the coffee made?" Liza testily returned her friend's question. "Are you completely witless and senseless? I was sound asleep until you kept leaning on my bell. How could I make coffee?" Liza's cheeks were glowing pink with her anger.

"Good. You're waking up," Valerie returned, absolutely unperturbed. "I'll make the coffee. You go get dressed. And hurry, or we'll miss the summer sales."

"I don't even want to go to the sales," Liza protested. "My wardrobe is fine. Remember, I just bought all those expensive and what you call 'boring' suits."

Valerie gave her a chiding look. "Every woman loves good sales. You can buy yourself another lacy slip or something," she bargained with her friend. "You have a real weakness for gorgeous underwear. Now go get dressed."

Liza sighed, and her shoulders fell as she accepted the inevitable. Valerie had been a smiling, pint-sized steamroller since they had played with their dolls together as children. And nearly every Saturday Valerie had awakened Liza around nine o'clock. She hadn't missed coming in years unless she was out of town or sick. She often pointed out that it was for Liza's own good.

"Nobody needs to sleep so late," she good naturedly volunteered many times.

"I do," Liza protested occasionally. But her protests did no good. For, though Liza was outspoken with business acquaintances and casual friends, she was very tolerant with those she loved. "You'd be a good top sergeant, you know," Liza threw over her slim, bare shoulder as she made her way back to the bedroom.

"I'm the wrong sex," Valerie smugly retorted.

Liza stopped in her tracks and turned slowly to confront her friend. Her eyes narrowed and she opened her mouth to speak.

Valerie scurried toward the kitchen, anticipating a long lecture. Liza followed her, her elegant gown swishing prettily around her slim ankles.

Before the righteous Liza could say anything, Valerie held up her hand to stop her. "Now wait," the tiny redhead protested, "I knew you'd be ready to argue with me just as soon as the words were out of my mouth. Don't say anything," Valerie warned. "You win. There is no reason why a woman can't be a good top sergeant. You've won your point without even opening your mouth. Now get dressed."

A disgruntled but resigned Liza drifted back to her bedroom to the whir of the electric coffee grinder as it noisily ground the beans for their coffee.

Over the next few weeks Scott Harburton dropped into Professor Wainright's office entirely too often for Liza's comfort. Even though they were brothers-in-law, she could see no reason for the psychologist to be in and out two or three times in a day, especially since the relationship between the two men was not particularly warm. Though smooth and cordial enough, Wainright was always a little guarded, defensive, around Harburton. And Scott's hawklike gaze watched Wainright closely, Liza was sure of that. But the really disconcerting thing for her was that he covertly watched her, too. Not only that, he was a little too solicitous when he talked to her, a little too flattering and a little too friendly.

With her characteristic frankness Liza did admit to herself that she had moments when the tall, attractive psychologist looked quite appealing to her, and she enjoyed his attentions, even though she felt they were basically insincere. Yet always she was aware of a basic lack of respect or regard for her as a person. She complained to Valerie about it one Saturday morning over coffee.

"I'll bet he's crazy about you," Valerie joyfully suggested. They sat at the tiny table in Liza's cramped but sunny kitchen, eating apple Danish and sipping mugs of steaming hot coffee. "You lucky thing, you," Valerie cheerfully continued. "I knew someone like him would come along for you sooner or later."

"But he doesn't *like* me," Liza protested. "I'm virtually certain he doesn't."

"Then why is he hanging around? It doesn't make any sense. Unless *he* has a journal that needs an editor, too."

Liza shook her head. "I'm sure it's not that."

"Maybe he's just waiting to ask you out, and he's nervous about it."

"Oh, come off it Val. You've seen his picture in the paper, haven't you?" Liza impatiently asked her friend. "He's always displaying some classy female on his arm. Ever since you began plopping the appropriate newspaper society page, displaying his latest exploit, in the middle of my desk I could hardly avoid his pictures."

"Publicity," Valerie easily explained with a shrug. "All popular authors have to have their pictures taken with the opposite sex. It sells books."

"Right," Liza dryly agreed, "and the fringe benefits are terrific."

Valerie giggled. "I'll bet women stand in line to have their chance with him."

"They are welcome to him," Liza firmly declared, a little surprised by the tinge of bitterness in her voice. "Every time he comes into the office, with his smooth

words and judgmental manner, I hate him a little
more."

"What would you do if he asked you out?" Valerie
asked, eyeing her friend speculatively.

"I'd say no," Liza answered, a little too quickly.

And that was exactly what she did say when he asked
her out the following week.

"Another time perhaps?" Scott smoothly inquired.
"Thursday night?" He leaned casually against her
desk. Perfectly creased gray linen trousers were pulled
taut over his muscular thighs.

"No, I don't think so," Liza politely replied. "I
don't believe I'll go out with you at all."

Scott's eyes narrowed momentarily as he considered
Liza and her response. It didn't make sense to him.
He'd tried most of his warm-up techniques on Liza,
but had gotten nowhere. Very few women had ever
turned him down. For anything.

He frowned and stood up straight, looking down his
aristocratic nose at her. "May I ask why not?"

His question was a combination of pique and intellectual curiosity. He felt like a befuddled schoolboy
addressing his teacher as he stood before Liza's paper-
laden desk while he waited for her explanation. In all
his secure and successful adult life he never remembered feeling quite this way before.

"I do not wish to know you better," Liza plainly
stated. Her face was serene and composed. Even
though her heart was beating like a scared baby bird's,
she commanded all the dignity of a reigning princess.

Her words hit him like a blow to his solar plexus. He
could almost feel his ego shrivel. It was a new experience for him. And his response was a verbal attack.

"Now I know where you worked before you came
here. You were fired from the diplomatic corps," he
wryly said as he gave her what was meant to be a chiding expression.

"I believe in speaking my mind," Liza revealed through a tight throat. "It is easier and kinder on everyone in the end."

"That's a debatable point," Scott swiftly returned, frowning in disagreement.

"But it is not one which I care to debate," Liza quietly stated. She picked up her blue pencil and put on her horn-rimmed glasses, and with a great force of will applied herself to her manuscript, thus effectively dismissing him.

The now angry and befuddled psychologist left her office shaking his head and wondering why Liza was so obstinate.

When Scott didn't come to the office the next day or the next, Liza hoped she had seen the last of him. And she dismissed the strange pang of regret that arose, unbidden, at that thought.

Professor Wainright had been rushing her mercilessly. The final deadline on the autumn edition of the journal was only a week away. Liza had been routinely working late into the night and arriving early each morning. Angela could carry some of the secretarial load, but the slim blond had no initiative or judgment, and often Liza found it easier to do a task herself than to pass it on to Angela.

Liza arrived bleary-eyed and tired one morning, carrying a heavy pile of the work she had done at home the night before. On her battered old oak desk, gracefully presiding over the neat piles of papers, there was a rose, a single red rose and a delicate white spray of baby's breath. The flowers were arranged in a shimmering cut crystal bud vase. They were just the balm for her weary spirit.

Her heart stopped. She had never had anything so beautiful in her plain, serviceable office before. It was like a bit of inspiring poetry set in well-worn, utilitarian surroundings.

Propped against the delicate vase was a small white card. Liza gently, almost dreamily, picked it up to read its message.

This rose is like you: beautiful despite your prickles. See you for lunch?

A large "S" was scrawled across the card in a strong, masculine hand. The fine white card stock was imprinted "Scott Brill Harburton, Associate Professor of Psychology, Graham University.

Chapter Two

Liza dropped the card as though it were molten steel. She stormed out of her office to see the receptionist, a graying, motherly woman.

"Mrs. Johnson, did you allow someone into my office this morning?" she demanded.

The startled woman blinked at her and didn't answer.

"You know I keep it locked so that none of my papers can be tampered with when I'm gone," Liza continued.

"But the gentleman was bringing you a rose, Miss Manchester, a beautiful rose. I thought you'd be glad to get it," Mrs. Johnson defensively replied.

The older woman was completely taken aback by Liza's fury. She knew Liza Manchester to be plainspoken. But Liza was also an even-tempered and considerate person. Despite her sometimes punishing work load, in the four months since she had worked for the University Mrs. Johnson had never seen Liza flare up in anger.

"Don't ever allow him to do such a thing again," Liza commanded in a voice that was near trembling. "Never, do you hear?"

And then she stalked back to her desk, back to the waiting rose. She picked up the elegant bud vase in her now trembling hand. She purposefully strode toward the wastebasket. She was determined to throw it away. She wanted only to get the offending rose out of her sight.

For a moment Liza held the rose and vase poised above the basket. But she couldn't let go. Despite her anger she couldn't drop the ripe beauty of the flower and the many-faceted glory of the glass vase. Whoever they came from, and for whatever reason, she told herself, they themselves were beautiful.

With a sigh of defeat Liza wearily put the vase back on her desk. Then, spying the note from Scott, she vented her rage on the small white card. With great satisfaction she tore it in half, then in half again, then again and again. "Prickles," she muttered angrily. "Prickles. He'll see how prickly I can be."

She tore the card as though she were tearing at Scott himself, cutting him into small pieces and throwing him away. Tiny pieces of white fluttered gracefully into the wastebasket. Liza frowned, then pulled herself up to her full height.

Never had Liza been so angry at a man. Not even her old boss with his lewd innuendos and grasping hands. Liza refused to allow herself to analyze why Scott upset her so. She was determined to forget the whole unpleasant matter. She wouldn't allow her day to be ruined by any man. Instead she plunged furiously into her work.

Throughout the morning the heady perfume from the velvety red rose drifted to Liza's nose. While she worked on the draft of Professor Wainright's lengthy explanation of obsidian arrowheads in the pre-Columbian Southwest, visions of her grandfather's garden crowded into her thoughts. She remembered her old, gentle grandfather. He was bent with arthritis, but always cheerful as he tended the red, yellow, salmon, and pink rose garden that flourished behind his house. Liza and her mother had lived with him from the time Liza was very young, just after her father had died.

With a stab of pain she remembered the day of her grandfather's fatal heart attack. He had died in the garden. He'd had a heart attack one fine summer's day.

Liza had been only nine, but when he left her, all the loving attention and caring concern had gone out of her life. Her mother had always been too busy struggling to support their little family. And nobody since had been as kind and generous to her as her stoop-shouldered, sparkling-eyed, big-hearted grandfather. No one had cared so specifically about her and her alone.

She had been his special little girl. His memory brought a painful lump to Liza's throat. Yet through the pain she remembered joy. She had loved just being with her grandfather, and just knowing he loved her.

Liza was aware of Scott Harburton's presence before he spoke. He filled the doorway almost as if he were bigger than life. He interrupted her thoughts of her grandfather, wrenching her from her bittersweet nostalgia.

She stared at him, her gray eyes enigmatic as she wrestled with her own changing emotions. Her own first reaction at seeing him was an odd pleasure. But she forced herself to stiffen against his disarming smile. She reminded herself that she did not like him.

"Ready for lunch?" he pleasantly inquired.

He was dressed in dark brown slacks and a beige corduroy sport coat with suede elbow patches. His ivory silk shirt was open at the neck, displaying his powerful, tanned throat.

She regarded him quizzically, as though she had not heard. Something about him was confused in her own brain.

"Ready for lunch?" he asked again. "I've just heard about a wonderful new Italian restaurant."

"No," Liza curtly answered after a moment. "No, I'm not."

She turned back to her work, pretending to concentrate on the papers that were to go into Wainright's report. But the words were a total blur to her. All she could focus on was Scott's disturbing presence.

"Shall I come back later? In an hour?" he asked. His manner was pleasant still. Accommodating. Reasonable. But Liza's reaction was not. She needed to have him go away.

"No, don't come back," she firmly stated, still looking down at her desktop. "I don't intend to have lunch with you. Nor do I intend to have anything to do with you, no matter how many flowers you send me. Go away."

Briefly Scott raised an eyebrow. He gazed down at her speculatively. He let out a deep breath.

"Are you going to make it difficult for me to make friends with you?" His deep voice was chiding again. He was treating her as though she were a disobedient child.

His attitude made her furious. "That's exactly what I'm going to do," Liza responded hotly. She threw down the pencil she had been gripping in tight fingers, and she glared up at him hostilely. "I'm going to make it very difficult for you. Impossible, as a matter of fact."

From his superior height Scott frowned down on her thoughtfully. He rubbed the back of his neck with one hand.

"You're either so entangled with your current lover that you aren't interested in another man, or you're afraid of starting relationships," he speculated. "Which is it?"

She felt her fury ignite like a bonfire. Abruptly Liza pushed her chair back and stood up, leaning across the desk to face him. Her face flushed with the heat of anger that burned within her.

"Afraid of relationships!" she practically shrieked,

"Afraid! I think you're making a faulty assumption. Maybe I wasn't plain enough the other day. I'll say it more clearly. I don't want to have a relationship with you. I don't want to get to know you."

Her heart was pounding wildly in her breast. Her breath came in short gasps. Again she realized that no man had ever made her so angry.

"You have no real basis on which to make that decision," Scott calmly pointed out. "You've barely had a chance to know me. Now, how about lunch?"

She blinked in surprise. She had done everything she knew to discourage him. Everything. And yet he just kept on trying. It was a nightmare right out of one of his positive-thinking psychology books. Liza had heard about them, even read some reviews about his philosophy. Think you can. Keep trying. Never give up. Basically she agreed with the thinking. But since she had met Scott, she had steadfastly avoided anything to do with the books.

"I do not like to eat lunch in a restaurant. It takes too much time. I always bring a sandwich from home. If I want to do something a little different, I go out and eat it on the lawn." Her words were forced through nearly clenched teeth.

"I'll remember that," Scott returned pleasantly.

An amused smile came to his lips. His total composure, his ability not to let anything she said bother him, absolutely infuriated Liza. She practically shook with rage.

He watched intently as Liza's eyes blazed angrily at him for a moment, then he turned on his heel and went out the door. When he reached the hall, he felt his composure slip. He let out an impatient sigh and raked his fingers through his hair. Liza Manchester was the most challenging woman he had ever met. And she stubbornly refused to be softened by any of his usually successful methods of ingratiating himself with a woman.

Was she so deeply involved in the relationship he suspected her of having that she did not want to disturb it at any cost? Or was it that she truly did not find him appealing? If she really didn't like him, one of his most important theories, the one he had developed and supported in his upcoming book, was shot to smithereens.

As though it were beyond his control to get her out of his mind, he remembered her long, shapely legs, and the sensual curve of her breast beneath her tailored suit. His mind's eye recalled her high color and the fire in her eyes as she told him off.

She was a paradox. A passionate woman in a prim business suit. She was a paradox and a challenge.

He sighed again in disgust and, frowning, stuffed his hands into his pants pockets. He grimly decided he might have taken on more than he had bargained for when he first heard about Liza. And he started quoting positive phrases to himself, phrases from his own book.

Jeffrey Childers eyed Liza's gift from Scott appreciatively later that afternoon.

"Exquisite lead crystal," he commented urbanely. "You have excellent taste."

His comment made it clear to Liza that he assumed she had bought the arrangement herself. His assumption annoyed her. Though Jeffrey had never sent her flowers, why should he assume no one else did? Yet she only thanked him coolly, unwilling to admit the rose and vase were a gift, lest Jeffrey ask the source.

Jeffrey Childers was the brilliant young rising star of the Sociology Department. He was intelligent, articulate, liberal, and academically successful. Liza had met him at the campus chapter of a national women's rights organization. He was one of the few men there when she came to her first meeting nearly five months ago. The subject of that meeting, appropriately for Liza, was

"Dealing With Sexual Harassment." She had joined the heated discussion and had spoken vehemently about her own recent problems. Jeffrey had talked with her afterwards at great length. And despite a continual air of almost professional detachment, he had invited her to lectures, concerts, and dinner dates fairly regularly since then.

He was young and attractive. Liza hated to admit even to herself that she found him a little too pompous and fairly dull. At least, she reasoned, they shared a common view on the role of women in society. They both believed the sexes were equal and should be treated that way.

Jeffrey had never even opened a door for her or held her chair. Instead he gave her high-sounding intellectual arguments on how such behavior was demeaning.

"When I do something for a woman that she could perfectly well do for herself, I'm transmitting an unspoken message to her. The message is, 'You are incapable. Weaker. You must depend on me.' It is an integral part of the reason women have never achieved equal status with their male counterparts. They unwittingly permit themselves to be demeaned by a cultural norm that, on the surface, is designed to display favoritism," he told her in his typically wordy, arrogant manner. "Never let a man do that to you," he warned.

After her own bad experience Liza had taken his warning quite seriously.

Jeffrey had established another rule. When Liza asked him out, which she did on occasion, she paid the bills. It felt a little strange to her at first, but as time went on she saw how reasonable the practice was.

This afternoon he absently regarded the graceful rose as he asked her out to the Social Sciences dinner. "I'm not sure who the featured lecturer will be," he informed her. "Someone from Psychology, I should imagine. We round-robin the after dinner speeches. It gives us all a chance to learn from others in the broader field."

"I'd like to come," Liza replied.

One of the chief reasons she enjoyed being with Jeffrey was that it gave her a chance to get a taste of the broader intellectual life at the University. She fully enjoyed it. She penned the date into her date book.

At noon the next day, Scott poked his head into Liza's office. She was completely absorbed in "Fossil Death Assemblages in the Santa Fe Basin" and barely came back to the present when he appeared at her desk.

"Lunch," he triumphantly announced, holding up a large picnic hamper. "On the lawn," he added with an incorrigible grin. He looked like a happy five year old displaying a new toy.

"You're impossible," Liza complained, shaking her head in dumbfounded wonder. "Can't you take no for an answer?" For a reason Liza could barely understand, she responded to his grin with a tired smile.

In her weak, work-weary state Liza had to admit that a picnic sounded appealing. She refused to speculate on how Scott's presence could add to or subtract from the appeal.

Despite her continual protests she had to admit that his dogged persistence was getting through to her. No man had ever kept trying and trying to take her out, no matter what she did. For most men her withering gaze was sufficient deterrent. Maybe Valerie was right. Maybe he did like her a lot. The thought softened her toward him.

"I cannot take no for an answer, especially with a beautiful woman. It would be the complete opposite of everything I preach or teach."

And before Liza completely realized what was happening, Scott had spirited her out of her drab office and out onto a secluded piece of lush green lawn behind the large, central library. He spread a colorful plaid wool blanket on the thick grass and plunked the lunch basket into the middle of it.

"Sit down, sit down," he easily ordered as he knelt down and dug into the deep basket.

Liza gracefully sat sideways. She regarded him quizzically as she struggled to pull down her trim navy skirt.

Recognizing her efforts, Scott frowned in mock disgust. "Nice legs," he said lightly. "You ought to be proud to show them off." Then, as though he understood how uncomfortable his remark made her, he quickly turned his attention to the picnic basket while Liza blushed out her embarrassment and felt strangely pleased.

"Chicken," he announced as he unwrapped a foil lined package. It was roasted to a perfect golden brown.

"Salad." Then he displayed hearts of artichoke on a bed of romaine and endive.

"Bread," he told her as he pulled out a crusty French loaf. "All for my lady's pleasure," he announced with a flourish of a large linen napkin.

"This is marvelous," Liza enthusiastically declared. "And I'm starved." She realized by her relaxed response that she had called something of a truce between them. It was definitely easier than fighting, she rationalized, smiling for no reason at all.

"They say hunger makes the best sauce," Scott teased. "If so, you'll love this meal."

He pulled a small plastic bottle out of the basket and poured from it into a paper cup. "Your beverage," he declared with a flourish as he handed the cup to her and poured one for himself.

Liza sipped it. "It's wine," she announced, blinking her eyes in amazement.

"Shush," Scott cautioned. "We could be thrown out for drinking wine on campus."

"Then why chance it?" Liza demanded indignantly.

"Drink it because it is delicious," Scott recommended without a qualm. "Drink it because I think you'll like it. It's the perfect complement for the meal." He drank from his own cup with enjoyment.

"But you and I could get into trouble for this," she nervously protested. "We could be suspended. Fired. Something," she added, now tense at the thought of losing her job. She wanted to stay at Graham. She liked the prospect of her new position.

"Do you ever take a chance on things, Liza?" Scott gently probed. "Do you ever taste the forbidden fruit? Steal a drink from a golden cup?"

"Now you're psychoanalyzing me," Liza answered testily. Her spine stiffened. "I don't like that. If I want to be psychoanalyzed, I'll make an appointment."

His eyebrows rose expectantly. His eyes twinkled with interest.

"With someone else," she quickly added.

"Drink your wine," Scott ordered, now frowning.

And Liza found herself obeying him. She sipped the delicate rosé, and it seemed to flow through her like a bit of molten sunshine, warming every part of her being. "It's good," she hesitantly admitted. "Very good. Delicate, yet heady."

"So are you."

Liza looked up at him with startled eyes. He was regarding her soberly, with perfect seriousness. An uncomfortable tension filled her. The smooth compliments Scott had first used had made her furious. But this was somehow more sincere, more acceptable. And she wasn't sure if he was changing, or she was.

"Eat your chicken," Scott gruffly ordered. And he proceeded to pick up a meaty drumstick.

Liza took a sizable bite of her chicken. They ate in silence, with Liza once or twice politely remarking on how good the food was. Scott said nothing. He just seemed to enjoy the companionable silence.

She was strangely afraid to look at him sitting across the blanket from her. Yet every inch of her, every nerve in her body was attuned to every motion he made, every little thing about him. She noticed that his tie was loosened and that his shirt sleeves were rolled up, displaying his powerful forearms. There were short, crisply curling, dark hairs on them.

Scott refilled Liza's wine glass, and with the second portion she felt herself grow light-headed. "I'm not going to get much work done this afternoon," she protested with a smile. "I'm far too relaxed for my own good."

"Do you have to work?" he asked softly. "There are many more interesting things to do on a beautiful afternoon."

His voice had a husky quality that sent tongues of flame throughout Liza's body. She had no doubt that his suggestion was seductive. And she also knew he was far too smooth and experienced for her. Scott could no doubt have any woman he wanted. And if he wanted to get her into his bed, he might be able to do it, whether she really wanted to go or not. Besides it was, once again, too much too fast.

Now that she considered it rationally, Liza didn't like feeling that Scott had manipulated her out of her office and onto the lawn. She didn't like being any man's plaything. She didn't want to be putty in any man's hands. That was too destructive for any woman, she was sure. And with Scott her change of attitude had been too close to being manipulated by him.

"I—I have to—to go," Liza choked out. In order to help prove her point she glanced down at her watch, as though she had a meeting to attend. "I have to go. Now." She stood abruptly, and would have fled immediately if she hadn't remembered her manners. "Thank you," she stiffly told him as he politely stood up to see her off. "It was delicious."

Then she turned on her heel and marched across the grass. She kept up a quick, determined pace until she reached her office and finally felt safe.

She couldn't see the intrigued expression on Scott's face as he watched her go. Was she as seemingly shy and as strongly opinionated with her lover? Or did she save that behavior for Scott alone?

Madge Wainright didn't come to her husband's office often. She was a busy woman who kept a hectic schedule of bridge luncheons, beauty shop appointments, and fashionable good works. But the problem she was worried about now was getting serious. She'd tried the indirect methods. Now she would take matters into her own hands.

She stood on the other side of Liza's desk. Her slender body was sheathed in a gold raw-silk designer's suit. Her neck and wrists were glowingly circled with seemingly dozens of delicate gold chains. Every bleached blond hair on her head was in its carefully styled place.

"Miss Manston." She distinctly articulated the words to command Liza's complete attention.

"Manchester. Liza Manchester," Liza corrected, holding in her irritation with the skill that comes from practice. Madge Wainright had never yet gotten her name right at first try. Nor had Liza ever had a truly pleasant interchange with her.

"Whatever," the anthropologist's wife impatiently returned.

"What can I do for you?" Liza carefully asked, determined to be her solicitous best at any cost.

She didn't like Madge Wainright. She was a spoiled, demanding, rich woman who seemingly cared for no one but herself.

"I think if you use your imagination you should be able to guess," Madge responded acidly. Her meticulously made-up eyes glared at Liza. Each individual eyelash spike was carefully curled and sharply pointed.

"What should I guess?" Liza inquired, mystified. Madge Wainright was up to something unpleasant, Liza was sure. She braced herself defensively.

"Don't play the innocent with me," Madge warned. Her expression revealed a barely controlled rage. "I may not be here every minute, but I have ways of finding out what is going on. Don't underestimate me or my power."

Liza was dumbfounded. Her mouth dropped open and she stared at Madge as though her boss's wife had lost her senses.

The blond woman's eyes narrowed menacingly. "I know you are working your way up toward success here at the University."

"I certainly am," Liza immediately retorted. She was filled with self-righteous conviction. "I'm doing my level best to do anything required to raise my position."

"That's exactly why I am here. To make it perfectly plain that for you the road to success is vertical, not horizontal."

Liza's brows drew together in puzzlement, and she did not answer immediately. She still wasn't sure what the society woman was talking about. And she wondered if everyone in the upper crust was so purposefully vague. It would be so much easier for everyone if people would just speak their minds.

Madge Wainright impatiently drew a deep breath. "I'll be plainer," she angrily promised, almost as though she had read Liza's mind. "I have good connections here at Graham. It will be no problem to get you fired."

"Fired?" Liza demanded, incredulous. "Fired? Why should I be fired?" In her anger she rose behind her desk and stood to face her accuser.

"Because, you ambitious secretary and would-be editor, you are exceeding job expectations on a grand scale."

The real meaning of Madge Wainright's accusation was just beginning to sink in when Liza heard the muffled click of an opening door. She looked past Madge's glowering face to the doorway to Professor Wainright's private office.

The professor's face drained of color as he saw Madge at Liza's desk. Then Liza saw a flash of blond hair in the inner office, followed by the muffled opening and closing of the door from Wainright's private office directly to the corridor outside.

Wainright visibly relaxed. And with a relieved smile he approached the still fuming Madge, who stiffened in surprise when she saw her husband.

"My dear," the balding anthropologist greeted his wife, "how perfectly marvelous that you dropped by." He put his arm around her and solicitously kissed her cheek.

Madge's furious air dropped immediately. She shed it as though it were a garment that didn't fit. "I just had to see you, darling," she gushed, "It's about Mother's upcoming charity dinner dance." The seemingly loving couple disappeared behind the professor's closed office door.

"Phonies," Liza silently fumed as she plopped back down in her chair. "A couple of smooth, sophisticated, selfish phonies. I don't ever want anything to do with people like that." It was a firm promise she made to herself.

Liza often had a delayed reaction to events. Her brain would process information a bit slowly, so that it would be well after a situation had passed that Liza would grasp its full import. It was only after she had gotten over her surprise at Madge Wainright's behavior change that she remembered the content of the woman's earlier remarks. Couched in only slightly subtle words, Madge Wainright had actually accused Liza of sleeping her way to the top, and of doing it with Carleton Wainright.

The horror of the accusation filled Liza with a hideous, seething rage. An angry pressure grew within her. She knew if anyone said one word to her she would explode. She was all the more incensed because exchanging sexual favors for advancement was something Liza had steadfastly refused to do.

Scott had guessed she would be angry, and had even tried to convince himself to stay away. But after Madge's brief report and her even briefer conclusion, "She's the one," Scott had to go see Liza. Some deep, inner compulsion drove him to her office like a lemming driven to destruction in the sea, he grimly told himself.

It wasn't until she saw his athletic form loom in her doorway that she remembered. Madge Wainright was Scott Harburton's sister. Liza's usually light-gray eyes turned the dark color of the sky before a storm as she gazed murderously at him.

He carefully adopted his most casual, friendly manner, smiling broadly at her as he walked to her desk and sat in a nearby chair. Even when he saw the dangerous sparks flying from her narrowed eyes, even then, he carefully retained his relaxed calm.

He would have started their conversation by saying something pleasant. He had been taught that that was what well bred people did. But Liza didn't give him a chance to exercise his highly developed social skills.

"Your sister has the tact of a charging bull-elephant," Liza angrily advised him, venting all her fury on him. Her cheeks glowed a warm rose. Her eyes blazed like a flame. And her breasts rose and fell dramatically, enticingly, beneath her pale blue silk blouse.

Scott's breath caught in his throat. He felt a strange, pleasurable tightening in his chest. Never had Liza looked so beautiful to him. And never had anyone dared to liken his stylish sister to a charging bull-elephant. A broad, satisfied grin slowly spread across his jubilant face.

"She has all the warm, human kindness of a striking cobra," Liza continued, practically sputtering out her rage. "And phony! I never saw anybody change her mood so fast. She is as cunning as a fox."

As she finished her tirade, Liza's eyes focused on Scott's face. She gasped in horror as she saw his amused smile. "And you sit there grinning at me like the Cheshire cat. You think this is funny," Liza charged. "It's not funny. It's not funny at all. It's piti-ful. Pitiful that your sister can be the way she is. Phony. Insensitive. Insulting. Your family is supposed to be full of community leaders. Big deals all over. Why, I'll bet if the rest of them are like your sister Madge that the world would be better off without them. Leaders? Big deals? A disaster I call it. A disaster. And you sit there grinning away like an oblivious idiot. Get out. Get out." She rose menacingly and pointed at the door.

He didn't move. Instead he gazed up at her, com-pletely bemused. She was magnificent in her fury. A passionate, intelligent, opinionated woman. He won-dered how she would be in bed.

"This is my office and I'm telling you to get out," Liza ordered. "Now get out."

Slowly he rose. A giddy joy filled him. He wasn't ten feet from her door when be began to whistle, some-thing he hadn't done since he was a boy. All the other women in his life had practically bowed down to kiss Madge's manicured toes. And his mother's. He couldn't wait until Liza met his mother.

It wasn't until he was almost back in his own office that the realization hit him. He had no idea whether

Liza was sleeping with Wainright or not. Scott knew only that Liza was impossibly angry with the tactless Madge.

The thought of Liza with Wainright chilled him like a blast of arctic air. And by the time he reached his own office he growled angrily at his secretary, "No calls," and slammed shut his office door.

For a long time Scott Harburton sat in his big, tan leather swivel chair and stared out his window, thinking black thoughts about his brother-in-law, Liza, and the world in general.

Jewel-bright Oriental rugs highlighted intricate parquet floors. Tiny, clear panes of leaded glass windows sparkled in the glow of the evening sun. The huge Great Hall of Graham University was filled to capacity with a noisy crowd of chattering people. They nibbled at the elegant array of imported cheese and crackers, sipped their drinks, and tried to outdo one another with brilliant, cocktail-party banter.

Liza had arrived early with Jeffrey, who enjoyed every moment of the sophisticated story-swapping and genteel one-upmanship cocktail parties guaranteed. She herself found most of the talk superficial and fairly boring, but she had long ago learned to smile beautifully at all the right times.

This evening she had defiantly worn her sexiest black crepe cocktail dress. Its clinging fabric artfully draped the feminine curves of her hips. And though the dress had a classic cowl neck, the delicate fabric clung closely to her generous breasts, dramatically outlining them. The only jewelry she wore was ornate gold drop earrings. Her makeup was appropriately and expertly applied. And she had finished off the effect with a generous spray of My Sin perfume.

Madge Wainright had accused her of being a woman who used her sex to further her career. Perversely, for the Social Sciences dinner, she looked the part. She hoped Madge Wainright would get an eyeful, and that Liza's very presence would make Madge furious.

However, her boss's wife hadn't arrived at the cocktail party yet. Instead her brother Scott stood halfway across the room from Liza, frowning thoughtfully. He was boldly inspecting her as he lounged casually against a huge carved stone pillar.

Liza could only see Scott out of the corner of her eye, but she was constantly aware of his intense scrutiny. Strangely his disturbing presence was more real to her than that of Jeffrey or the friends with whom they talked.

Absently she listened to the University comptroller tell about the latest disastrous foul-up of the University computer. "When you want something done wrong, rely on the computer," he dryly commented.

Liza smiled appropriately and sipped her drink. She stole a quick glance over her left shoulder. Scott was still watching her with an intense, brooding expression.

Her skin tingled lightly with a mixture of pleasure and fury. She stared at her own drink trying to decide what was happening within her. Scott seemed to have some strange power over her. The realization made her angry.

Resolutely she held her chin high as she slowly turned her head. She was determined, at least, to stop his insolent inspection of her with one of her withering looks. Then maybe she could forget about him for the rest of the evening.

Her cool gray eyes glinted like the frozen sea in winter. Her classic oval face froze in a look of contempt. Even her dark blond hair, pulled back in a severe chignon, contributed to her attitude of scorn. She looked every inch the forbidding female.

Scott countered with a wry smile. His eyes twinkled in amusement, as though he knew a wonderful secret about her.

Furiously she snapped her head back to face her own group. Jeffrey was talking, a long-winded tirade about something timely, she was sure. She tried to listen, but couldn't. She was too intensely aware of Scott to even hear what Jeffrey said. She promised herself she wouldn't look at Scott again that evening. But when she did, a voluptuous, raven-haired woman was brazenly kissing him on the lips.

Liza felt the air rush out of her body. It was as though she had been kicked hard in the chest.

The rest of the predinner conversation was a blur to her. She merely made the appropriate nods and smiles while her own mind kept repeating the same question over and over. Why should she react to Harburton so strongly? She hated it when he paid attention to her. But she also hated the fact that he had been soundly kissed by another woman.

They were late getting into the adjoining dining room. Jeffrey had been so intent on what he was saying that he barely realized that everyone else had left to find places at tables.

In the immense dining hall the small leaded-glass windowpanes glowed a gentle apricot with the last light of the setting sun. Overhead three huge chandeliers of sculptured bronze sparkled with hundreds of tiny lights. A mammoth fireplace dominated one wall. Centered on another was a long table with a central podium: the speaker's table. Snowy-white linen draped the large array of round tables that were set with sparkling crystal and silver and lustrous china.

"We'll have to sit in front with our backs to the speaker's table," Jeffrey lamented. They were the only seats left.

After they were seated Liza furtively scanned the crowd for Scott, almost before she realized what she was doing. It was instinct that drove her to locate him. When she didn't see him or the raven-haired woman she told herself she was relieved. However what she actually felt was more like disappointment. She told herself it was wonderful not to have him near. Yet there was something else, something inside her that told Liza that Scott was still close by. She still had the peculiar sensation of being watched.

Before she could think, Liza swung around in her chair. Scott Harburton sat directly behind her, chatting pleasantly with the University president's white-haired wife. They were seated at the speaker's table. The black-haired beauty from the cocktail party sat at his other side chatting pleasantly with the University provost. Liza's jaw dropped as she stared in amazement.

Immediately Scott looked her way. A smile played around the corners of his broad mouth. His eyes danced merrily as he observed her stunned reaction.

She snapped her mouth shut, abruptly turned forward and sat in rigid anger as her heart pounded furiously and her temples throbbed.

Liza struggled her way through the meal. The chicken Kiev was sawdust in her mouth. She barely finished eating it. And even her favorite dessert, peach melba, slid down without her even tasting it properly. She waited only for the chance to escape from Scott's constant scrutiny. His eyes had been on her through the whole meal, she was sure. She had felt them.

The University president stepped up to the podium and greeted the crowd. Through the hall there was a scraping sound as chairs were turned so that everyone could have a good view. Liza tried to position her chair so that Scott was not in her line of sight. But it was impossible. He was right in front of her. She had to look at him, and she couldn't avoid his penetrating gaze. His eyes seemed to beckon her, possess her, while bearing some strange resentment, too.

"Wonderful to have you all here," the white-haired

host began. After the ritual few jokes and the usual pleasantries, the University president gave a brief speech about the plans for the coming year, and then went on to introduce the evening's speaker.

As he did, a grim foreboding that had gripped Liza when she first saw Scott at the speaker's table grew into a real horror.

"You know our speaker best as an established scientist, a top-notch clinical psychologist who has written dozens of scholarly papers, though he is now only thirty-six years old. He joined Graham's faculty after receiving his PhD nine years ago. And since that time he has been voted the best-teacher award, and was one of the youngest people ever to get tenure at this institution."

A terrible knot formed in the pit of Liza's stomach. Her dinner rested inside her like a leaden weight.

"He hasn't been with us this past year," the University president went on, "because he took a leave of absence to write his newest book. No doubt he will manage to promote it right to the top of the best seller list, just as he did with *Think You Can*. I'm sure you have seen our speaker on television interview shows, and even read about him in the gossip columns. He's become quite a celebrity," the president continued.

Liza prayed that she would not have to stay in front of him, listen to his speech, and be subject to his sardonic glance. She wished she were invisible. Or gone. But since she could be neither, she merely glared at Scott, doing nothing to hide her own displeasure.

"With his own success he is living, walking proof that what he writes about in his books works, and works well. His psychological prescription for all people everywhere is a healthy dose of positive thinking and a firm faith in the almost boundless potential within each individual. Scott Harburton has proved that you can do anything if you only think you can. His new book, due to be released very soon, is on women. It promises to be most controversial." Then with a sweep of his arms he announced, "Ladies and gentlemen, Dr. Scott Harburton."

The applause was enthusiastic. And as Scott got up to stand at the podium, he looked taller, broader, and more overbearing than ever to Liza.

His twinkling blue eyes sought her out first. It was almost as though he were seeking her approval. Then he trained them on the larger audience.

Liza felt a tightening in her already knotted stomach. An embarrassed flush brought bright color to her cheeks. And she nervously clutched her hands in her lap.

"Ladies and gentlemen," he confidently began, "I know you will be pleased to know that the latest scientific research conclusively proves that men and women are different."

Light laughter rippled through the hall. Even usually stolid, serious Jeffrey laughed.

Scott was a good speaker. He held his audience with bright anecdotes and smooth delivery. And he made several points that disturbed many of the radical feminists. They positively infuriated Liza, who now was convinced she knew why she had experienced an intensely negative reaction to Scott from the first moment she saw him. Everything he said was completely opposed to what she believed.

He explained scientific testing techniques and experimental results. The statistics were impressive, even to diehards like Liza.

"Our testing, our laboratory experiments have proved conclusively that women, all women, respond positively to courtly gestures." Scott elaborated further. "Every woman, every relatively normal, living, breathing woman in our society, loves the attention of the traditional courting behaviors. When a man opens a door for a woman, or sends her flowers, or holds her chair, he is silently saying, 'You are someone special. I want to take care of you in a special way.' When he does those things, women who are clinging vines and women who are radical feminists both respond positively, even if they don't admit it at the time. Is it cultural? Or is it inbred?'' He shrugged his broad shoulders. ''That is for scientists to decide after far more research has been done. I can only suggest a couple of reasons for you to think about.''

Scott paused and looked around the room to give emphasis to what he said. ''The first possible reason is one that most feminists will have the least trouble dealing with. It is that every person, male or female, likes to be treated as though he or she is special. I love it when a woman offers to get me a cup of coffee. And I think I would love it if a woman, a special woman, sent me flowers. Anyone here care to try?''

He was eyeing Liza as a shimmer of laughter traveled through the audience. She blushed and shifted herself uncomfortably in her chair.

''The second reason is biological, or at least that is my best guess,'' Scott continued. ''The male robin gathers the worms and protects the nest from predators. The male lion guards the females and the cubs. When our earliest ancestors lived in caves, and indeed in any primitive society, the men fought off the fierce saber-toothed tigers while women nursed their babies. Without the mothers and their milk, infants died. The women and children had to be protected, or the species would not survive. Whether we like it or not, despite the relative safety of modern times, we are still carrying the genes of our ancestors.''

Again Scott paused to give the audience a chance to digest what he had said. It was a moment before he continued his speech.

''What does all this mean to us today? What does

this mean in the era of unprecedented tension between the sexes?"

He dropped his voice to a conspirator's whisper. "Gentlemen, it means you should court your women. Open their doors. Buy them perfume. They'll love it."

He returned his voice to normal. "It goes without saying that intelligent adults will work for equal pay for equal work. They will insist on having a woman recognized as a complete person, not just a sexual object. But never think that when a woman gets her equal pay it does not mean she cannot get roses, too. And, women, relax. Stop fighting the way men long to treat you. Do yourselves, and them, a favor. Let them love you and take care of you in small, special ways. It's only natural." As he said the last, his gaze was once again on Liza.

Liza left the banquet that evening absolutely furious with Scott. She cleverly manipulated Jeffrey away from the crowd that surrounded Scott after his speech. She was incensed that Scott had looked completely unperturbed to be the center of a heated discussion. His ego was intact. In fact it was solid as granite. And his amazing intellect appeared to relish the mental sparring with his colleagues.

Jeffrey wasn't nearly as cool as Scott. In fact, the usually urbane professor positively sputtered. "How could an intelligent, educated, twentieth century man say such a thing? It is a betrayal of the women's movement. Surely he must not care about political realities."

"Maybe he was telling the truth as he saw it," Liza suggested softly. She was both horrified and surprised by her own reaction, which was to defend Scott's thesis.

"How can you even say that? How can you suggest that his theories are true? It would be the death of everything you have been fighting for. The death, I say!"

Jeffrey's normally calm approach to life had blown away like a leaf in the wind. He wasn't even thinking any more, Liza was sure. Instead he was reacting. She uncomfortably wondered if he was reacting to what Scott had said, or to Scott himself.

Though Liza had defended Scott to Jeffrey, when she was alone at home, her position flip-flopped. She fell into a troubled sleep that night only after hours of tossing and turning while she fussed and fumed.

"No woman wants her doors opened and her arm held as though she were some weak, namby-pamby, incapable person," she grumbled as she furiously pummeled her pillow for the twentieth time. Her poor pillow was a sad substitute. What she really wanted to attack was Scott Harburton himself.

"His opinions sound good to me," Valerie pronounced the next morning. She had waked Liza in the usual Saturday fashion. They shared coffee and rolls in the kitchen while Liza heatedly related the contents of Scott's speech.

"Valerie, sometimes you exasperate me," Liza charged. "Just because you haven't had a problem with sexual discrimination, you think it isn't a problem for anybody. Women need to be free of their oppressive chains. Open your eyes," Liza demanded. "You're missing the obvious."

"Turn it around," Valerie lightly suggested as she daintily licked the last crumbs of her sweet roll from her fingers, "You're missing things too. Just because you haven't been properly courted, properly appreciated by a man, you think it isn't a pleasure for any woman. That Scott of yours is right. Besides, he doesn't want men to keep women in chains. He only wants to see that they are properly cherished. As people. I'm for that," Valerie enthusiastically declared. "And you would be, too, if you were honest with yourself."

"I *am* honest with myself," Liza angrily retorted. "Anyone will tell you that. Very honest. And he's not 'my' Scott," Liza firmly told her friend. "I have absolutely no interest in him."

"I think you're making a mistake," Valerie chided. "Scott Harburton is a very sexy man. And rich. What more could a woman want? Relax for once. Let yourself fall in love. It could be heaven with someone like him," the snub-nosed redhead cheerfully counseled her all-too-intense and serious friend.

"I haven't got time to fall in love," Liza quickly returned. "I've got too many goals that are more important. Career goals. And if I did fall in love, that supercilious psychologist would be the last man on my list. I loathe him," Liza grimly reported.

Valerie was unperturbed. "They say hate is just a step from love, you know," she smugly said.

"It's a step I'll never take," Liza soberly promised. "Not with him, anyway."

"Don't be too sure," Valerie warned her friend. "Scott may have something to say about it all. And you just may not have any choice."

The beginning of the next week was dismal and gray. Clouds filled the sky and rain misted down lightly.

That morning Liza was reluctant to leave her warm, cozy apartment. But thoughts of the journal deadlines and her own eventual success drove her on. She dutifully belted herself into her trench coat, popped up her umbrella, and headed toward her office, a ten minute walk from her apartment building.

A hushed, almost eerie atmosphere had fallen over the campus. Even the students walking to class kept their voices to a loud whisper instead of their usual exuberant chatter. Gargoyles moodily peered down from the gables of the gray gothic buildings.

Liza was lost in the otherworld feeling of the day

when a voice spoke behind her, jarring her back to reality.

"I was hoping to run into you." Deeply masculine tones came from directly behind her. Scott Harburton.

She groaned her displeasure and hurried on without acknowledging his presence, just as though she had not heard. But her blood raced and her heart pounded wildly in her temples. Flight seemed her only salvation from his disturbing presence. She labeled her emotion anger, intellectual anger at him for his unwelcome opinions.

"I'll walk with you to your office," he said in a throaty whisper somewhere behind her right ear. "It will be easier to talk there." He was either completely unperturbed by her intended disregard, or completely oblivious of it.

Liza swung round to confront him. Her wide umbrella caught a sudden gust of wind. She struggled to keep hold of it, nearly crying with the effort and frustration. Nothing seemed to go her way when Scott was around. Nothing.

He was hatless and the drops of rain nestled in his dark, curling hair like a shimmer of stars. The collar of his trench coat was turned up against the wind. And she abruptly realized that he seemed completely at home in the rain. Completely at home and disturbingly handsome.

To save her own sanity, to stop the disturbing reactions her body seemed always to have when he was near, Liza knew she had to make him leave her alone. "No," she sharply cried out, "you'll not come to my office."

And she swung around and marched away. As she did, she carelessly splashed through a shallow puddle in the wet sidewalk. She blamed Scott for her wet feet.

When she got to her office, he was still behind her. She stalked past the astonished Mrs. Johnson, who watched Liza's furious stride and angry face. Scott casually strolled after her, his long legs easily keeping up with her rapid steps.

Liza shoved her dripping umbrella into the corner of her office and shrugged out of her wet trench coat. After shaking it furiously, she hung it in her tiny coat closet. Then she whirled to face Scott. Before she could begin her angry tirade, he spoke.

"Did you know that your hair curls beautifully in this foggy, foggy dew?" he asked. His voice was deep and husky. There was an appreciative gleam in his eye that banked the fires of Liza's fury.

She glared at him as she self-consciously smoothed wayward wisps of honey-blond hair into the tight bun at the back of her neck.

"And your complexion is magnificent," he finished softly.

He stood close to her now. Again she could see the droplets of rain glistening in his vibrant dark brown hair. An incredible bittersweet ache stirred deep within her. She fought it.

"Go away," Liza harshly demanded.

Scott raised his eyebrow only a fraction. He allowed no other expression to show on his strong face.

Liza's heart fluttered in her breast. For a moment she felt utterly lost. With an excruciating act of will, she regained control of herself. She lifted her chin defiantly and faced him squarely.

He regarded her thoughtfully for a long moment. He studied her, examined her as though she were a new psychological phenomenon. Her heart caught in her throat. Vainly she fought for control of her body. It wouldn't come. She trembled inwardly, and worried that any moment she would be visibly shaking.

"You're a puzzle to me, Liza Manchester, a gorgeous puzzle," Scott announced finally. His voice was low and amazingly gentle. "I don't understand you."

His statement, his admission, made Liza feel like jelly inside, all soft and quivering. She fought with herself until she could once again channel her emotional reaction into anger. It was her only defense against him.

"That's quite an admission for a world famous psychologist," she caustically remarked. "You're supposed to understand everybody."

He laughed lightly. The laugh was both directed at himself and at her perception of him. "Is that what you think?" he probed gently. "That psychologists are supposed to understand everybody."

Now he was smiling an apologetic half-smile. His eyes twinkled a bit, and Liza realized he had a dimple, quite a nice dimple, in his right cheek. She didn't answer Scott's question. She merely stood staring at him, strangely fascinated by the newly discovered dimple.

Scott moved closer and sat casually on the edge of her desk. He studied her with still twinkling eyes.

Because she couldn't look him in the eye, Liza concentrated on the way his trousers were pulled taut across his muscular thigh. His legs would be hard to her touch, she decided. Firm and powerful. Then the realization of her own wayward thoughts brought a rush of embarrassment to her. As she scolded herself she heard him speak again.

"Psychologists try to understand people," he revealed in a soft, nearly seductive voice. "They don't always succeed. Just like I'm not succeeding now. I surely don't understand you," he confessed.

Liza again found refuge for her confused emotions in her own cutting anger. "Well, at least you have the sense to admit that you're not all-knowing where I'm concerned," she proclaimed with satisfaction. Her clear, gray eyes were lighted with triumph. She stood up straight and proud.

"Thank you," Scott returned with an amused smile. His dangerous cobalt-blue eyes were twinkling wickedly.

Liza was taken aback. She certainly hadn't wanted her words to be taken as a compliment. She had to set the record straight, convince him once and for all that there was nothing between them but serious disagreements.

"We're incompatible," she declaimed. "Intellectually," she hastily added when she observed his wry smile. "It was very clear to me when I listened to your speech. We're poles apart in our beliefs. That makes me not want to be with you."

"Actually I guess I overestimated you," Scott admitted. His critically assessing look caught Liza off guard. She suddenly felt open and vulnerable. "I didn't realize you were such an emotional coward. You run away from me, or dismiss me, every chance you get. You're afraid to get to know me, and you rationalize that fear any way you can. Now you say its because we're intellectually incompatible. That's rubbish."

His tone was soft, but his accusations stung Liza to the core. She ached just as though she'd been dealt a physical blow. But her reply was prompt.

"I certainly am not an emotional coward. You are a poor judge of people," she defiantly maintained. "Ask anyone here. I stand behind my beliefs, even when hardly anyone else agrees with me. I have a reputation for integrity," she proudly proclaimed. "And I do not feel that spending time with someone who strongly espouses a wholly different viewpoint is reasonable or sensible. Once again you are wrong, Professor Harburton," she loftily concluded. Yet his accusation, his assault on her was so like Valerie's that Liza was hit doubly hard. In response she stood all the straighter.

"No," he patiently pointed out, "this time you are the one who's wrong. If you had any faith at all in your own convictions, a real exposure to someone of different opinions wouldn't shake those convictions at all. You'd just have to say you didn't like the experience. Say that honestly. Instead you're avoiding any confrontation. You're running away like a scared child,'' he accused her.

He was thoughtful for a moment. "Why don't you look at spending time with me in the nature of an experiment," Scott suggested. He nodded his head, serenely pleased with the idea. "Yes, look at it as an experiment—a living laboratory to test your own ideas. It's very sound scientifically," he argued. "I'll look at it the same way. You see, I have a theory about you, and I'm a scientist. I'd like to prove my theory right or wrong. Of course you may be too inhibited to be open to such a test," he boldly accused.

His accusation raised her ire. Liza took a deep breath, then let it out slowly. She stopped for a moment to clear her thoughts. Could Scott be right? Was she inhibited? Could she be avoiding him because she wasn't really convinced of her own position?

Whatever else was happening, she couldn't allow him to accuse her of cowardice. "All right," she finally agreed, "all right, I'll view any time with you as something of an 'experiment' as you call it." She lifted her now solemn gray eyes to look into his. "After a while I'll tell you whether all the things you do that I hate are still objectionable to me. And I'll tell you honestly."

Scott watched her with a gravity that revealed that he understood the effort it took for Liza to take this stand. A glow of admiration lighted his gaze. But Liza didn't see it. She had dropped her eyes. She was staring down at the desk top, wondering why she already felt defeated.

"Dinner, then?" he suggested softly.

She recoiled at first. She hadn't meant to date him. Just to be around him. Yet this was the first challenge.

She had to meet it. "All right," Liza agreed, her voice barely above a whisper. She still did not look up. She didn't face Scott, who was beginning to disturb her on so many levels.

"I'll pick you up at seven," he promised. "We'll dine at the Faculty Club."

Liza felt somewhat relieved. The Faculty Club was familiar. She had been there many times with Jeffrey. The atmosphere was sophisticated but relaxed.

"The Faculty Club would be nice," she agreed.

"Good. See you at seven."

He disappeared out her door. Moments later, from her window, she could see his tall form striding through the gray mists that enveloped the campus.

Late that afternoon, after her work was finished, Liza got an attack of what she honestly admitted were the jitters. She convinced herself that she had made a mistake making a date with Scott for that evening. She needed some time to pull herself together before seeing him again, no matter what she had agreed to about scientific experimentation.

She determinedly leafed through the University directory until she found his office phone number. She dialed it with hands that were close to trembling.

"Dr. Harburton's office," a pleasant sounding woman answered.

"Yes," Liza said awkwardly. "Yes. I'd like to talk to Dr. Harburton. Please."

"I'm afraid I can't put you through right now," the secretary's voice immediately reported. "But I will be happy to take a message."

Liza sighed with relief. She hadn't wanted to talk to him anyway. It was better to leave a message. "Please tell him that I will not be free tonight after all," Liza said slowly, distinctly, so that there would be no mistaking the meaning. And she left her name and phone number.

"I'll give him the message, Miss Manchester," the voice promised.

As Liza hung up the phone, a weight fell from her shoulders. She should have never agreed to go with him in the first place. The whole idea was ridiculous, ridiculous and deeply disturbing.

Chapter Three

When she got home that evening, Liza peeled off the gray linen skirt and ivory silk blouse she had worn all day. With relief and satisfaction she pulled on her faded jeans and a bright yellow T-shirt that had shrunk to skin tightness. Across her full breasts a message was written in navy blue Old English letters: "When God created man She was only joking."

Deftly she pulled the pins from the neat bun at the back of her neck. With long, slender fingers she quickly combed out her hair which fell well below her shoulders, cascading down her back in a glorious display.

Barefoot, Liza padded around her apartment, delighting in the artistically decorated rooms. The apartment had a homey air and a casual comfortableness that she enjoyed.

She pulled a large beige cushion off the brown and rust tapestry-print couch. Pillowing her head she stretched out on the floor, her fingers absently playing with the soft tufts of the rug as she read the latest issue of a publication specifically aimed at women in the professions.

"Sexual Harassment" was the lead article. And as she read it, she vividly recalled the smallest details that began the horrid experience she had had with her last boss. The furtive, then bold glances. The seemingly accidental brushing of his hand on her hip or breast, the first casual references to meeting after hours. And then the demands. They were blatant. Unmistakable. Put out or get out. She had left.

Liza knew it was a story that happened over and over to women everywhere. The article she read merely confirmed her already certain knowledge. The battle between the sexes would never be over, Liza sorrowfully concluded. She frowned in disgust as she put down the magazine and got to her feet to go to the kitchen. She was just thinking about cooking some pork chops for dinner when the doorbell rang.

Valerie, she immediately decided. Her best friend dropped by often during the week. Valerie's apartment was close by, and many evenings, instead of cooking lonely dinners, the two of them went out for pizza or hamburgers.

As usual Liza buzzed her caller in without greeting her on the intercom that connected to the lobby. She waited by the open door to her apartment while the elevator hummed its way up to her own apartment. She hadn't wanted to cook anyway, she realized. It would be good to go out. And it would be nice to have some friendly chatter.

But it wasn't Valerie who emerged from the elevator to pause in surprise at the picture Liza made. It was Scott, and he looked as shocked to see her so casually dressed as she was to see him at all.

Her hair framed her face and draped luxuriously over her shoulders. Her gracefully round hips and full breasts were sharply outlined by the close fitting jeans and T-shirt.

Scott stopped in his tracks for a moment. A look of near incredulity briefly passed over his face. But he recovered himself quickly and walked to Liza's doorway.

His generous mouth turned down in a frown of honest puzzlement. His dark brows drew together and his blue eyes narrowed speculatively as he studied her delicately youthful features and her clear, glowing complexion. Then he made a quick survey of her pleasantly rounded figure.

"Are you Liza Manchester or her teenage sister?" Scott asked, incredulous.

"What kind of question is that?" Liza angrily demanded.

"You're Liza," Scott returned, giving her a look of mild disgust. Then he ignored her indignant gaze, walked past her and into the apartment.

"You aren't supposed to be here. I left a message with your secretary. I told her I was too busy," Liza protested. Her lower lip jutted out petulantly. Her hands were firmly placed on the curves of her hips, and she looked like a paradoxical mixture of an outraged child and a fully developed woman.

She stood by the still open door. Scott turned to face her. "I was at meetings all afternoon," he told her with a shrug of his broad shoulders. "I didn't go back to the office to pick up my messages."

He walked over to the sofa and watched Liza expectantly, as though waiting for her to make the next move. He was dressed in gray flannel trousers and a navy sport coat. His navy and gray striped tie contrasted with his crisp white shirt. He was obviously dressed for their civilized dinner out.

Liza still stood by the open door, her hand firmly clasping the knob. "You haven't been invited in," she caustically pointed out.

"You're not busy," he countered. Frowning slightly he settled comfortably on the sofa. "You were just trying to get out of having dinner with me. It's that emotional cowardice of yours again," he gently scolded.

She glared at him furiously, angry that he had found her out.

"One thing I've already learned about you," Scott casually announced, "is that you always tell the truth.

You were right about your reputation for integrity." One side of his mouth turned down in a disarming half-smile.

Liza slammed the apartment door shut with a bang that rang through the small living room and echoed in the hall outside. His comment had come just as though he had been reading her mind. She scowled at him.

"You are the most objectionable man I have ever met," she declared as she stamped her foot angrily. "You won't be discouraged, or put off, or take no for an answer. You just keep coming back and coming back. You must have the most colossal ego in the Western Hemisphere," she charged.

She was hoping that at last her rancor would have its effect on him, send him away as it had other men. But she was disappointed.

"Oh, its not ego that keeps me going," Scott easily admitted, still unperturbed by Liza's outburst, "it's curiosity. Intellectual curiosity. You see, other men might just look at you as an attractive and appealing woman. They'd study your figure and wait only for their chance to take you to their beds."

Liza fumed at his blatantly sexual reference to her body. It was just another way men used women. Casual sex, sex without love. Jaws clenched angrily, she waited for him to finish. Then she would attack his views again.

"I'm sure I'd be as eager as any man to have you in bed with me," Scott explained coolly. "But I'm different from other men in some ways. I look at you as a challenge, a test, an experiment. Everything I have learned as a psychologist leads me to believe your independent, radical feminist attitude is nothing but an effect of never having been properly cherished, properly cared for. For me, you are a piece of research. And I pursue research ruthlessly. My ego has nothing to do with it," he loftily concluded.

Yet while he spoke he wondered at his own words. Why, if he was so interested in her intellectually, did he have trouble keeping his eyes off her body, her curvaceous, luscious, totally female form? Why was it that repeatedly throughout the day he imagined himself making love to her? Somehow there had been a subtle change in his mind. Now when he thought of "woman," any woman, Liza's picture flashed, unbidden, in his brain.

Liza stood staring at him, openmouthed and unable to speak. She wished she had something to throw at him. Something heavy, like the couch. It was a moment before her fury subsided and the impact of his argument really registered with her. But when it did, she drew herself up to her full height and answered him.

"You may try to unlock the secrets of other people's brains, but I think you are dismally lacking in logic. You want to be nice to me, care for me, do things for me, show me how happily I'll respond to that outdated kind of behavior. Well, you can start by leaving me alone. That's what I want to have done for me," she pointedly told him. "I want you to leave me alone. If you do anything else you are just being a high-minded, intellectual-sounding, male chauvinist pig."

Her cheeks blazed bright pink. Her eyes sparkled dangerously. Her chin lifted defiantly.

"You *are* an emotional coward," Scott softly declared as he stood up. There was no hostility in his voice. There was only a seductive gentleness. You're scared of something, and you're not even sure what it is," he told her as he walked across the room to where she stood.

When he got close to her, Liza had a ridiculous desire to weep, though she wasn't at all sure why she should feel that way. She had done very little weeping in her life.

"You're wrong," she weakly protested as she looked up at him. He was well over six feet tall and towered over Liza's taller-than-average height.

"Prove it," he gently challenged. "Come to dinner with me."

She couldn't understand why his physical closeness should affect her resolve the way it did. But there was something enticing, inviting, and exciting about being near Scott. It made part of her want to be with him. She wanted that more than anything in the world. Her body and her emotions wanted to be with him even if her logical brain said no.

Liza looked down hopelessly at her own informal jeans and T-shirt and shrugged helplessly. It was a silent protest and an appeal, both. Though she said nothing, Scott instinctively understood and responded.

He immediately loosened his tie, pulled it off and carelessly stuffed it into his pocket. He undid the top button of his shirt. Then he grinned, a broad, happy grin, and she saw his dimple again. For a moment she watched it and her heart stopped.

"How about pizza?" he suggested. "You won't even have to change." He didn't tell her that he liked looking at her just the way she was. He didn't tell her that her skin-tight T-shirt was affecting his pulse rate in an exciting way.

He was standing so close to her that his warm breath fanned her forehead. She couldn't look up at his face, so she concentrated her attention on one of his white shirt buttons instead. From where she stood, his chest and shoulders looked incredibly broad. They filled her whole horizon.

"I like pizza," she agreed, feeling surprisingly meek.

"You'll need shoes," Scott suggested.

Liza could hear the hint of a smile in his voice.

She giggled awkwardly as she looked down at her bare feet, toes curling into the woolly carpeting. Then she ran off to rummage around the floor of her bedroom closet for her worn running shoes.

When they left the apartment he opened the door for her.

"Part of the experiment," Scott drolly insisted as Liza began to protest.

How silly, she thought. And then she thought that if Jeffrey could see her he would scold. She was perfectly capable of opening the door herself. But instead she watched, as though it were all a surrealistic movie, while Scott smoothly maneuvered himself ahead of her to deal with the big glass door to the outside.

The rain had cleared, and the summer night was warm and a little muggy. As they walked to the parking lot of Liza's building, Scott's hand rested lightly on the small of her back. His touch was sure and firm and oddly comforting, even though she realized that he was supposed to be guiding her with his hand.

How ridiculous, she thought. She knew the way to the parking lot better than he did. After all, this was her building. She sighed. Jeffrey was right. She herself was right. This sort of behavior was silly.

The pizza parlor was dimly lighted. On every surface candles flickered from their wine-bottle holders. Red checkered cloths covered each table.

The dinnertime rush had ended. There was just a scattering of people throughout the large, low-ceilinged room. Scott smoothly piloted Liza to a secluded table near the back. As she felt his sure, strong fingers holding her bare elbow, she remembered how effortlessly he had managed to open first the car door for her, and then the door of the restaurant. Now he held her chair and seated her at the table, making her feel awkward.

As he sat across from her at the small round table, Liza opened her mouth to object to his courtesies. But the words died in her throat as he spoke.

"You didn't make a lot of small talk coming over in the car," Scott told her with a disarming smile. "And you didn't say a lot of things designed to intrigue or impress me. That's refreshing."

Liza was totally appalled by his unexpected compliment and by the rush of delightful warmth that flooded her body. She hadn't said anything in the car because she didn't want to. She had no wish to impress him, and intriguing him was the furthest thing from her mind, she insisted to herself. During the entire trip from her apartment to the pizza parlor she wondered how on earth she had agreed to go out with him at all. Yet he had managed to turn her silence into a good point. He had complimented her. Liza was bewildered but strangely pleased, too.

"Too many women never learn the fine art of being quiet with a man," he added, further confusing her feelings. Then he picked up a menu and studied it.

Liza followed his lead, hiding behind her own menu and wishing that she understood what was happening to her and with her. She was hardly aware of the printed words that swam before her eyes. But she was keenly aware of the tall man who sat across the table from her. His slightest movement impressed itself deep in her consciousness.

He broke her thoughts with a question. "Shall we have a large deluxe pizza, everything on it?" he inquired.

"I don't like pepperoni."

"I don't like it much either."

Liza felt ridiculously pleased. Neither of them really liked pepperoni. It was a small, silly thing to have in common, but nice all the same.

While they ate, Scott asked her question after question about herself. Liza talked openly to him about her happy childhood with her grandfather in the little bungalow he owned on the southwest side of Chicago. And she told him how her retired grandfather had time for a garden and a small girl's troubles, while her mother worked busily all the time.

She talked about school carnivals and Girl Scouts and how she had always wanted to go to summer camp, but they never had the money to send her. And she realized that Scott Harburton was a good listener, and she hoped it wasn't because he had been trained as a psychologist. She desperately wanted to believe that he was actually interested in what she said.

"It sounds as though you all along have been unconsciously preparing yourself for an editorial job," Scott commented after Liza had given him the long list of night school courses she had taken. "And I'll bet you'll be very effective."

"I thought you'd say, 'for a woman,'" Liza dryly commented.

A low chuckle broke from his throat. They had finished their pizza, and Scott had paid the bill. He helped her out of her chair and took her elbow to guide her to the exit.

"You're as prickly as a cactus, aren't you?" he teased.

Liza stopped still in her tracks. She faced him, disappointment filling her eyes. Everything had been going so well between them. But now his comment cut her to the core.

He frowned, regarding her solemnly. With a roughened index finger he lightly traced the curve of her jaw. Concern and apology were evident in his expression.

The gentle touch of his finger to her cheek sent a flood of warmth through the whole of Liza's body.

"No," Scott whispered softly, just loud enough for her to hear, "no, not a cactus. More like a rose. A beautiful rose. Soft, lustrous and fragrant."

Liza recalled the red rose he had sent her. And the

message that came with it. "Beautiful despite your prickles."

His voice was low, almost a caress. His eyes were lighted with a glow that warmed Liza to her very soul. Her spine turned to jelly as she listened to him in rapt fascination.

"But you've definitely got thorns," he told her, giving her a gentle smile. "And you're a woman who sends mixed messages."

At the last his voice was lightly teasing again. But Liza reacted with hurt. And when she was hurt, she lashed out.

"Mixed messages? What do you mean?" she demanded as he ushered her through the maze of tables in the dimly lighted restaurant and outside into the warm, humid evening air. "How do I give you mixed messages?" she queried defensively.

As he lowered his gaze to focus on her breasts, her breath caught in her throat.

"The words on your T-shirt, 'When God created man She was only joking,' is a put-down to men," he told her as he unlocked the passenger door of his white Mercedes sports car. He helped her inside, then casually got into the driver's side.

"The way the words are pulled tightly across your beautiful breasts..." he paused meaningfully and examined them in profile. An appreciative light gleamed in his eyes. Liza squirmed uncomfortably, wishing he would look away. "Well, the outlined breasts are a definite come-on. The combination makes you, your face, your body, your person, a mixed message."

Without any more explanation, he inserted the key in the ignition lock and turned it. The powerful engine of the sports car purred to life.

"The T-shirt shrank," Liza weakly protested. "It fit fine when I bought it. It was even loose."

He took the wheel firmly in his strong, tanned

hands, then turned to her briefly before he put the car in gear. "You're still wearing the T-shirt, even if it is seductively tight," he concluded. "That's a definite statement."

Then he trained his eyes to the rearview mirror, smoothly maneuvered out of his parking place, and joined the traffic on the busy street.

Brightly lighted signs whizzed past Liza's shoulder. She felt almost as though it were a carnival atmosphere. And, she thought miserably, she was the side show. The mixed-message lady. She vividly recalled the glowing approval in Scott's eyes as he openly admired her moments earlier. And Liza was glad it was dark. In the dimly lighted interior of the car, Scott Harburton could not possibly tell that she was blushing.

When he dropped her off at her apartment, Scott smoothly pulled Liza into his arms. It happened quickly and seemed completely natural to have his firm lips wedded to hers and his big hands spread possessively across her back as he pressed the fullness of her breasts against his hard-muscled chest.

When Liza remembered the kiss later she burned with embarrassment at her own instinctive response. Her arms had immediately slid around his neck and her fingers were lost in the crisply curling hair at the back of his neck.

Her heart had raced and her body warmed to his until her blood turned to fire. She had clung to him, savoring the taste of him and the hypnotic movement of his lips as his body indelibly imprinted itself on her own.

Slowly his sensuous hands had begun an exploration of her waist and hips. Then he lightly moved up her rib cage until, stepping back slightly, he quickly, thoroughly, caressed her breasts, sculpting with his hands and commiting them to memory, even as his lips lifted fractionally from hers.

Liza felt herself straining toward him as a flower leans to the light. Her senses were drugged, her mind reeling, and she was enveloped in a cloud of pure sensation.

The glow that surrounded her from the kiss kept her out of touch with reality. She hardly realized that Scott had gone until she watched the elevator doors close and swallow him. And then she felt bereft, as though a part of her had left with him.

As he rode down the elevator Scott's breathing was ragged. His heart still thudded in his broad chest. Kissing Liza had been a headier experience than he had even imagined. He was glad he could put some time and distance between them. Liza Manchester was a problem he needed to think through.

Later, in her bed, Liza relived the kiss and her body flooded with warmth at its intimate intensity. Then, with an agonizing wrench of consciousness, she recalled what Scott had said to her earlier that evening. She was an experiment to him, an intellectual exercise. Pain tore through her as though she had been stabbed with a saber.

After the pizza dinner Liza was convinced she didn't want to see Scott again, no matter what. He had stirred up feelings inside her that she hardly knew were there. They were so strange she had trouble identifying them. She knew only that they were different and uncomfortable.

There was a peculiar tension within her whenever he came near. She had an awareness of him that was like radar blips on a darkened screen. The closer he came, the faster the blips. She firmly told herself that the tension was a result of the intellectual war that raged between them. And after literally hours of quiet analysis Liza concluded that the heightened awareness that she likened to radar blips was caused by her intense dislike of Scott. The tension was a natural result of anger, she decided.

She refused to think about the shared kiss. Refused even to acknowledge to herself that it had happened. Yet every time the phone rang in her office, she thought it might be Scott. Even not considering the kiss, there had been something between them that night, something companionable, something caring, something her very soul needed as a flower needs the rain. She wanted to see him again, she finally admitted to herself.

From her second floor office Liza could hear the frequent creaking of the massive old oak doors that were the entry to the Social Sciences building. The doors opened dozens of times an hour, admitting students, professors, and other University staff members. Each time Liza heard the whining groan of the aged hinges, her heart stopped and she waited breathlessly for the sound of Scott's footsteps to come down the hall to her office.

In several days there had been no word from him. And though she again told herself that she didn't want to see him, the fact that he didn't even call made her ridiculously angry.

Emotionally she had swung from a furious loathing to a breathless anticipation. That had been the pattern of her days. She realized that she had gotten precious little done. There were several letters that she had scheduled herself to send to reviewers. They sat untouched on the pile on her desk. And there were travel plans to work out for her boss—he was due to go to a conference in St. Louis soon—but she couldn't keep her mind on airline tickets, either.

"That's enough," she scolded herself aloud as she impulsively threw her pencil across the room. "You're going to take yourself in hand and get to work. No more of this mind-wandering nonsense."

Resolutely she grabbed a manuscript from the top of her pile. She leafed through it until she found the part she wanted to read, and began to read it for the third time that day. Once again the letters blurred before her eyes. Their meaning escaped her. She could have been reading a grocery list or an ancient Greek tragedy. It was all the same to her. Her usually good powers of concentration abandoned her completely. They had flown like a carefree bird on a warm spring day.

Every nerve within her tightened. Liza was frantic. Would she be permanently disabled by her fury at Scott Harburton? Would she never get her powers of concentration back? Would she never, ever get any work done?

She pushed back her chair, slammed down her papers, and frowned at the open doorway of her office. It seemed terribly empty to her.

"He's in New York," Valerie pertly announced when she saw the scowl on Liza's face. The petite secretary plopped down on the chair opposite Liza's desk. There was a folded magazine in her hand.

Liza's scowl deepened as she stared mutely at Valerie.

"New York. You know. The Big Apple. N-e-w Y-o-r-k," she spelled it out.

"Oh," Liza dully replied. "So what?"

"So that's why he hasn't called," Valerie offered brightly.

"I don't care," Liza snapped, wondering how Valerie would be able to tell Scott hadn't called her. Liza had carefully not discussed Scott with her friend. Valerie's well-meaning matchmaking had been going on for the last few years; she seemed determined to find Liza a proper man. Liza seemed equally as determined to have no part of Valerie's projects. Though Valerie didn't have a steady boyfriend, she had an inner conviction that her prince charming would come in his own good time. It was Liza she was worried about.

"Oh, come on," Valerie chided, "you do, too, care. You can't fool me. I've known you for ages, remember? You've been walking around as though the world ended days ago. The moment Scott and you were together last, to be precise."

"It's all this work," Liza replied, sweeping her arm across the paper-strewn desk.

"Nope," Valerie retorted, cheerfully refusing to be swayed by Liza's explanation. "You positively thrive on hard work and deadlines. It's a whole lot more than that. I think you've finally fallen for a guy. Fallen hard. And it's your bad luck that he has a new book coming out. He's going to be out of town. A lot. And there will be a lot more pictures like this in the magazines and newspapers."

She thrust the slick magazine under Liza's nose. On the "People in the News" page there was a picture of Scott with the black-haired woman on his arm, the one who had been with him at the Social Sciences dinner. "Best Selling Author's Steady Beauty," the headline read. The woman was identified in the caption line as Monica Grant, daughter of one of the directors of Scott's publishing house. Scott gazed into her eyes as Monica stared up at him with unconcealed adoration.

Liza's stomach knotted tightly and she felt a cold chill creep over her body.

"I thought so," Valerie gloated in satisfaction. "You have fallen. Hard. That's wonderful."

"You couldn't be more wrong," Liza protested angrily. "And even if you are right, how can you be happy about it? You sound happy—no, delighted—that the man about whom I allegedly care is involved with another woman. Exactly what kind of loyalty would you call that? What kind of friendship? Are you some kind of a sadist or something?"

Valerie smiled with delight, bubbling over with the joy she felt. She completely ignored Liza's foul temper and furious expression. "Oh, this is going to be wonderful," she enthusiastically predicted. "You are both going to be so happy. I can't wait."

"Valerie," Liza called in angry exasperation, "calm down. Let's get something straight here."

Valerie shook her head, and her short red curls bounced prettily. She sprang out of the chair, and joyfully clapping her hands, she headed for the hall.

"Oh, it's just great," she called over her shoulder.

"Valerie, come back here."

Liza's sharp order followed her friend's disappearing form, but it had no effect. Valerie didn't come back.

Liza moaned, then held her head in her hands. She could feel a headache developing as she despaired of ever talking reasonably to the impulsive Valerie.

Liza was glad Scott was in New York, she resolutely told herself that evening. She had wanted a quiet time, a dinner alone at home. Yet when the phone rang, she dashed to it eagerly and picked it up with trembling hands.

"H-hello," she ventured.

The voice on the other end was male, but not Scott's.

"Oh, it's you Jeffrey," Liza said as her body sagged visibly with relief or disappointment. She wasn't sure which.

"How about dinner tomorrow night?" he asked.

"Oh, all right," Liza agreed unenthusiastically.

They talked for a few moments before they hung up. After replacing the phone Liza stood still as a statue, with her hand grasping the receiver. She realized that although she had dated Jeffrey steadily in the last few months, she had hardly even wondered when or if he would call.

He was intelligent, reasonably undemanding, and would allow Liza her freedom. Beyond that he was rather pleasant to look at and he had good manners. Certainly his position at the University was secure, and he had real possibilities for advancement. Yet she could think of him as nothing more exciting than nice.

The restaurant was crowded when Liza and Jeffrey arrived. It was the closest really good place to eat near campus. The food was excellent continental fare.

"Do you have a reservation?" the tall, gaunt-faced headwaiter inquired.

"Why, no," Jeffrey responded a bit defensively, "I didn't expect you to be so crowded tonight. It's only Wednesday."

"It should be about forty-five minutes before we'll have a table," the waiter disdainfully replied. "You may sit in the lounge if you like."

Liza wondered whether the curiously pinched look of the waiter's nose was natural. Or did he regularly use a clothespin to achieve its almost bizarre, pointed effect? She stifled a little giggle as she thought of him, tall, stick-like, and terribly formal, walking through the elegant dining room with a common clothespin on his nose.

She was still struggling to hide a smile when Scott Harburton nodded at her pleasantly as he escorted the voluptuous Monica Grant to the headwaiter's station. Seeing them shocked Liza's whole being. Her heart stopped. Her breath caught in her throat. And her eyes were riveted to Scott's broad back as he stood in front of her.

"Ah, Dr. Harburton," Harold, the headwaiter, brightened visibly as he identified his new customer. "So nice to have you here." He picked up two large, burgundy colored menus and led Scott and his companion to a waiting table.

Monica Grant drifted into the dining room in a cloud of expensive perfume. Her hips swayed suggestively and her tight fitting orchid dress accented her tiny waist. Her perfectly arranged long black hair fell nearly to the center of her back.

As she turned to take her seat, her well-developed breasts were contoured in a close fitting bodice. Her makeup was perfect, as though it had been done with a professional hand. Every eyelash, each stroke of blusher, seemed to have had special care lavished on it. Reluctantly Liza admitted the effect was stunning. It was a little overdone, but stunning.

She hardly realized that she had been staring at Monica. Her eyes were round with amazement. But first she sensed, then she saw, Scott watching her. There was a sardonic gleam in his eyes and a hint of a smile on his lips. He seemed to be mocking her.

Liza flushed to the roots of her hair. Her palms grew moist. Her heart raced. She wished she had worn something besides her simple, light-blue linen dress. She felt too unsophisticated and vulnerable.

"Let's go someplace else," Liza impatiently complained, "I don't want to wait for nearly an hour to eat." But, most of all, she knew she wanted to escape, get away from Scott. She couldn't relax, not at all, while he was near. And as for his date Liza had unusually uncharitable thoughts about her.

"But where else is there close by?" Jeffrey pleaded. We'll have to spend time driving in any case."

"I'd rather be moving in a car than cooped up here," Liza snapped back.

He gave her a small frown of disgust, but she was enormously relieved when he agreed. They went out the door into the fragrant evening air.

Liza took a deep breath, a breath of freedom and relief. *I shouldn't be anywhere near Scott,* she thought resolutely. *He makes me too angry.*

It wasn't until she and Jeffrey were seated in a comfortable restaurant a few miles from campus that he brought up the subject of Scott. "He seems to date the sort of woman his philosophy appeals to," Jeffrey commented disapprovingly. "His date looks like the sort who is eager to trade his protection for her favors."

"You'd think a psychologist could see through somebody like that," Liza complained bitterly. "There probably isn't much to her besides her looks."

Monica Grant was the kind of woman Liza detested. She obviously used her physical attraction to make her way in the world. Liza, especially since her heightened awareness of the inequality between the sexes, considered that immoral and degrading to women everywhere.

"Scott Harburton deserves a woman like that," Liza bitterly pronounced.

"Right," Jeffrey agreed, a bit too enthusiastically.

Liza suddenly realized that even Jeffrey was anything but immune to Monica's charms. In fact he appreciated her physical beauty more than he would ever admit, Liza was convinced.

"I've never trusted psychologists, anyway," Liza complained to Jeffrey as they began their soup course. "They are full of theories that contradict each other."

"It's because they practice such an inexact science," Jeffrey loftily explained. "There is no precision to it. No surety. All they can do is guess. Now take mathematics. There a rule is always a rule. And in simple math, two times two is always four. It is so comfortingly predictable. Statisticians approximate, but on a sound mathematical basis. And sociologists," he added, importantly referring to his own specialty, "use exhaustive techniques to gather their data, then process it with scientific thoroughness. Yet psychologists think they know something. They even tell other people how to run their lives."

Jeffrey looked sidelong at Liza. A satisfied smile broke out on his face. "It's good to know a woman like you who can't be swayed by sexist nonsense." He looked like a self-confident cat licking his lips as he contemplated Liza. "Of all the women I know, you, Liza, are the least likely to fall for charm and flattery and all the other manipulative, phony stuff. You're too honest and independent. You're immune."

Liza wished the words, intended as a compliment, sounded less like a slap in the face. "Is that the kind of woman you admire?" she asked Jeffrey. "Honest and independent. Is that what you look for in a woman?"

"Of course," he smugly replied, "but be sure to add intelligent. Empty-headed women are a bore."

But Liza uneasily remembered Jeffrey's reaction to Scott's date. And she was sure he was either fooling himself, or her.

They were just beginning their after-dinner coffee when Jeffrey made a suggestion.

"I think it is time we began sleeping together." He said the words in passionless tones and followed them with a casual sip of his coffee.

Liza blinked in surprise and stared at him mutely. The thought of having an affair with Jeffrey had never seriously occurred to her. She enjoyed the undemanding kisses they shared, and had easily escaped from any further intimacies with him. She had never encouraged him because she didn't particularly want him to make love to her.

"I've taken some time to analyze our relationship," he explained, "and we are certainly compatible, both intellectually and emotionally. The physical dimension is the only one that is now lacking. In order to have a genuinely fulfilling relationship, we should also interact on that level."

Liza couldn't believe she had heard him correctly. Jeffrey seemed to be asking her to be his lover, but he was asking her logically to "interact physically" with him. His approach was totally intellectual. She was too surprised to be insulted by it.

"Well?" Jeffrey demanded.

Liza took a comforting sip of coffee and used the motion to pull her thoughts together.

"Isn't it a bit soon?" she suggested, looking for an easy way out of the whole subject. She didn't want to tell him the real reason for her reluctance: She just didn't find him very exciting, not even enough to consider an affair.

"We've been dating for months," Jeffrey argued. His voice was tinged with impatience. "Most normal adults nowadays don't wait that long before becoming lovers."

Liza frowned. She knew Jeffrey was right. So many of her acquaintances, especially in the women's movement, were quite candid about their numerous affairs and even their one-night stands. They declared it was their right to enjoy free physical expression as long as no one got hurt.

Liza was largely silent in discussions of sexual freedom. She was only partly convinced that the liberated lifestyle was reasonable. Her personal reservations told her that it was her right not just to follow the current way of thinking, but to decide things for herself.

"Why are you hesitating?" Jeffrey probed. "Surely you can't say that the thought was a bolt from the blue. I'm a normal male and you are a physically attractive woman."

Liza didn't want to hurt Jeffrey. He had been a pleasant companion. She didn't want to tell him that he didn't interest her much. She smiled at him apologetically and felt like a coward when she replied.

"I guess I just don't do anything without thinking it through," she told him. "It's just not in my nature," she explained, hoping her words would put him off.

Jeffrey frowned. "Okay. Think about it," he agreed somberly.

Liza could see his disappointment. She felt like ending his misery, just saying no, but she couldn't. Was that because something was telling her to say yes?

"I'm going to St. Louis next weekend. To a big Social Sciences conference. Come with me," he suggested. "There are several sessions on women's issues that you would be very interested in, I'm sure."

Again Jeffrey sounded completely unromantic and passionless. Liza could hardly believe his unemotional, detached attitude. It took her a moment to answer.

"I'll think about it," she promised. She wished she could think of something else to say.

Jeffrey's lips were pleasant against hers as he kissed her in the hall of her apartment later that night. His searching hands traveled up and down her back, resting finally on her hips, pulling her closer to him.

Liza had no doubt about his desire. Usually with any man she found the knowledge quite pleasing, and she told herself that maybe she should let him go on. Maybe if Jeffrey were her lover she would lose the strange feelings she was having about Scott Harburton. Once her body was mated to Jeffrey's, Scott would disappear into the background. Maybe Jeffrey was her answer after all.

His tongue pried her lips apart and thrust deeply into her mouth. And though Liza stayed pliant in his arms, she felt strangely uncomfortable, she felt invaded.

It wasn't because she hadn't been kissed like that before. It was more that she had never really considered it. What on earth was Jeffrey doing inside her body? Had she invited him? Did she want him?

She was relieved when the intimate kiss ended and his lips traveled to her cheek. He whispered eagerly into her ear, his voice impatient but confident.

"Tonight."

Liza pulled away, shaking her head. She said the first thing that came to her mind. "I have a headache."

"Oh, really," Jeffrey retorted, "that's a bit of a cliché, isn't it?"

"It's true," she countered defensively. "It started over dinner."

He frowned uneasily, then his face lighted with with an idea. "It's probably sexual tension. There's a sure cure for that," he offered hopefully.

"It's more like sinus trouble. I think the weather is going to change," she countered.

"Maybe you're not as liberated as you appear."

It was an accusation that stung her. Liza sighed impatiently. "Let's discuss this some other time," she wearily suggested.

"Tomorrow night," Jeffrey tried.

Liza shook her head. She desperately wanted to buy some time to think things over. "By the time you go to St. Louis, I'll let you know how I feel," Liza solemnly promised.

"All right," he reluctantly agreed, "I'll give you some time to think about it."

Later that night, in the quiet sanctuary of her bed, Liza's brain was consumed with thoughts of Scott and Monica. Scott obviously found the dark-haired woman attractive, or he wouldn't take her out.

"Let him go out with any woman he wants. He deserves what he gets. I don't want him to find me attractive," Liza firmly told herself. "I only want to prove to him once and for all that women don't want to be treated like weak-willed, dependent ninnies. I want to prove to him that they only want a chance to be true equals."

Yet she could not explain away the ache she felt. It was a painful, festering wound in the area of her heart. And it was all because of Scott. She did not spend one moment of her restless night considering Jeffrey's proposition that they have an affair.

The next morning Liza was surprised to discover an exquisite porcelain figurine of a ballerina on her desk. The china dancer was dressed in a classical, pink full-skirted dress. She pirouetted gracefully atop the latest draft of an article Liza was proofreading. Tucked beneath the round pink base of the statue was a note.

> The ballet is in town. I hope you'll be free. I'll stop
> by about seven.
>
> Scott

The ballet. Liza had spent so much of her energy working toward success, concentrating on her own advancement and avoiding sentimentality and emotionality, that she had pushed the natural poetry in her soul back to a far recess of her mind. She simply didn't let it come out. Yet she responded with instinctive pleasure to music. And if any sight delighted her eye, it was the ballet.

Had Scott known? Had someone told him? Or did he merely make a lucky guess? Liza hardly cared. It didn't matter. And despite her admittedly angry feelings about him, she was starved for the sounds of the orchestra and the drama of the dance. Using the same force of will that pushed ballet to the background when her career beckoned, Liza pushed away all thoughts of Monica Grant. Tonight Scott would take her to the ballet.

By ten minutes to seven Liza was ready to go. Her hair was neatly caught up into its customary bun, but pulled back more severely than usual. She had left her makeup to a minimum, using only a touch of mascara and some lipstick. She didn't want to be accused of trying to attract Scott Harburton. In fact, if anything, she told herself she wanted to have the opposite effect. She had even resisted wearing jewelry. She didn't have much, since she only bought the very best and she couldn't often afford it.

She nervously smoothed the close fitting skirt on her black crepe, scoop-neck dress. She inspected her stockings for runs. She studied her delicate, high heeled strap sandals, considering whether to change them for something more serviceable, less fashionable. Less seductive. But she didn't have time.

The buzzer rang, and Liza jumped nervously. It seemed to take hours for the elevator to bring Scott up to her floor, hours in which Liza was only conscious of the deafening sound of her own heart beating in her ears. Despite the fact that she desperately tried to discipline herself not to react to him, Liza thought she would strangle from the nervous tension that grew around her heart. The tension was just beginning to turn to anger when the elevator doors slid open, and Scott strode out into the corridor.

Chapter Four

He seemed taller than ever, and even more virile, in his formal dark suit. Every hair was in place and his grooming was immaculate, yet he had an untamed quality about him, an air of sexuality that sent Liza's heart racing even as she scolded herself, again remembering that his date with her was something of an experiment to him. Yet she could not still her furiously beating pulse, nor deny her happiness at seeing him.

He carried a white box Liza recognized as a corsage box. "Good, you're not wearing jewelry," he commented, smiling as he handed her the box.

Liza opened it to discover a delicate corsage of four pink tea roses.

He studied her critically and frowned. "On your shoulder or in your hair?" he asked.

Without waiting for her answer, he pulled out a single rose and gently placed it into her coiled hair. The other three he gently pinned on her shoulder. As he did, his warm breath lightly fanned her temple.

While he stood before her, she felt frozen, immobile. Any movement of her body, any nuance of expression seemed impossible to her. It was as though all parts of her were made of lead and uncontrollable by her own weak will.

She stared at his immaculate white shirt front, unable to look up, unwilling to see his face. Then she felt a gentle pressure beneath her chin as he raised her face to his.

For a moment she stared, bewildered, into his commanding blue eyes. Her pulse raced as, slowly, easily, he lowered his lips to hers, brushing them lightly but firmly with his own.

An electric charge traveled through Liza. She could feel its tingle from her lips to her fingertips. The back of her knees, even her toes, responded with an aliveness that she hadn't known before. And somewhere deep within the center of her being was a wild and sensual stirring.

Too soon the kiss was over, and he stood looking down at her through eyes that glowed with a light Liza hadn't seen before.

"You're beautiful, Liza," Scott told her. His voice was husky. It caressed her as though she were wrapped in a velvet cloud. "You don't know that you're beautiful, but you are. Someday you'll know. I want to be there then."

She blinked, trying to bring herself back to reality.

He kissed first one eyelid, then the other. Again her breath stopped as she felt the soft pressure of his lips against her skin. The wild sensations started again. The sensations that traveled straight through her.

He put his large hands on her shoulders, his tanned thumbs caressing momentarily the creamy skin exposed by the scoop-neck. Then he spun her around. "Get a wrap," he advised her, his tone now businesslike. "It's going to be chilly tonight."

Floating in a soft pink cloud of dreamy illusion, Liza took Scott's arm as he led her to his waiting car.

The dreamy quality was continued with the ballet. Sitting just a few rows behind the orchestra, Liza felt she was almost a part of the elegant dancers. She was that close.

Always careful with her money, Liza had never allowed herself orchestra seats. Instead she had eagerly leaned forward from a balcony seat, hoping to get the very best view for her money. Yet if she could have watched, she would have seen herself still in her characteristic pose, leaning forward even now to bring herself closer, closer to the experience on the stage. Often her body swayed rhythmically with the smooth strains of the music.

"That was marvelous," Liza enthusiastically declared as they joined the crowd to leave the theater. "Just marvelous."

Scott smiled at her without speaking for a long, heart-stopping moment. "I don't believe I've ever been with anyone who appreciated and enjoyed ballet the way you just did. It was something just to watch you," he revealed. "You were so wrapped up in it that you were almost a part of it yourself."

"You—you watched me?" And she realized that she had been so entranced by the performance she hadn't even noticed.

"Not all the time," Scott chided. "After all I did come to see the ballet. And I did see it. But you were a captivating sight too," he observed with an appreciative glint in his eye.

Liza pulled her black shawl tightly around herself. She straightened her spine and lifted her chin as they walked out of the theater doors and toward the parking garage. Scott watched her show of dignity with an amused twinkle in his eye.

He took her to the top of the John Hancock Center, to the cocktail lounge there. They settled confortably at a small table by the window. The city lights sparkled beneath them like a fairyland. The dark room and sophisticated atmosphere contributed to the sense of unreality.

"It's almost like we're floating up here," Liza commented as she surveyed the view. "As though we're not really in a building at all, but instead we're all in a highly structured cloud."

"Liza Manchester, you've got a delightful imagination," Scott remarked.

Liza shifted her weight uncomfortably in her chair, but had no time to respond before the waitress came for their order.

"What would you like?" Scott smoothly inquired.

Liza shrugged uncomfortably. She couldn't think of anything she wanted. And she drank so little alcohol that she hadn't any idea what would be the proper thing to order.

"Bristol Cream on the rocks with a twist for the lady," Scott told the waitress. He watched Liza for a sign of approval.

She nooded in agreement, relieved to have him make the choice.

"Scotch on the rocks. Chivas," Scott told the waitress, who then disappeared.

As Liza watched her go, she had a moment of complete panic. What in the world would they talk about now? She had never been good at making small talk. And she felt sure Scott expected her at least to hold up her end of the conversation. Monica would, she told herself unhappily. A desolate wave of misery washed over her. She felt she would drown in it when Scott spoke.

"Did you take ballet lessons when you were a girl?" he asked.

"Only for a year," Liza answered, almost wistfully. She felt some old pain surface, and she hurried to push it back.

"You move gracefully, as though you had a well trained body. A dancer's body."

It was a compliment, a very large compliment. And Liza knew it. She was ridiculously glad Scott had noticed, noticed what she had learned even as a nine year old, a thing she had learned so well that she carried it with her to stand and walk with pride and grace and dignity.

"Now, class," Madame Aubert would say in her musical, French-accented English, "your body, it is a most marvelous creation. Stand straight. Stand proudly. Carry yourself well."

And Madame Aubert, well over fifty, and firm and lovely still, would stand before the ballet class clad in her leotard and tights and demonstrate proud bearing. "You owe it to all the generations of your ancestors, right back to the beginning of time," she preached.

Liza had learned from Madame, and learned well.

"Why did you only take lessons for a year?" Scott probed, bringing Liza back to the present from her fond memories of Madame Aubert's ballet class.

"Why?" Liza asked. "What do you mean?" She was annoyed by his intrusion into her past. He certainly didn't belong there. Yet she could think of no earthly reason not to answer his question. Instead she stalled.

But Scott would not be put off. "Why did you stop taking dancing lessons? You seem such a natural for them."

"My grandfather died," Liza bluntly responded, as though that were explanation enough. When she said it, the familiar ache started again.

The waitress came, carefully setting their drinks in front of them. Scott took a quick sip of his Scotch, but seemed more interested in Liza than in his drink. His full attention was focused on her.

"Why would your grandfather's death keep you from taking ballet lessons?" he queried.

"I guess it does sound strange," Liza admitted, a small, sad smile coming to her lips. She took a leisurely sip of her drink. "It's good," she pronounced, nodding at the glass in front of her. "I've never had sherry on the rocks before. And the lemon-twist is a nice touch."

Scott frowned. "I don't need a psychology degree to tell you're trying to avoid the subject of your grandfather and dancing lessons, now do I?" His expression was teasing, but there was an understanding there too, and a kind of sympathy.

"Once you suggested that I was an emotional coward," Liza reminded him.

He nodded.

"Well, you were right," she blithely admitted. "I am."

"Okay," he laughed bitterly, "I guess I asked for that. But I must say I haven't seen many people as honest as you are." He waited patiently, not rushing her. As he expected, she finally opened up.

"My mother and I lived with my grandfather," Liza began slowly. "My father died when I was very young. My grandfather was a widower. And retired. He was wonderful to me." Liza smiled a bittersweet smile, a smile that was both beautiful and vaguely tragic. "I suppose he spoiled me. But whatever he did, I adored him. When I was eight or nine, he insisted that no young lady grew up with any grace at all if she didn't have ballet. My mother was too busy for such silliness."

Liza realized she was getting into more detail about her early life than she usually liked to do. But for the first time in a long time she felt free to talk about herself. And, strangely, she felt Scott cared.

"Grandfather started me in ballet. He took me to the lessons every Tuesday and Thursday after school. We took the bus downtown for a year, maybe a little more. And to me it was a magical year." Her eyes glowed warmly with the happy memories. "Madame Aubert, the teacher, was like a fairy godmother to me, opening whole new worlds. I adored her. Then my grandfather died. He just fell over in his garden one afternoon. A heart attack. My mother had no time to take me to ballet class. And she said we had no money, because when Grandpa died we didn't get his pension, only his house. So that was that. The ballet was over.''

Liza smiled grimly. She studied her drink, carefully focused on it, knowing only that she couldn't, wouldn't, mustn't look at Scott. She was too close to tears. Sympathy from him might make her cry. She couldn't remember when she had cried last, and certainly never in public.

In the car on the way home, Liza wondered if Scott would try to kiss her good night. He had kissed her earlier, stirring up emotions that had been dormant within her. What would happen if he tried that again so soon? She hardly had time to put up her armor against him. In fact, it was worse than that. Their chatter had been friendly all evening. She talked easily and felt more comfortable than she ever had with anyone else, except maybe for her grandfather years ago. It made it even harder to put up her defenses against him.

He smoothly opened all the doors for her. She did have to admit that he could make her feel marvelously special in the process. Her reaction sobered her. Was she being sold the same bill of goods that had kept women in bondage for generations? She decided she would consider the question. Later.

At her doorway he didn't try to kiss her. He only took her hand and held it in his own for a moment.

"It—it was lovely. Thank you," Liza choked out. She was filled with unreasoning tension. It took all her courage to look up at him. But desperately she wanted to see his face. She wanted to see if it betrayed any emotion about her, any emotion at all.

It didn't. It was an unrevealing mask. He merely looked at her for a long moment, studied her regular features with a quiet and approving satisfaction. Then he simply squeezed her hand lightly, and was gone.

As she stood in the hall and watched him disappear

behind the sliding doors of the elevator, Liza thought her heart would break. She felt she was losing him forever, and an incredible pain welled up within her.

"Oh, no," she protested in a hoarse whisper. Then she escaped to the refuge of her apartment, firmly closing the door behind her.

Scott frowned deeply as he rode down in the elevator. And when the doors opened on the first floor, he didn't get out right away. Instead he stood still, lost in thought.

Finally, he muttered an oath and strode angrily out the elevator doors. He cursed himself because he had not kissed Liza. But it had taken a supreme act of will not to. He had to prove to himself that she had no control over him.

Scott had always been in perfect control of his own reactions where women were concerned. The women he dated were sophisticated, knowledgeable, and generally easy to forget. They were almost always rich, well educated, and beautiful. They lived by and understood the social and ethical mores of the rich and famous. They were smooth, polished, and full of easy, polite phrases. They all fitted into a pattern, a pattern that neatly fitted into his life.

Liza, on the other hand, spoke her mind and let the cards fall where they might. She was bright but not highly educated, kind but not filled with phony politeness. And she didn't fit into any mold or pattern Scott knew. None at all.

He simply would not allow her to affect him in any unusual way. He wouldn't allow it at all.

Professor Wainright called Liza into his office. There were two reasons why she was sure it was about the editorial assistant position. First, he had been late in making the decision and, as a result, had largely avoided Liza the last week or so. And second, he had the puffed up air of authority that he always assumed when he had an announcement to make.

She settled herself comfortably in the big wing chair across from his desk. Automatically she tugged the hem of her tailored skirt lower on her leg.

"As you are no doubt well aware, the decision I have had to make about the editorial assistant's position is somewhat overdue." He cleared his throat and fiddled uncomfortably with some papers on his desk for a few seconds, avoiding looking at Liza.

It was her first clue that the coveted position might not be hers. Her body tensed. Her breaths grew shallow. She clutched her hands tightly in her lap while she nervously waited for more.

"It has been a most difficult decision for me to make," he revealed with a self-indulgent sigh, "really most difficult. You've done an admirable job. Really quite admirable. But..." he paused, and his features feigned a compassionate look that froze Liza inside. Wainright shrugged apologetically.

"But what?" Liza demanded frostily. Her somber gray eyes bore into his, issuing a challenge.

He smiled briefly and took his time. His whole manner was that of superior to underling, king to peasant. Liza was sure he was trying to make her squirm. She was just as certain that he would never do it. She stubbornly lifted her chin and straightened in her chair. She would be ready for whatever he said, and for whatever manner he used.

"My dear," he purred with seductive gentleness, "we both know you don't have the necessary job qualifications," he advised her. "A truly prestigious journal demands an editorial assistant with a college degree. And while you have done a marvelous, perfectly marvelous, job, you wouldn't want the journal itself to suffer because of your educational lacks, now would you?"

How clever he was, Liza angrily thought. No matter how she answered the question, the answer would be wrong. She decided not to answer it at all. Instead she countered with her own statement and question. "Months ago when I started doing the work, you offered me this chance for advancement. At the time *I* pointed out that most journals had degreed workers. You," she accused, her eyes narrowing, "countered by listing half a dozen well known journals that have non-degreed staffs. 'The job qualifications wouldn't be a problem,'" she quoted him, her voice tinged with sarcasm.

"Oh, my dear, I know this is a blow to you. And I'd had no idea things would work out this way," he solicitously replied. "You see, I alone do not make the choice. The editorial board is the decision-making body. They are set on having a person with a degree. I really have very little to say about it except thank you. You helped in an emergency, took over, and did a superb job. Absolutely superb. I don't know what I would have done without you. I truly don't."

"You'll find out soon," Liza warned.

"Oh, I do hope not," Wainright replied immediately. "I hope an increase in rank and higher pay will induce you to stay on as my secretary. I've gone through quite a lot of trouble to pull strings in personnel. And you won't have to wait a year for your first vacation. You'll be eligible after only six months."

"I see," Liza returned icily. She scolded herself for not feeling more appreciative. She grudgingly admitted Wainright had done what he could for her. She told herself she should be grateful.

"You will also be able to complete your degree with greatly reduced tuition," he added. "Soon you'll genuinely qualify for an editorial position. In the meantime you'll get valuable experience working here, assisting the new editorial assistant."

Professor Wainright smiled with satisfaction. He was proud of the neat piece of work he had done to keep Liza happily in his employ, despite her predictable disappointment.

"And who will be the new editorial assistant?" Liza queried.

"Ah, my dear. In that we've been very lucky. There is someone right here, someone who could easily slip into the position, someone who has all the proper qualifications. I'm sure you'll be as pleased as I am that Angela has accepted the position."

"Angela?"

Liza was dumbfounded. The temporary secretary was barely adequate to do the tasks Liza had passed on to her. And she'd never thought it was because Angela was overqualified for the job.

"Angela's degree is in physical education. She is an out-of-work gym teacher," Liza countered, hardly believing it was possible that the inefficient blonde could be considered seriously for *any* position.

"She can rightfully put B.S. after her name," Wainright said solicitously. "You can't."

Liza had no answer for that.

After a moment, during which he let her get used to the idea of Angela getting the job she had wanted, Wainright spoke again.

"You'll be an absolutely invaluable help to her," he confidently predicted. "It is crucial for her to learn exactly how things are done. And to have your help on a continuing basis. See how important you are, my dear?"

The last was a soothing balm over her hurt. She was valuable, important, needed, despite her disappointment.

"I see," Liza choked out. Then she stiffly rose and left Wainright's office to go back to her own. She felt numb with shock and wanted only to be left alone.

Jeffrey was waiting for Liza when she got back to

her office. Impatiently he glanced at his watch. He frowned.

"It's four forty," he told her.

"I'm sorry, Jeffrey," Liza automatically apologized. "It's been a hard afternoon."

"We have to hurry if we're going to make the plane."

"The plane?" Liza parroted dully.

"To St. Louis. You did decide you'd come with me, didn't you?" Jeffrey demanded.

"No. No. I'm sorry. I didn't decide," Liza told him. And she realized that she hadn't even thought about Jeffrey Childers or his proposition for days.

"Then decide now," Jeffrey insisted. "There's still time."

"I can't," Liza grimly concluded. Her face was ashen, her eyes dull.

"You can't decide or you can't come?" Jeffrey probed.

"Both," Liza finally concluded. Her voice held neither enthusiasm nor conviction. She wished only for Jeffrey to go away, disappear, evaporate, so that she could be alone.

Her strained manner finally registered on Jeffrey's consciousness. "Are you all right?" he asked.

Liza looked up, somewhat surprised by his uncharacteristic concern. "No. No, I'm not." Liza promptly replied.

"Can I do anything?" Jeffrey offered.

Liza thought she detected a note of reluctance in his voice. But she was pleased by his offer.

"No, I don't think you can help. But thanks for the offer," Liza answered, convinced in that moment that she wouldn't ever bring any problems to Jeffrey to talk over. She just didn't feel that close to him. And if she didn't feel that close to him, how could she even think about an affair with him?

Jeffrey could hardly conceal his relief when he

learned she would not take up his valuable time. "We'll talk when I return," Jeffrey promised, patting her shoulder reassuringly and giving her a quick, almost brotherly kiss.

When he finally left, Liza slumped into her chair to wait out the endless fifteen minutes until five o'clock, until she could close the office.

Liza was compulsively straightening pencils when Scott casually sauntered into the office. He stopped short when he saw her. His usually smooth tanned brow knitted into worried lines. His broad mouth turned down in a frown.

"What's the matter?" His voice was soft, concerned, but the question was a demand.

Liza bit her lip hard to keep the tears that shimmered in her eyes from rushing down her cheeks. She had been composed ever since the horrible news, composed and contained until Scott appeared. Then all the emotions of the day welled up in her at once and she could hardly control herself any more. She stared up at him, silently pleading not to be questioned further.

He studied her for a long moment. Then he asked, "Is Wainright in his office?"

Liza mutely nodded yes.

"Don't leave till I get back," he curtly ordered, striding purposefully to Wainright's office door.

Liza looked at the clock. Four fifty-seven. "I'm leaving in three minutes," she choked out, determined not to stay one minute longer than necessary.

Many secretaries would have left early after receiving bad news like Liza's. But Liza stubbornly would do nothing less than her job, despite her personal feelings.

"I'll be back," he promised.

And he was.

Scott was grim-faced, even though he himself felt somewhat relieved at what he had learned from Wainright. Instead of enjoying his own, partial good news, he focused all his attention on Liza's needs.

"Come on," he gently ordered, grasping her hand to pull her out of her old wooden swivel chair. "We're getting out of here."

Liza didn't even check the clock. She just gathered up her purse and gratefully followed him.

As they got into their seats for a breath-stopping ride on the American Eagle roller coaster, Liza glanced quickly at Scott. Her eyes were bright, her cheeks glowing with excitement.

"You're trying to cheer me up with all this craziness, aren't you?"

Beneath them the bright lights sparkled in the velvet dark of the night. The carnival atmosphere of the Great America theme park was an enchanted fairyland.

"Very perceptive," he agreed with a teasing smile. "And you don't even have a degree in psychology."

Liza giggled her pleasure. She felt like a carefree teenager in love for the first time. Everything about Scott seemed magic at that moment.

His face was suddenly incredibly precious. Each plane, each individual feature so etched itself on her heart that she knew it would be there forever. His deep-blue eyes glowed with a caring warmth, but now she sensed more, too. There was a primitive force that she had never seen before.

Liza's pulse raced and her breath caught in her throat just before the giant attraction lurched and sent them spinning wildly through space. Her body, her mind, her heart itself, were consumed with dizzying emotions. At times she felt she would burst with the joy of it all.

By the time they left the theme park Liza felt delightfully happy and mellow. They strolled hand in hand with the last of the late night visitors over the acres of nearly barren parking lot. She contentedly breathed the soft summer night air as they made their way to Scott's waiting Mercedes. But as they neared the city, the pain of losing her coveted promotion that afternoon came back to her in a rush. And even the shared joy of the evening could not chase it away.

She said nothing to him but he immediately picked up the change in her.

"I gather you're coming back down to earth," Scott gently said when they had been driving in the car for nearly an hour.

A tear slowly slid down Liza's cheek.

Scott said nothing more. He merely reached across the seat to take her smaller, strangely cold hand into his.

Liza liked the lightly calloused touch of his big, comforting hand. And she wept silently but without shame as they drove the last few miles to her apartment.

"Where's your teapot?" Scott called to Liza as she retreated to the sanctuary of her bathroom to wash her tearstained face.

"In the cupboard over the stove," she returned.

"And the tea?"

"In the canister on the counter. It's marked 'tea.'"

When Liza finally emerged, her face washed and her hair freshly brushed, two steaming mugs of tea waited on the antique cobbler's bench she used as a living room coffee table.

"I don't want to talk about it," Liza bleakly warned as she sat down next to Scott on the sofa. "It always takes me a while to work things through. The reality should hit me tomorrow night or so. Right now I'm mercifully numb."

As though he had been doing it for years, Scott wrapped his powerful arm around Liza's shoulders and cradled her against his massive chest. "You don't have to talk," he assured her, then he kissed her on the top of her head, his lips nuzzling gently her silken hair.

Tears flowed again. Tears of frustration, futility, and defeat. Scott gave her his handkerchief. She wiped her eyes and blew her nose, then sipped her tea. The cup was burning hot against her lips. The scalding sensation was momentarily distracting and Liza was grateful.

Scott stayed until Liza was cried out and calm, though neither one of them had said a word.

"Th-thank you," she finally whispered, half apologetically as she handed him his now damp handkerchief.

"It was my pleasure," he softly replied. His deep voice soothed her.

With a tanned finger he tilted her somber face to his. Slowly his firm lips descended to hers while his big hands softly caressed her shoulders.

His kiss was light and undemanding, yet Liza could feel a surge of energy and warmth flow from him to her. With it she felt the beginning of the renewal of her own strength.

He kissed her for a long time. Liza leaned toward him fractionally, and he pulled her to him in what she sensed would develop into a crushing kiss. Yet he checked himself and pulled back.

"I'll talk to you tomorrow," he hoarsely promised before he turned to go.

For a long time Liza stared at the door that had closed behind him. Her thoughts were a heady jumble of elation and despair.

The doorbell rang. In the fog of her sleepiness, Liza first ignored it. Insistently the buzzer sounded again.

With a leaden arm Liza pushed back the covers. She inched her feet to the floor and slowly rolled to a sitting position. Her eyes were still half-closed, her hair cas-

cading around her shoulders in pleasant disarray, and
her face looked puzzled, uncomprehending.

Again the buzzer blared.

"I'm coming, I'm coming," Liza complained, blinking her eyes to unsuccessfully bring them to focus. "Why do I have such an early-bird friend?" she muttered to herself as she wearily trudged to the bell. It had to be Valerie.

Without bothering to call down over the intercom, she pressed the button. She didn't even take the time to get a robe to cover her revealing nightgown or to put slippers on her bare feet. Sleep still fogged her sight, and it took her a moment to realize that it was not Valerie who came through the door she finally opened. It was a tall, broad, and muscular man. It was Scott.

Chapter Five

Battered jeans rested low on Scott's slim hips. He wore a navy T-shirt that revealed the rippling muscles of his broad chest. Slung over his shoulder was a navy Windbreaker. Worn deck shoes covered his feet.

The sight of him only intensified Liza's sleepy haze. It was as though he were a living part of her dream. There was a sensual aura that surrounded him and seemed to overwhelm her with a flood of heady sensation.

He was more virile, sexier even, than he had been in his formal suits. And in her half-awake state, Liza was particularly vulnerable. Her breathing grew shallow. Her heartbeat speeded up dangerously. She stared at him, bewildered.

His husky voice drifted through the hazy void to her sleepy head. His words were smooth, like silk, enveloping her, caressing her.

"You're charming, absolutely charming."

She stood motionless, waiting to puzzle the situation out, waiting in a fog of sleep and sensation to understand.

He inspected her from the tips of her bare toes, as they dug snugly into the thick carpet, to the top of her disheveled head. He studied her trim legs. They disappeared beneath the knee-length pink gown she wore. Its delicate fabric betrayed the outlines of her hips and breasts beneath. His eyes glowed brightly as he focused on the rosy tips just visible beneath the film of pink.

As though in a hazy, romantic dream Liza found herself lightly leaning against Scott. His face came in and then went out of focus as his lips lowered slowly to hers. She felt the hardness of his muscular chest as her breasts sensuously moved against him.

A deep, primitive, anguished groan escaped from his throat. His powerful arms gathered her close, then crushed her to him. He held her as though he never wanted to let her go. And she gloried in the surges of pleasure that pulsed through her body as he buried his face in her neck, then wildly trailed kisses beneath her ear and across her cheek, finally claiming her lips with a fierce intensity that left her gasping.

A surge of hot emotion traveled through Liza. She felt her nipples harden as her breath left her body. A delightful tingling spread over every inch of her skin, while a stirring deep within her sent tongues of searing flame through her whole being.

She was still half-asleep. And his kisses drove her into a sensuous trance. Her body was nothing but glorious feeling. But somehow her brain flashed a warning. Then the realization of his power over her sobered her. Her senses were reeling and her body felt as though it were made of lead as she slowly inched away from him.

"I'm getting dressed," she announced, her voice shaky with emotion. She dazedly stumbled to the bedroom. She closed the door and leaned against it until her heartbeat returned closer to normal.

"Wear jeans," he huskily called through the closed door. "And rubber-soled shoes." Seconds later he added, "Bring a jacket."

It was all she could do to follow directions. Mechanically Liza stumbled around her room gathering her clothes.

"Ready?" he asked, as she emerged wearing jeans, a

pink oxford cloth button-down shirt, and her running shoes. Her hair was more carelessly pulled back than usual.

"Where's your jacket?" he demanded as he inspected her.

"Why do I need a jacket?" she asked, in a complaining tone, "It's not cold."

"Don't argue," Scott counseled. "Get a jacket."

She groaned, but turned back to her bedroom for her jacket.

"Where are we going?" she asked through a yawn as he pulled the white Mercedes into traffic.

"Sailing," he revealed. "It's a ride yet. You can sleep until we get to the harbor."

"I will," Liza agreed immediately. And she closed her eyes and fell back to sleep, grateful that she could. She wasn't sure whether she was still sleepy or whether she merely needed to escape Scott's overwhelmingly sexual presence. The feelings he stirred in her were new and too powerful to deal with so early in the morning.

Scott chuckled in amusement as his eyes lightly caressed her sleeping face.

The water sparkled as though a thousand diamonds floated upon it. The sky was cloudless and incredibly blue. Scott's thirty-five foot ketch swiftly cut through the small blue waves that splashed against the hull. The sail loomed above them, a huge, billowing white sheet that swelled with wind. The Chicago skyline stretched along the western horizon, displaying its dramatic skyscrapers to perfection on the clear, sunny day. To the east was open lake, a vast, undulating body of water that rolled to the Michigan shore.

Liza's hair broke loose from its pins and long blond wisps waywardly blew in the breeze. She took a deep breath of the fresh air and sighed her appreciation. She lay on the long canvas cushion which lined the seat of the cockpit. She was glad she had her jacket. Even on a hot summer morning the wind was chilling.

"You finally awake?" Scott teased, the tiny lines at the corners of his eyes emphasizing the twinkling, deep blue. He looked as carefree as a young boy, and Liza's heart stopped as she watched him, while the wind whipped at his hair and plastered his navy jacket against his broad chest.

"Nobody could sleep with the wind blowing like mad and the sun shining so hard you could probably see it if you closed your eyes," Liza answered dryly, hoping to hide how deeply the sight of him was affecting her.

Scott laughed. It was a deep, hearty, happy laugh.

He was comfortable with her. He liked her. She sensed that from the gentle way he had cared for her last night. And she could hear it in his conversation. At the very least they were friends. She hugged herself in satisfaction and pushed away disturbing thoughts of Monica Grant or any other woman who might make a claim on him.

"Cold?" Scott asked as he watched her crossed arms clutched across her breasts.

Liza shook her head. "Just happy." And she realized she was hugging herself in her joy.

"There's makings for coffee in the galley," Scott suggested. "And things to munch on for breakfast."

"Are you hungry?" Liza asked him as she lazily stretched to rouse herself from her relaxed state. She stretched as gracefully as a cat. Scott watched her with appreciation, a little surprised by his own quick reactions to the sight of her. Sometimes all it took was a toss of her head or a provocative twist of her body to arouse him. It was the little things about her, the things that were unique to Liza, that affected him. Her eyes flashing defiantly. The proud tilt of her chin. Her rich, infectious laugh.

"No, I'm not hungry," he quickly answered, shaking his head and smiling at her. "I ate a big breakfast. It's my favorite meal. I never leave home without it. But I wouldn't mind a cup of coffee."

"You eat? In the morning?" Liza grimaced. She wrinkled up her nose to show her disapproval. "Why would anybody do that?" she indignantly asked.

"Not everyone is like you in the morning," he teased. "Despite the fact that your delectable body is incredibly sexy draped in pink wisps, you still look a little like a furry animal just coming out of hibernation, a baby bear who hasn't quite figured out that it's spring yet."

"Do I?" Liza giggled, ignoring his reference to her body and concentrating on the last part of his comment. "I guess that's pretty much how I feel. And I'm practically incapable of making any big decisions before noon," she volunteered.

"I'll remember that," he promised with a meaningfully raised eyebrow.

Liza regarded him suspiciously. As often happened the sexual undertones to his words were obvious. And they filled her body with a delightful warmth that left her strangely weak.

"Can you make coffee at this hour?" he asked, glancing at his watch. "It is after eight."

"That's about all I can do," Liza called over her shoulder as she climbed down the ladder and into the cabin.

The galley was in the prow of the boat, past the two bunks which were built with highly-polished mahogany and brass fittings. The tiny, superbly equipped kitchen area was also fashioned of mahogany, with brass pulls and stainless steel fixtures.

An automatic drip coffeepot sat on the open counter in a clear plastic housing, gimballed to keep it from sliding with the motion of the boat.

Liza filled the top part with tap water. After a quick search through the cupboards, she found the coffee and filled the drip basket. Then, while the machine sizzled a bit, then dripped, she investigated the cabin. She rubbed her fingers lovingly over the smooth, satiny wooden surfaces. Polished mahogany drawers and panels hid neat compartments for stowing all the gear needed for a long voyage.

When the coffee was ready, Liza brought it up to Scott.

"I tasted it, it's all right," she quickly promised as she passed him the hot, steaming mug. "I hope you like it black."

"I do," he affirmed as he took the mug in his hand.

They were silent for the better part of an hour, just enjoying the sun and the water and the occasional gull that swooped overhead. Liza again stretched out on the long, padded seat of the cockpit and let her mind wander to all manner of pleasant things. The ballet. Her grandfather's rose garden. Fireworks on the Fourth of July. Snow at Christmas.

Occasionally she could feel Scott's eyes upon her, watching her, following the curves of her body, studying the delicate planes of her face.

It was a pleasant feeling, and enticingly intimate. There was a bond between them in those moments, a closeness that Liza had never known before, not even after she had been dating a man for a long time.

Occasionally the thought came into her mind that this was all part of Scott's experiment. That he wouldn't have had anything to do with her if he wasn't trying to prove a point. But Liza resolutely kept pushing those painful thoughts to the back of her mind, just as she had always thrust her hurt feelings away and concentrated on the business at hand. It was particularly easy for her to do on this sun-drenched day on the lake.

"Did you get this boat from the royalties on your

book?'' Liza asked, her tone musing. She was lazily contented and thoroughly warmed from the bright sun.

"No," Scott answered, his voice suddenly guarded, as though he were uncomfortable with the subject. But he did answer her question.

"I've always had a boat, ever since I was a teenager," he revealed. "I learned to sail in Michigan. My family always summered at my grandparents' house." He pointed to the Eastern horizon. "It's a wonderful house. Just about there."

Along the far distant shoreline Liza could not even see the faintest tracings of the green of trees. But she knew they were there, east across the swelling waves.

Liza lazily repeated the word. "Summered. You must have a rich family."

"Just because I had a boat?" Scott asked, a bit irritably. His annoyed tone surprised Liza. She knew she had hit one of his raw nerves, even though she wasn't sure what it was. "Lots of middle class people have boats."

"It's not the boat," Liza protested. "It's the word, 'summered.' Rich people 'summer.' Middle class people 'vacation.' That's semantics. I got a smattering in a course I took once," she easily explained.

She kept her voice purposefully casual and her eyes focused on the horizon rather than looking at him. Yet she sensed a disturbed look on his face.

"Do you prefer rich men?" he asked. The discomfort was now evident in his voice, as was the control he exercised to try to hide it.

Liza shrugged. "How would I know? I never knew any before."

And with that she closed off the conversation by closing her eyes and settling herself into a feigned sleep. But she was disturbed, deeply disturbed. Scott seemed defensive about his money, and even his background. Had that money brought him problems? Maybe even woman problems?

Liza couldn't imagine a woman caring whether Scott was rich or poor. She was still thinking about that when her body, weary from its almost sleepless night, finally took over. Liza slept.

"Hey, I thought you said nobody could sleep with the wind and the sun like it is," Scott complained. His irate voice broke into Liza's dreamlike trance. She slowly opened one eye, turned her head slightly, opened the other and blinked her eyes until she focused on him.

"I was wrong," she easily admitted. For she had slept, and slept soundly. And she had no idea for how long.

"It's lunchtime," Scott announced. "Why don't you fix something to eat?" He sounded even more impatient than he had earlier when they were discussing his boat.

Liza just lay still for a moment, waiting to wake up a bit before she made any drastic movements. She felt delightfully lazy and didn't want to disturb herself unduly.

"I'm hungry," Scott's plea interrupted her reverie.

"You're bossy," Liza protested without moving an inch. She still lay in the sun, perversely enjoying the fact that her inactivity was making Scott angry.

She tried to hide the little smile that appeared on her lips. And she closed her eyes, so as to keep him from seeing the twinkling lights in them. She was enjoying this, the first upset she had ever noticed Scott have. He was usually so calm, so in control. And he was upset now about his lunch, or lack of it, of all things.

Liza could call him insensitive or authoritative or any other high sounding, critical name, and he could hold his cool with perfect aplomb. But to have his lunch late? It seemed to upset the elemental man.

"All right, so I'm bossy," Scott gruffly admitted. "Now will you get me some food?"

"You didn't ask me if I was hungry," Liza petulantly revealed. "And I thought you were supposed to be pleasing me, catering to me. Not ordering me around. How in the world are you going to succeed in this experiment, as you call it, if you order me around?"

"I didn't order you," Scott quickly protested. "I asked you to fix something."

Liza turned to him, her eyes wide. "But what if I don't want to?" she complained. "Why is it always assumed that the woman should do the cooking? You are a capable human being and, in point of fact, the host on this expedition. Why don't you cook?"

"Damn it, woman, I'm steering the boat. Do you know how to do that? Can you tack into the wind? I'll give you the wheel if you think you can. Then I'll cook. Otherwise, get below. I'm starved."

Scott took a deep breath. She watched his already mighty chest expand, pulling his knit shirt taut. Then he let out an impatient sigh that made Liza giggle softly.

"Look," he explained with savage precision, "I don't give a damn about any social commentary now. I'm hungry. Now what do I have to do to get some food?"

"Just say please," Liza loftily informed him.

"Please, Liza, could you fix me—no, fix us both some lunch?"

"I'd be delighted to do exactly that," she pertly replied. Then she pulled herself up from her reclining position and for the second time that day she made her way into the sanctuary of the cabin.

Liza hummed to herself as she worked in the efficiently designed galley. She loved to cook, and enjoyed taking plain fare and dressing it up, presenting it beautifully. The soup and sandwiches she brought up on deck were carefully prepared, and even garnished attractively.

"I didn't realize anything this good could come out of that little galley," Scott appreciatively offered, after he had eaten more than half of his lunch. "All I've ever been able to do is open a can."

"You had a rather nice assortment of cans to choose from," Liza told him, returning the compliment. "It just took knowing which ones and how to combine them."

She had heated mushroom soup, adding just a hint of sherry, which she found in the liquor cabinet. The canned ham she had cut into paper thin slices. Then she had spread a generous layer of carefully seasoned chicken salad over the ham and carefully rolled it up. She had also made sandwiches of hearty cheese spread with olive butter.

"So, you like to cook," Scott appreciatively commented. "I would never have guessed it. I've always pictured ardent feminists as practically allergic to all forms of domestic arts."

"For shame, Dr. Harburton," Liza gently scolded. "You should know enough about human nature to know not to catalog people. Each individual has his or her own very unique characteristics."

Scott frowned. Somehow it made his dimple appear briefly. His deeply tanned brow furrowed slightly, and he looked very much the average man, confused beyond reason by a woman's thinking.

"Well, I still say most feminists don't like to cook," Scott persisted as he appreciatively finished the last of a sandwich.

"How many do you know well?" Liza challenged. "How many have you gone out with? Or even dated regularly?"

"Not many," he admitted ruefully as he began eating a ham roll.

"Why not?" Liza demanded, her brows raised in censure. "Feminists are every bit as attractive and available and as datable as any other woman. Why do you avoid them?"

"I don't purposefully want to avoid them," Scott protested. "I just don't seem to want to date them."

"And why not?" Liza persisted. "Do they injure your male pride? Your sensitive ego? Do they disturb your equilibrium as they tell you they are your equals in every way?"

"They're not my equals in every way," Scott testily returned. "I wish people would begin to get that straight. For one thing, I have yet to meet a woman who is as strong as I am, or as strong as most men, for that matter. Men's bodies are equipped to do different tasks. And on the other hand," he continued, seeming to enjoy his chance to spout his opinion, "I have yet to see a man who could have a baby. Men and women are different, biologically, chemically, emotionally. Science has yet to find the causes for the differences, but let me tell you, they are definitely there."

"So why would that keep you from dating a woman who believed she should be your equal intellectually or under the law? Surely you don't object to that. Is your ego so delicate you have to keep women down?" Liza challenged.

"Of course my ego isn't that delicate," Scott insisted. "I don't think my ego has anything to do with it. Or at least not that much. What I don't like about the radical feminists that I've met is that they try to prove their own superiority by downgrading men. Every time I've taken a militant feminist to dinner, she has spent the whole time trying to prove how she's better than I am. We don't talk pleasantly, we don't enjoy each other's company. No. Instead she has to prove something. She has to prove her superiority. If I can manage to avoid a woman like that, I do."

"But then why did you start this whole silly 'experiment' with me?" she asked thoughtfully as she finished the last of her cheese sandwich. "You're stuck with a feminist now, whether you like it or not. And I'm some kind of a guinea pig. We're both in bad positions. What, Doctor, are you trying to prove?"

He frowned and rubbed his chin. Then his deep-blue eyes roamed her figure as though it were his right. And though she was clad in jeans and a shirt, Liza felt she was being mentally undressed by him.

"It was your legs that started all this," he began slowly.

"My legs?" she asked, incredulous, glancing down with disbelief at her jean-covered limbs. "What could my legs have to do with your proposition that women truly like to be smothered with outdated courtesies?"

"Your legs, and the delectable curve of your hip. Your whole body," he went on, paying no attention to Liza's question. His eyes still lingered on her figure.

Liza squirmed uncomfortably. "So you look at me as a sex object," she caustically concluded.

"I sure do," Scott agreed wholeheartedly. "I look at most women that way, for openers. Sometimes that develops into something, sometimes it doesn't. But it's a good start."

"At least you're honest," Liza commented dryly.

"There's more," Scott ventured, and waited for her nod to go on. "You intrigue me. You're a walking paradox. Your face is beautiful and from the chin down you are, to put it bluntly, stacked. You are absolutely voluptuous."

Liza's irritation was evident from the frown on her face. "What does that have to do with women's lib?" she demanded.

"Oh, everything," Scott smoothly answered. "You are the very personification of traditional womanhood. That is, until you open your mouth and spew rigid feminist doctrine or glare frostily at a man. You seem so determined to be judged as a person that you forget that you're also a woman. You just try to push that fact away, as so many other feminists do. And you say you want no part of being treated like a cherished woman. But you have no idea how being cherished feels. Try it, you may like it,'' he speculated hopefully.

The corners of his mouth turned up slightly, and Liza raised her chin haughtily and glared at him. Scott smiled as though he knew a secret that she did not. Then he trained his eyes on the horizon, leaving Liza to her own unsettled thoughts.

Later that afternoon Scott perched Liza next to the wheel of the sleek ketch and showed her how to steer the boat.

''This is fun,'' she enthusiastically reported. She loved the feel of the wind in her hair and the firm pull of the mahogany wheel beneath her hand. She also loved the feel of Scott next to her as he showed her how to steer. When he left her side she had a distant feeling of loss.

Scott stretched out on the cushion where Liza had slept earlier. Hands behind his head he watched her intently as she steered the craft.

''How do you feel about dinner dances to raise money for charity?'' he asked after a long, thoughtful silence.

''You mean the kind you see pictures of on the society pages of the newspaper?'' she asked. ''The kind where women dripping with diamonds hang on to the arms of men in tuxedos while they all sip imported champagne?''

He nodded.

Liza shrugged. ''I don't know. I've never been to one,'' she admitted honestly.

He was quiet again for a long moment. His eyes were trained on the gently rolling waves when he asked the next question. ''What do you know about my family?'' He still didn't look at her.

She frowned thoughtfully before she spoke. Some-

how she sensed that what she was about to say was
terribly important to Scott.

He waited expectantly, his breathing nearly suspended, for her to pronounce what he half suspected
would be an indictment of his family's way of life as
well as his own. He had no idea why the opinions of the
honey-blond woman who sat at the wheel of his boat
meant anything at all to him. She was often an annoy-
ance. She had opinions that countered his, and she
stated them quite clearly. Yet he eagerly awaited her
opinion on him and his way of life in a way which mystified him completely.

"Your family is well connected, influential, rich,"
Liza tentatively began. "They seem to have been so for
several generations, at least, and they show every indi-
cation of staying in the forefront of new developments
in the University, the city, and, for all I know, the na-
tion as a whole."

"I do have a cousin who is a congressman," Scott
offered, not at all sure whether she would be pleased
with the information or more critical because of it.

Liza nodded noncommittally. "That's about all I
know," she concluded.

Scott's eyes narrowed thoughtfully. His brow wrinkled. He had wanted her to say more, and she didn't.
It left him with an unsettled, almost angry feeling. But
then, he thought uncomfortably, Liza was not a
woman to do what he wanted when he wanted her to
do it. She wasn't a woman who was predictable, who
was anxious to find out what he wanted to hear, and
then say it. No. Liza was a very different kind of
woman. A woman who was honest enough to speak
her mind. Somehow the only thing he was sure of now
was that she was not telling him everything she knew
or thought.

"You do know more," he challenged. "You've been
working for my brother-in-law for months now. And

you've had some contact with my sister," he added with a wry smile.

After yesterday's disappointment Liza didn't want to think about Carleton Wainright, not at all. However, that didn't stop her reaction to Madge.

"Your sister. Oh, I almost forgot that Madge is your sister."

It was incredible that she had forgotten, she told herself. But to her Scott stood on his own and had no connection to other people in her experience. Liza frowned solemnly as she inspected Scott's now familiar face. Mischief filled her as though a playful spirit had skipped across the water to the boat and immediately taken up residence in her soul. She almost giggled aloud.

"I must say there are certain similarities between you and Madge," she offered with mock seriousness. "Something about your eyes. The high cheekbones. The inflated ego. The autocratic manner. The regal disdain. And the temperament. I think you have something of the same temperament."

He grunted his displeasure.

The last statement sobered her, for she knew in many ways it was wrong. Madge had a viper's tongue, and Liza had been hurt when it had been used on her. For all his other faults Scott had never been mean or cutting or even unduly angry.

Liza had been baiting Scott and she knew it. For some reason she had liked the idea. But her mood switched again as she watched him shift uncomfortably on the cushion. For a fleeting moment his face displayed his unhappiness before his expression was once again masked by the rigid control he usually used to seal his feelings off from the view of the rest of the world. In that instant Liza was lost. She knew only that she never wanted to see Scott in pain as long as she could prevent it. She quickly changed the thrust of her conversation, now desperately wanting to please him.

"Really, you're nothing like Madge," she offered, hoping to see him relax in response to her statement.

He didn't. Instead he frowned in disgust. His deep-blue eyes stared moodily at the horizon.

"Actually my whole family is much like Madge. Spoiled. Rich. Expecting to lord it over people. I'm that way too," he admitted. Then he let out a long, unhappy sigh.

"You're not," she corrected him vehemently. "You aren't petty and nasty and mean." And as she said the words she knew how true they were. Scott Harburton, for all his faults, was a good man who meant well, a man who valued people rather than used them. She could also see that he didn't view himself that way. That knowledge hurt her, too.

Her feelings left her somewhat confused as to why he needed to use her to prove his thesis. But she was certain that whatever else was going on, her basic sense of him was right.

"I think maybe we've all had too much money too long," he revealed. "It makes us think an awful lot of things are our due, our right. Maybe we're arrogant because there is no other way that people who grow up with all the advantages can be."

"That's nonsense," Liza argued vehemently. She hated to see him downing himself, hated to see the pain it caused him. "You're arrogant. Sure. I think you'd be that way if you didn't have a dime in your pocket and had never heard of the upper crust. It's just you," she explained, hoping to help.

"Thanks," he glumly replied. "You really know how to make a fellow feel good about himself."

Liza's heart sank. Despite all her good intentions it was another one of those open-mouth, insert-foot moments for her.

"The dinner dance tonight is a command performance," he explained, and Liza got the feeling he was explaining more for his own benefit than for hers. "Everyone in the family is expected to be there. It's Mother's favorite charity. Something to do with some disease or other. I don't know if Mother is even sure what it is, even though she is on the board of the organization. It's the sort of time when the whole family turns out to make a good appearance and provide the rest of the assemblage with scintillating conversation."

Liza said nothing, waiting for him to say something more, although she wasn't exactly sure what it would be. "And unless I have a really good excuse for not being there, something like your boss, my esteemed brother-in-law, has arranged by going out of town to a professional conference, I'm sure my mother will give me a lecture about not upholding my part of the family image or some such thing."

The picture of opinionated, assured Scott being lectured to by anyone, much less his mother, was almost incredible to Liza. The lighthearted, mischievous spirit filled her again and she giggled.

"What's so funny?" he demanded irritably.

"You are," she teased. "A big, successful psychology professor who would rather go to a party that is a bore than get a lecture from his mother."

"My mother is an awful lot like Madge," he testily offered in his own defense.

"Oh, dear."

"And these things don't come every week. Only a couple of times a year," he hastily added.

"I see," Liza responded, trying now to be gentle. "And, besides, I'm sure your position in society carries with it its responsibilities," she added. "Noblesse oblige and all that."

"Thanks," he dryly replied. "You're a peach."

Liza grimaced. She realized now that she had managed to hurt him. She had never wanted to do that.

Her emotions traveled up and down like a child on a teeter-totter when she was with Scott. She knew it, but was powerless to do anything about it.

"Maybe it isn't all that easy being rich," she speculated, offering an olive branch for a possible peace.

Scott said nothing, nothing at all. He just watched Liza, watched her for a long, considering time. Then he pointed at the eastern horizon, toward the distant Michigan shore, and gave her an order.

"Keep the boat heading that way," he said. "Keep the wheel steady—pretty much like driving a car. Call me if you're worried or the wind kicks up. I'm going to take a nap."

He closed his eyes and leaned his head back against the cushion. To Liza he looked strangely tired.

"Shouldn't we be heading back?" she uncomfortably suggested as she settled herself next to the helm. She determinedly gripped the unfamiliar wheel and pretended it was indeed a car she was driving, despite the choppy lake surrounding them. "What time is your dinner dance?"

"Have you got a date tonight?" he asked, neither changing position nor opening his eyes.

"No."

"Good. Sail east toward the Michigan shore," he gruffly ordered. "Right now, if you don't mind, I'd like a little rest. Remember, I've had a lot less sleep than you have."

"Aye, aye, Captain," Liza saucily replied.

Scott grunted uncomfortably, but made no other response. In mere minutes his breathing was regular, and Liza thought he was fully asleep.

He wasn't sleeping, though. Not at first. Instead, while his body relaxed, his mind went into high gear. And all his turbulent thoughts centered on Liza. He finally decided that she was refreshingly different from any woman he had known before. When they had an affair, as they surely would, it would be like none other he had known.

With that satisfying thought, he slept.

Chapter Six

Liza felt a delightful pleasure, as though she had been offered a gift, a precious gift to savor, because she could watch Scott as he slept. The worried look had gone from his face after he had rested for a while. And in sleep he looked comfortable, composed, as though he had come to some peace about whatever things were bothering him when he began his long nap.

She studied his face, memorizing each plane, each line. The healthy tan made his features somehow bolder, though she didn't understand how that was possible. His face was strong, his forehead broad, his chin square, his lips firm. She settled her eyes on him for a long moment. It brought back the exquisite sensations that filled her when he kissed her. A delicious thrill crept through her body as she remembered his touch, the pressure of his body against hers, and the hungry seeking of his mouth.

His body was long, lean, and powerful. For all his suave manners and sophisticated background there was much of the elemental man about Scott Harburton. His emotions, his reactions, were primitive and they touched the basic, human, excitingly female responses in Liza. But there was more to her feelings about him than that. She was comfortable with sharing her thoughts with him. As comfortable as if he were her best friend. And she was grateful that he knew instinctively not to bring up the subject of her job loss until Liza herself did. And she also knew that when she did want to speak her mind, he would be a wonderful listener.

She studied Scott so intently and for so long that though she steered the boat toward the gray-green line of trees on the horizon, she was hardly aware of where she was going. She just automatically followed the direction that Scott had given her, enjoying the way the craft cut through the surging waves as the wind carried them on. But when the faint line of trees became very distinct indeed, Liza was suddenly aware that they were nearing shore. She had no idea what to do next.

"Scott," she called, wishing somehow that she did not have to disturb him, but distinctly concerned about where the boat was heading. "Scott," she called more insistently.

He stirred sleepily, but did not open his eyes.

"Scott," she tried again. There was a touch of alarm in her voice this time. "Scott, we're getting close to shore. I don't know what to do."

He opened first one eye, then the other, focusing on her. A slow smile started on his relaxed features. It grew to a welcoming grin.

"Hi," he said huskily. Then he quickly checked the horizon, assessing the position of the boat. "You're doing fine," he assured her. He closed his eyes again.

"I'm doing fine?" Liza questioned, trying to keep the sense of panic and unreality out of her voice. "How could I be doing fine? As far as I can tell the sun is lowering to the horizon behind us, which means we are heading east. That means that shoreline ahead of us is Michigan. And here we are, it's getting later and later and we're nowhere near Chicago. How on earth can you say I'm doing fine?"

He blinked his eyes open and sighed heavily, "When

are you going to relax and trust me?" he asked.
"You've done very well. We're very close to where I
wanted us to be."

She frowned in disgust.

"You're going to be a good sailor."

"That's great. But how about letting me in on the
secret? We are close to where you want to be. But what
about me? I don't even know where we are or what we
are doing."

He reluctantly sat up, swinging his legs off the
cushion and dropping his feet into the cockpit. "I'm
abducting you for the weekend," he explained quite
casually.

After an initial moment of shock, she regarded him
warily. "Abducting me?" she questioned, her eyes narrowing. "You're just casually abducting me without
even talking to me about it? That is absolutely ridiculous. And where, for heaven's sake, are we going?"

He raised his arm and pointed to the horizon just a
little north and east of where they were. "My family's
summer house is just about there. We're on our way
there."

"You can't just take me there," Liza insisted. "I
have some opinion about what I do. You have no right
to just high-handedly whisk me off to parts unknown,
just because the spirit moves you. I should have something to say about it. Why don't you ask me these
things? Why do you insist on telling me afterwards,
after you have your plans made? It shows how insensitive you are to a woman's position. If you considered
me your equal, you'd never try this high-handed stuff.
You would find out what I want instead of telling me
what I am going to do."

Scott took a deep breath and let it out slowly. "I did
do that, didn't I?" he mused. "It's the old arrogance
coming out." His eyes sought hers. They were as deep
and as blue as the lake itself. And they looked squarely

into hers, wanting to conceal nothing, wanting only to have her understand. The look was an apology. And his apology completely disarmed her. All her anger vanished.

"Next time just talk to me before you make a plan, like abduction," she suggested. Then she realized what she had said. He had said something about abduction. What exactly had he meant by that? Again her eyes narrowed and she challenged him. "Just exactly what do you have in mind?"

He moved across the cockpit and took the wheel from her, setting their course slightly to the north.

"My family has this big old house on the lakeshore. It's been our refuge for over thirty years. I spent most of my boyhood summers there. I'd like you to see it."

"What about your party?" Liza asked. "Your mother?"

"You let me worry about my mother and my party, okay?" The wind ruffled his short, dark hair, and he had a contented expression on his face as the boat sped toward shore.

"When—when will we get home?" she questioned as the details of the world and time flooded back to her brain.

"Tomorrow."

"Tomorrow?" Liza parroted in surprise.

He nodded.

"You'll miss your party for sure."

"Right."

She regarded him suspiciously. "We're going to spend the night there?"

"It's much more comfortable than the boat," he explained logically.

Liza could practically feel the wheels of her brain turn as the pieces of the picture fell into place. "Are you planning to sleep with me tonight?" she warily asked.

"Of course," he admitted easily. "I've been planning to sleep with you for a long time now. This is a really wonderful opportunity to leisurely begin an affair," he pointed out casually.

Liza blinked in her astonishment. It was too much like the way Jeffrey had approached her. Too cut-and-dried. And there was no love in his voice. That fact stabbed her cruelly. She felt herself chill to a rigid, icy stiffness. When she spoke her voice was brittle.

"How do you know I want to have an affair with you?" she demanded. "How do you know I'm ready to get that involved?"

"You're ready," he answered with complete assurance. "You've been ready since the first time I kissed you. Your body gives you away. You don't have to say a word."

Instinctively she knew it wasn't she who wasn't ready for lovemaking. It was Scott. She knew without a doubt that he wasn't ready for what she felt for him. Without wanting to put a label on her own feelings she continued her argument, hoping to stave off a confrontation, a confrontation that would be disastrous to her.

"I thought you said this was your family's house. That everyone went there. It seems like a very public way to start an affair," she suggested coolly.

He raised his eyebrows in delight. "Ah, that's why this is the perfect weekend. Everyone, but everyone, is at the big charity affair. No one would think of missing it. So no one could possibly come to the beach house."

Liza's heart sank. "I think we'd better turn the boat around and go back," she stiffly choked out.

Scott eyed her suspiciously. He couldn't imagine what was wrong with her. He'd been predicting women's behavior for years now. He knew when a woman reached a certain pliancy in his arms, when she returned his kisses with a fervent ardor, the way Liza did, that she was ready to go to bed with him. There had never been any problem before. One step had always followed the other the way summer follows spring.

She would come around, he told himself easily. Liza was just obstinate. It took her longer to come to terms with the inevitable. But she would. His blood quickened. She was stubborn but passionate, too. She would be fantastic in bed. He continued to sail toward the shore.

"I want to go back to Chicago," she insisted. "Now."

Scott decided to use logic on her. "Look, it's late. We'll never get back to the city before midnight. If we go to the beach house we can get some steaks out of the freezer and fix up a good dinner. We can relax and have a quiet time of it, and sail home leisurely tomorrow."

"And in the meantime you will overwhelm me with your manly charms," she speculated uneasily.

"Not if you don't want me to," he easily responded. "I won't do anything you don't want me to do."

"Promise?" she asked.

Her question was asked in a childish manner. Liza herself was even aware that her lower lip was stuck out slightly, and her suspicious gray eyes watched him as though he were an untrustworthy adult.

"Promise," he confirmed with a reassuring smile.

It was an easy promise for him to make. He was virtually certain he would be thoroughly enjoying Liza's delectable body before the night was over.

"We'll have to swim for it," he advised her after dropping anchor a safe distance from an untouched stretch of sandy beach. Magnificent dunes rose sharply from the smooth shore, and atop them was a thick growth of dune grass and clusters of deep-green trees.

"I'll sink before we get there," Liza protested. "I'll never swim the distance in my jeans."

"Strip," he suggested, pulling off his own shirt and beginning to unzip his own jeans.

Liza blushed scarlet and abruptly turned the other way.

"I'm wearing a bathing suit," he dryly reported. She felt herself relax.

"I'm not."

"There are some down in the cabin," he informed her somewhat impatiently.

"You keep women's bathing suits on board?" she queried, her eyebrows raised in mild censure.

"You never know when they'll come in handy."

She was about to say something cutting about wondering why he should bother, when he gave her instructions.

"There are several to choose from. In the forward compartment over the port bunk."

She began to go down the short ladder to the efficient cabin.

"You are a good swimmer, aren't you?" he asked, almost as an afterthought. "I could swim to shore and get a dinghy to bring back out here."

"I am an excellent swimmer," she called testily over her shoulder. "A very good swimmer indeed."

Liza easily made it to shore. The only discomfort she knew then was exposing her briefly clad body to Scott's critical gaze. The white bikini she had selected had been the most modest suit available in the cupboard Scott had indicated. At least its concealing triangles were fractionally bigger than those of the other suits.

As she waded out of the water the white fabric clung to her body as though it were a second, nearly invisible skin. Her high, full breasts were barely covered by the flimsy material. And in the cool brush of wind that greeted them as they climbed onto the broad beach,

Liza's nipples hardened, thrusting provocatively against the material.

She struggled to walk in front of him, to avoid his penetrating gaze that sent wild bursts of sensation to the very core of her being. From over her left shoulder she heard him speak.

"It's up there," he told her, indicating the low dune which rose directly from the flat beach.

Liza could see a house surrounded by trees. A huge, white Victorian affair with many gables and a two-story porch that wrapped around three sides.

She didn't know what she had expected. A cottage maybe. Most people who had a place on the beach had a three or four room affair. The house toward which they walked was bigger than most houses she saw in the city.

Liza's feet sank into the soft, warm sand. It squeaked cheerfully as they walked toward the long flight of wooden stairs that trailed up the dune to the house.

"So this is where you summered," she said as they neared the broad front porch. "It looks more like a hotel than a house."

"In some ways it was a hotel," he informed her. "We would have most of the family out here for some part of the summer or other. And everyone had to have a space to sleep. Certain of the rooms were assigned to certain family members. And then there were some that were just set up as dormitories for whomever stopped by. My grandparents very deliberately used this place as a way to keep our big, fairly busy family together. You see, they had six children. And when the children all went their own ways as adults, this place sort of acted as a magnet to draw everyone back together. It was a very smart thing for them to do."

"Your grandparents mustn't have been as bad as I thought," Liza said aloud as she remembered her earlier feelings about the things that Scott might have missed in his privileged growing-up period.

"My grandparents were the best thing that ever happened to the family. When I have children, I hope I can build a family every bit as close as they did."

Scott surprised himself. He hadn't thought of having children in years. At least not for ten years. He had watched his own parents' disastrous marriage, and when he was still in his twenties he decided the whole process was too destructive. Too stressful. He didn't want to risk the kind of misery in his own life that he had watched his parents deal out to each other ever since he could remember.

Something had been wrong between his father and his mother. Something he didn't have any perspective on at all. He might be a psychologist, he told himself, but he had no idea what was happening in his own family. His gentle father sought refuge in his work, while his socially active mother busied herself with bridge and shopping.

His grandmother had been the solid one in the family. She had come from a working-class background. She had been a lowly clerk in one of the businesses Scott's grandfather had managed, an offshoot from one of the family's many real estate interests.

She had been filled with common sense and good humor and a fierce independence that never let her get sucked into the phony social climbing activities of so many of her contemporaries. At the same time, his grandmother had been loved and appreciated by almost everyone she met, whether they were bellhops in the elegant hotels the family frequented, or members of the social register.

Liza's bare feet burned on the carefully painted green boards of the porch floor. Wicker furniture was strewn almost randomly along the broad stretch. The house itself was welcoming and casual despite its impressive size.

"I've got to get the key," Scott called over his

shoulder as he headed toward a dilapidated shed that stood about a hundred feet to the side of the house.

But no sooner had he started off than the front door swung open and two laughing figures merrily darted out. They were blurs of bare skin to Liza's incredulous eyes.

Scott watched with narrowed gaze as his brother-in-law, Carleton Wainright, chased after small, blond, practically naked Angela. She wore a bikini bottom and no top. Her bare breasts looked surprisingly small, but she moved provocatively, and Wainright hauled her back against him, his pale, slender hands grabbing her breasts as he pressed her back against his own chest.

One of his hands quickly moved down over her abdomen, lowering itself to the minuscule wisp of fabric that was her only protection from complete nakedness. His face was buried in the curve of her neck.

"What in hell are you doing here?" Scott demanded in a loud, authoritative tone.

Wainright froze. Slowly he released Angela, who did nothing to cover herself. Instead she stood inches from Wainright's side and turned her inviting gaze on Scott.

Liza was stunned speechless. She could do nothing more than gaze on the ludicrous scene in absolute disbelief. Later she could vaguely recall Scott harshly ordering them to leave. A few minutes afterwards she heard a car engine start and the crunch of gravel beneath rubber tires. By then she had sunk into one of the old-fashioned wicker rockers on the porch. She was in shock.

The pieces of the puzzle began to fall into place for Liza. She had always been relatively naive. She always assumed people had the best morals and motives until it was proven otherwise. She had even been willing to believe that she had been mistaken about what she thought had been Wainright's passes. To say nothing of looking at Angela only as an ineffective worker. Angela had something else going for her. She had no need of superb secretarial skills or any editorial skills at all.

Liza sighed. She knew herself well enough to know she would never be any different. She would always be sadly surprised by people with hidden motives. The best she could do was to put up defenses against those people who had proved themselves unworthy and those people whose motives she had reason to suspect.

"I never did like him," Scott angrily revealed when he returned to her. "I didn't like him when Madge brought him home to meet the family. He always reminded me of a weasel. Cunning. Clever. Calculating. Determined to get to the top at any cost. And I think marrying Madge was a big step for him," he added bitterly. "She was his ticket to fame and fortune. And you know what the creep said in his defense?" Scott asked her.

He didn't wait for her reply. "He said Madge didn't understand him. That she never had. He told me that I couldn't blame a fellow for finding a little recreation when he had a wife as cold as Madge is. He's saying that about my sister, for heaven's sake, and he is trying to use the argument to gain my sympathy. I should have torn him limb from limb," Scott grated out through clenched teeth.

Liza could see the veins in his neck throbbing. His massive chest rose up and down as he breathed angry deep breaths. After a time he stilled.

"Madge wasn't always so difficult," he soberly revealed as he sank down into the chair next to Liza's. "In fact she was pretty delightful as a kid. That is some of the time she was. Other times she was a holy terror, but in an okay way. It must be a pretty lousy feeling to wake up one day and discover that some jerk married you for your money and position, and that now he would get his kicks sleeping with whomever he pleased. How the hell do you deal with something like that?"

"I don't know," Liza answered gently. "It would be awful."

"Oh, no," he muttered in disgust, turning his now sad eyes on Liza. "I've been so upset about what Wainright has done to Madge that I forgot all about what he did to you. That bastard is the one who didn't give you the promotion. He gave it to his bare-breasted baby instead."

"That's right," Liza glumly agreed. "I always wondered why their dictation sessions were so long. Now I know."

She looked out across the porch, out over the low dune that rose up from the beach, and watched the water lapping peacefully against the sandy shore. The sun was just beginning to set and the western sky looked as if it had been draped with millions of yards of apricot chiffon. A huge glowing orb of deepest rose burned intensely within it.

She looked at him solemnly. "At least I don't have him in my family," she sympathetically stated.

Scott stood up and eagerly pulled her to her feet, too. And as naturally as though he had done it for years, he pulled her into his arms, hugging her tight. His bare chest and legs felt strangely comforting against her. Yet even in her state of shock and sadness she felt her body warm to his.

"Liza you're a wonder," he declared. Then he kissed her soundly on the lips. She reveled in the feeling of her barely-clad breasts pressing into his chest. Her hips and thighs burned with a new fire. A wave of delightful dizziness claimed her.

He dragged himself away from her, sensing that this moment was not the one to begin their first explorations of true intimacy. But his heart thudded in his chest. He knew the time would be soon.

"I'm going to cook you a really good dinner. I hope you like steak."

"Are you a good cook?" she inquired. "Most male

chauvinist pigs aren't, you know." Her eyes now danced with teasing lights.

"My good woman, when will you learn not to classify people according to your own preconceived notions of how they should behave. Don't you know enough to realize that people are all different?"

He was throwing some of her own counsel of the afternoon back at her.

Liza giggled. "Call me when you want help. In the meantime, I don't suppose this whole huge house would have a change of clothes for me. Something a little more decent to wear? I feel as though I'm on display."

"You are," he affirmed with a wicked grin. "Most definitely. And I love it."

She felt a rush of pleasure fill her with a heady warmth. But she persisted. "Clothes. Something to cover my nakedness."

He gave her an exaggerated frown, obviously not pleased to be helping her with the problem. "Try the second floor, the middle bedroom in the front," he suggested, "My cousin Patricia and her husband Bart stay there. She's about your size."

Patricia had no designer jeans or exquisite, expensive clothes in her dresser drawer. Instead, in casual array, were T-shirts that carried messages like "Friends of the Park" and "La Rabida Run." There were simple shorts that carried the Sears label and rugby shirts that had neither alligator, nor fox, nor any other animal displayed on them. A box of Pampers stood in the corner, and a sturdy toy box was carelessly shoved beneath the crib that sat in an alcove formed by a small gable.

The bedroom had the same casual atmosphere as the rest of the rambling house. The furniture was quite ordinary, the decorating merely coats of paint, much of it needing to be redone. The only clue that rich people owned the house was its gargantuan size.

"I think I like Patricia," Liza declared as she padded barefoot into the big old country kitchen. The kitchen wasn't at all fancy. Instead it had a huge stove, one which she was sure had been designed for a restaurant, and a rather battered round oak table in the center. The counter tops looked as though they could be redone with Formica, as they were worn. But she suspected it would be years before they were taken in hand. The only shiny new concessions to the elegant world in the whole kitchen were the sparkling chrome-and-glass microwave oven, and the new Krups coffee maker.

"I think you would like Patricia, too," Scott confirmed as he lifted the lid on a saucepan and stirred the contents. "She's my favorite cousin. How do you like your steak?"

"Medium rare," she reported easily.

Scott was wearing tight jeans and no shirt. His broad chest was muscular and had a light tracing of dark hairs that arrowed provocatively down past the waistband of his jeans. He was barefoot. A white kitchen towel was casually stuffed into his pocket. He wiped his hands on it then gave Liza his full attention.

She was wearing a pair of navy running shorts and a tan T-shirt with Beethoven's picture on it. She had selected the T-shirt carefully. The huge picture of the famous composer covered the front of her quite well. It was not so blatantly obvious that she was not wearing a bra.

"I liked you better the other way," he said honestly.

Liza blushed uncomfortably. She was relieved to hear the phone ring. She started toward the source of the sound, glad to be able to busily avoid further comment from Scott.

He rushed past her. His hand reached the kitchen wall phone inches ahead of her own, grabbing the instrument.

"I'm expecting a call," he explained. And immediately he had the receiver to his ear. "Hello," he said. "I'm not going to be able to take you tonight," he explained in a moment. "I'm out of town, and I'm not going to be able to get back before the dinner tonight. Sorry."

There was a pause. "I know it's a rotten thing to do to you. But look, my cousin Howard is just in from Baltimore. I've already called him. He'll be glad to take you. He was kind of expected to go anyway. And he'd be much happier to be there with you than alone."

There was a period of silence while Scott listened. "Look," he finally said, "he's thirty-six, filthy rich, and just divorcing his second wife. What more could you want?"

Again there was a short silence. "Well, I'm not going to be there," he said flatly. "Howie will call you in about half an hour. Okay? No, I'm not doing some final revisions on anything. I'm working on a whole different project," Scott revealed. "You'll know all about it when the time is right," he promised.

"Monica Grant?" Liza asked as soon as he hung up the phone. She could not bear not to know who his date for the night had been. She held her breath as she waited for his response.

"Yes," Scott answered, nodding. "Jealous?" His dark brows rose speculatively. He enjoyed the prospect of Liza being jealous. He enjoyed it very much.

Liza refused to answer. "Am I the project?" Liza questioned after he was back working busily at the stove. She tried to make her inquiry sound casual. However just the sound of the idea, the thought that she and Scott were really on the "experiment" basis after all bothered her deeply.

He turned from the onions he was lightly sautéing and smiled at her. "You're my number one priority now," he assured her in a voice that was meant to be comforting. It was not. Instead she was unsettled, completely unsettled by the very thought.

Liza didn't even offer to help. Instead she wandered out of the kitchen and seated herself in a huge old wicker rocker on the porch. She was engulfed in deep, depressing thoughts. Amid the dim realization that she had once again lost a job because of sexual harassment, as indeed was the case, she concentrated on the thing that bothered her even more. If she was Scott Harburton's number one priority now, what exactly was he trying to prove with her?

The dinner was delicious, but Liza ate without enthusiasm. She felt as though her whole world existed under a dark cloud. Scott tried a few times to make conversation, but stopped after discovering she hardly responded at all. Then he made a confession.

"You know the reason I came to your office in the first place was to help Madge," he revealed. "She thought you were the little flirt who was taking her husband from her. She'd had problems with him before, and always, one way or another, she had been smart enough to block any serious developments. That's why the last few secretaries were fired. Wainright couldn't keep his hands off them. This time Madge wasn't sure what was happening. You looked so businesslike to her. With your tailored suits and no-nonsense hairdo, she couldn't be sure it was you putting up with any funny stuff. She asked me to find out."

"So that's why you were so hostile to me at first," Liza said, hardly masking her anger. "You thought I was a home wrecker. Or at the very least a most cooperative secretary." She glared at him furiously.

"I was wrong," he said defensively. "But I didn't know that at first. I could tell beneath all that tailored exterior you wore like a shield that you were a very sexy lady. I had to do a little more investigating. So I got to know you.''

''All the time you were thinking I was probably an easy mark,'' she said in disgust. Her gray eyes were dark, like the sky before a storm.

''I made a mistake,'' Scott apologized a bit impatiently. ''So don't hold it against me forever. Everyone makes mistakes.''

''I lost my last job precisely because I *wouldn't* sleep with my last boss,'' she revealed frostily. ''It seems I can't win no matter what I do.''

He didn't say anything. He merely sat quietly at the big kitchen table, watching Liza.

''Well, I guess this is the end of our relationship,'' she suggested without enthusiasm. ''You found out what you wanted to know.''

Her food lumped in her stomach. Her throat closed tight. She bit her lip hard to keep back the tears that threatened to overwhelm her now. The pain that welled up within her was frightening in intensity. She didn't want to end her relationship with Scott. She didn't want it to ever end.

''Don't be silly,'' Scott responded lightly. ''I'm not about to let our relationship end yet. There's still too much for us to find out about each other. We can have a really satisfying affair. Besides, I have still got something to prove. I fully intend to prove to your opinionated brain that women enjoy being taken care of in the old-fashioned ways, that they like being cherished. Our experiment is still on,'' he informed her.

It wasn't at all what she wanted to hear. She didn't want him to be seeing her because of some silly experiment. And she didn't want to know that he wasn't ready to have their relationship end yet. It was the word ''yet'' that put her off. It meant he fully expected to have it end one day. And if that was what he expected, then Liza never wanted things to get started.

She chewed her perfectly cooked steak as though it were no more than a dry hamburger. Her whole life, she told herself, was currently under a large black cloud. Nothing was right. Not her work life, not her personal life, nothing. She finished her meal in gloomy silence.

Liza helped Scott do the dishes, and after wiping the last pot and putting it carefully away, she faced him squarely. Her gray eyes were without their usual sparkle. Her face held not the hint of her usual good humor.

"It's late. And I'm tired. I think the wind and the sun and the lovely shock I got here were all too much for me. I just want to go to bed and pretend I haven't got a care in the world. The farthest thing from my mind right now is any sexual exploit," she warned.

"Okay," Scott agreed, resigned to the truth of her words. He knew Liza well enough not to argue with her at this time. She had withdrawn from him, and it would be a while before she would voluntarily come back. What he didn't quite understand was why it hurt him the way it did. What he really wanted her to do was to turn to him in her misery, turn to him and let him soothe away her problems. But she wasn't open to that. She wasn't open to him. That hurt. It was a new hurt, different for him.

"Why don't you sleep in Pat and Bart's room," he suggested.

"Thanks," Liza gratefully said, giving him a small, sad smile just before she drifted out of the kitchen and toward the stairs.

"My room is the last one on the right, if you change your mind about sleeping with me. Or if you just want to talk," he suggested after another moment.

His last words pleased Liza for some ridiculous reasons that she didn't completely understand. She walked up the stairs with a strangely contented smile on

her face. Despite the strain and the odd basis of their
relationship, so many things told her that he cared for
her as a person.

It was a start.

Scott read until nearly midnight. The thought of going
upstairs was unsettling to him. He wasn't sure he could
just pass Liza's door without opening it, going in, trying
to make love to her.

He wanted her, that was sure. He ached to have her
in his arms, in his bed. Yet despite his best predictions
about women in general, despite his years of knowledge and his largely satisfactory liaisons with women,
Liza eluded his understanding and his grasp.

He muttered an oath and angrily put down the science fiction book he was reading. He stretched his arms
over his head and gazed out the open window into the
velvet dark night. A soft summer breeze blew in, carrying with it a faint perfume of wild flowers.

He knew he wouldn't sleep. He wasn't tired enough.
He would only lie in his bed and think disturbing
thoughts about Liza who slept only a few thin walls
from his door. Releasing a loud, resigned sigh, he
strode out the door for a hopefully exhausting hike
across the dunes.

The breeze blew in Liza's window, too. It filled her
nostrils with its heady fragrance. It seemed to seep into
her pores and claim her yearning body with its glorious,
sensuous promise of romance.

She stopped the tossing and turning that had kept her
from sleep since she had first lain down on the big
double bed that Patricia shared with Bart while their
baby slept, just barely hidden from their view, in an
alcove nearby. She wondered what it was like for married people, lovers who trusted each other and turned
to each other for solace, for understanding, and for the

incomparable joy that came when their bodies joined. The thought stirred such a wave of intense emotions within Liza that she could no longer stay in bed. Instead she threw back the covers and got up. She stripped the light nightgown from her body, and grabbed for the Beethoven T-shirt and the navy shorts. She pulled them on eagerly and darted for the door.

She tiptoed across the hall, not wanting to disturb Scott's sleep. She lightly ran down the steps and darted out the wide front door. Her target was the beach.

The moon was full and silvery bright. The stars shone like jewels, almost close enough to touch. Liza ran down the beach with the wind blowing in her hair. She stopped short at the water's edge, loving the feel of the small, silken waves as they broke on her toes.

The water was smooth and inviting. Hesitating only long enough to assure herself there was no one else on the beach, Liza pulled her clothes off and darted into the sapphire-blue lake. The water was cool and lovely as it caressed her tingling skin. It languorously kissed every inch of her as she floated easily in the water. She swam for a while and then leisurely walked along the shore. She felt deliciously daring, exposed as she was, naked, and facing the world. She wondered how it would be if Scott were with her, how he would like the sight of her, the feel of her, beneath his pleasantly rough hands. She had had to swim vigorously and long to rid her body of the fierce tension that had gripped her, the ache that she knew could be satisfied only by him.

It was with a sense of real loss and regret that she later pulled her clothes back on and walked up to the big house and her lonely bed. She thought seriously of going to Scott, giving herself to him to experience the pleasure of his lovemaking. But she knew then that she would be utterly lost. That nothing of herself would be reserved. Just as surely she knew that would be a certain death to her.

From his perch on the low dune, Scott had watched Liza for nearly an hour. The ache in his loins grew to alarming intensity as he watched her cavort in the waves like a carefree nymph.

He had left the house to get relief from the intense pressure he felt, his intense desire for Liza. But instead of finding relief he found nothing but more frustration.

Scott was frowning deeply when he finally climbed the stairs and walked past her closed door to his own bedroom. Somehow he wasn't able to control his relationship with Liza the way he was used to doing. That realization kept him awake in his bed and muttering muffled oaths until the light of dawn began to turn the eastern horizon pale gray. His last thought before he slept was that the gray of the morning sky was very like the gray of Liza's eyes.

Chapter Seven

For nearly half an hour Liza had been lying in the dreamy, trancelike state that was neither wakefulness nor sleep. A warm, gentle breeze blew in through the wide-open window. It lightly caressed her skin. The morning sun bathed her in a delicious warmth that fed her sensuous lethargy.

Slowly she lifted the light covers, easing them aside. She lay still and felt strangely, delightfully expectant. Her firm, rounded body was covered only by the thin film of her blue silken gown.

There was a soft knock on the door, then a moment's pause.

Through half-opened eyes she watched him. Dressed only in skintight jeans he strode barefoot through the door he had boldly opened, and into her room.

She neither moved nor spoke. The only sign of recognition was her breath catching in her throat, her heightened pulse and the rapid rising and falling of her breasts.

Wordlessly he came to her. As he neared she felt a warm pleasure rush through her like a wild river of delight.

He stood at the side of the bed for only a fraction of a second as his hungry eyes thoroughly raked her enticing form, only subtly concealed by frothy blue silk. A soft moan escaped from his throat. He dropped to the

bed, lying next to her. He scooped her into his powerful arms and buried his face in the hollow of her throat.
With a gasp of delight she held him to her, glorying in
the smoothness of his skin as she memorized each inch
of his broad, muscular back with her searching hands.
She lightly rubbed her sensitive breasts against the hard
wall of his chest. She was claimed by a fierce longing,
coupled with an incredible weakness. At that moment
her body was no longer her own. It was his to do with
what he wanted.

He smelled of crisp after-shave, and his springy hair
was damp beneath her caressing fingers.

His mouth sought hers as though it were his right.
His warm, moist lips coaxed hers open, and as he
plundered her mouth, his hand slowly explored her
shoulders, her side, and then caressed and cupped her
throbbing breast. His eager tongue searched out every
inch of her open mouth, and she felt a momentarily
satisfying completeness that ignited new and more insistent fires deep within her.

"You were beautiful last night in the moonlight," he
huskily whispered in her ear. His soft, warm breath
sent a sensuous shiver through her. He wanted her. It
gave her a sweet thrill.

"I—I couldn't sleep," she explained, suddenly too
shy to look up at him, to meet his eyes. She was fascinated, yet afraid of what she would see there. Instead
she studied the strong, tanned column of his throat.

"I couldn't sleep either," he confided. "Especially
after that. I'm a normal, healthy male, you know."

"I'd say extremely healthy," she teased, smiling up
at him for a brief revealing moment. His eyes glowed
with desire. And something else, something warmer
and more personal.

"You—you didn't—you didn't try..." her voice
trailed off as she wondered what she would have done
if he had come to her last night. Her heart beat fright-

eningly fast and her breathing became strangely shallow.

"No," he explained in a voice barely above a whisper. "You drew a line. I won't cross it. Not until you decide the time is right. It's too important." And as he said the words he realized how completely he meant that. Whatever he did with Liza was getting to be more important than anything he had done with any woman before.

He kissed her lightly on the lips while his workroughened fingers gently traced the curve of her jaw. Slowly he caressed her shoulder, urging the delicate strap down, lowering her gown until her breast was exposed. He rubbed it gently, teasing it briefly before lowering his open mouth to cover it.

She lay still while her body basked in the bevy of wild sensations that coursed through her. His tongue flicked lightly over her, sending great surges of pleasure traveling through her whole body and echoing the tantalizing sensation in her deepest core. She had a yawning ache, an incredible desire to open herself to him.

"We'll be fantastic together," he promised throatily while his hand moved beneath the gown and languorously traced slow, ever-widening circles on her bare stomach.

"You seem awfully sure of what's going to happen," she teased, laughing lightly to ease her own tension.

"I'm using all my best positive thinking on it. I'm picturing success: you lying naked in my arms, making love with wild abandon. You next to me, glowing with satisfaction after we've made love."

His fingers strayed to her inner thigh. He briefly traced its curve, shooting a surge of heady, breathtaking sensation through her. "We'll have a wonderful affair."

The words chilled Liza. They snapped her out of her sensual, dreamy state. She stiffened. Scott felt her do so, and pulled back, frowning quizzically. He wasn't sure what else he'd have to do to make love to Liza. But he knew something had happened between them to tell him that this lovely Sunday morning was probably not the time.

Liza's passion had been overlaid by a churning misery that was strongly akin to fear. She wasn't sure what she wanted from Scott Harburton, but she knew it wasn't an affair. Most affairs had no commitment. Most affairs ended. Liza knew her feelings well enough to know that she couldn't bear that. It would be better if it never began.

"Wouldn't it be a disaster for you to have your name publicly linked with mine? I mean, I don't believe in the things you advocate. And with all the publicity you attract you might have problems—" He covered her mouth with his. Again her blood flamed. His lips dropped to caress her breasts again. His tongue lightly circled the rosy mound.

"I can deal with any problems you cause me," he huskily assured her. "Besides, I expect you'll come around someday after I've sent you dozens of bouquets of flowers. You'll finally admit that you like it."

He smiled. She saw the dimple in his cheek. Impulsively she raised her fingers to touch it. She returned his smile, loving the dancing joy and pleasure lights that glowed from his deep-blue eyes.

"What if you're wrong and I'm right?" she challenged impishly, trying hard not to be only aware of his gently stroking hand on her thigh. "What would you do then?"

He frowned thoughtfully. "As a scientist I would have to accept the evidence and be glad I found the truth. As a lover"—he drew his brows together deep in concentration—"I'd be damned disappointed to find out you really don't want me to do things that bring me pleasure, too."

He said nothing for a long moment. He looked into her eyes, silently asking the question that had been in his mind since he met her. He read her answer: a sadly reluctant no. Whatever else was going on, Liza was not ready to make love with him.

"Come on," he finally said with a resigned sigh as he swung his long body to a sitting position, "breakfast is getting cold."

He stood up and pulled her out of bed. Her shoulder strap was still down, her breast exposed. Gently he pulled up the strap.

"There. You're decent. Come on." Pulling her by the hand he led her toward the deck.

"I can't go downstairs like this," she protested, holding back.

"You were out there last night with nothing on at all," he argued.

"Yes, but, I didn't think anyone could see me," she defensively pointed out.

"You were wrong," he told her matter of factly. "Now come on. You look ravishing." He began to pull at her again.

She stood her ground. "I want to take this nightgown off."

"I'm all for that," he enthusiastically replied, glad to use humor to release some of his own almost unbearable tension. He turned to give her his full attention.

"I want to get dressed," she emphatically told him.

"You're full of ideas that foil my plans," he complained, frowning his displeasure.

"I see you're beginning to understand me," she smugly retorted, grinning up at him like a mischievous child. She, too, was glad of the light repartee. It was a welcome relief from her knotted emotions.

"I think I'd better go read one of my own books," he revealed with mock disgust. "You're the challenge of my career."

She laughed musically, joyfully, as she watched him go.

The trip home on the boat was a quiet, peaceful time. Liza couldn't remember ever feeling so contented. Despite their lack of physical union, there was something vital between her and Scott, something real, something that was growing as important to her as her own breathing.

With him she felt a spectrum of emotions that hardly seemed possible to experience with a single individual. Despite the tension between them they were so in tune with each other that often words hardly seemed necessary. When she laughed with him it was a happier, more joy-filled laugh than she shared with anyone else. When he kissed her, caressed her, her body thrilled in a way that she had never known before.

Briefly a chilling thought filled her mind. When he hurt her, left her, then her soul would plunge to new, excruciatingly painful depths.

She pushed the thought away. She let it go, let it blow away on the warm summer wind that propelled the boat across the huge blue lake. She would deal with that pain when it came.

"Are you going to go to work Monday?" Scott asked gently as he dropped her off at her apartment.

She nodded glumly. "I have to. At least to give my two-weeks' notice."

"It won't be easy."

"I'm pretty tough," she assured him with a falsely bright smile.

"I know that. I just don't like to see you hurt," he told her just before he kissed her goodbye. "I'll be thinking about you."

As though to prove the truth of his words, Liza got a

big bouquet of yellow roses delivered to her office the next day. The card with it merely said "Scott."

The golden presence brought a glorious glow to Liza's otherwise dismal day.

Professor Wainright didn't come into the office until very late in the morning. By that time Liza had already called Valerie's aunt in personnel, asking for a different assignment. She was virtually assured that something would come up within the next two weeks. So, when Wainright did finally get in, Liza went into his office and gave her notice.

"I wish you'd reconsider, my dear," he replied with false warmth. His thin-lipped smile did not reach his eyes. "There is no real reason for you to go. I've gone to a good deal of trouble to have your position upgraded to the very highest level. You won't find another secretarial job as good as this one."

"I'll take my chances," Liza dryly answered. "I don't want to work for you anymore."

She sat in a velvet covered wing chair on the opposite side of Wainright's big mahogany desk. The office furniture was elegant, quite out of place in the generally shabby offices of the world-famous University.

Most professors cared little for how their offices looked. They were absorbed in their work, not in the decor. Wainright, on the other hand, bought his own furniture from his wife's family's ample funds. The result was elegant, if a bit ostentatious.

"You're leaving just because of what happened over the weekend?" he asked with raised eyebrows. "Come now, we are both adults. You were at the beach house for the same reason I was. You can hardly criticize my behavior," he smoothly suggested.

His remarks were a bit too close to the truth for Liza's comfort. She squirmed uncomfortably in the sumptuously upholstered chair, remembering how close Scott had come to making love to her, just as Wainright had planned to do with Angela. She felt embarrassed and uncomfortable until she remembered the one critical difference between the two couples' plans.

"Professor Wainright, you are a married man," she angrily retorted. Slowly, word by word, she expressed her outrage at being classed with him. "There is absolutely no way you could decently have *any* clandestine relationship with Angela or any other woman. No honorable man so lightly dismisses his marriage vows."

It felt good telling Wainright off. Liza felt the cleansing freedom of truth wash through her being.

"That isn't all," she continued, now glaring at him as she spoke, "You used my skills to do your editing job, and then turned around and gave the permanent assignment to Angela. Why? Not because of Angela's qualifications. Oh, she has some on paper, a bachelor of science degree. But Angela is a useless worker. She can barely follow directions. She couldn't think her way out of a paper bag. However I'm sure that she passes the test in bed, and that was the unspoken but critical qualification. Now you want me to stay on as your secretary. My guess is you got me a big raise so that I won't complain about being assistant editor in fact, while Angela sits in the editorial office polishing her fingernails. I do the work, she gets the glory. Forget it, Professor," Liza flatly told him. "I won't play that kind of game."

"Ah, my dear, I can understand your disappointment," Wainright said with an elaborate show of sympathy. "But all is not lost. I'm quite certain that Angela will not hold her new position permanently. When she leaves there is no reason why you cannot step into her office."

He was like a weasel, Liza decided, remembering Scott's comments, a cunning, highly polished, well educated weasel. His eyes were small and beady and shifted about the room as he talked.

"In the meantime you will be paid for what you do."

"And what will that be, Professor?" Liza asked warily. "Are you planning on another game of musical beds?"

"Why not?" Wainright asked with a shrug. "My celebrated brother-in-law never keeps any woman for long. And you, my dear, are certainly not even of the same type as the women he is used to. He won't be interested in you for much longer," he confidently predicted. "Stick around and you'll find you've got some nice insurance with me."

It took a moment for the meaning of his words to penetrate. When it did, it took her another moment to answer. Then Liza spoke slowly and distinctly. She wanted Wainright to have no doubt about her reply.

"Professor, I don't want anything that you have to offer. I do not want the editorial job. I do not want you as a lover. There is nothing you could say or do that would make me change my mind."

His eyes narrowed and he regarded her maliciously. "It would be very easy to make your affair with Scott public. The scandal sheets would eat it up. With the publication of his new book you'd be a real minus, militant feminist that you are. It's my guess he'd be better off not being seen with you right now. Certainly Monica Grant must feel that way."

Liza had only the vaguest idea what Scott's new book was all about. However she didn't want to endanger its success in any way.

"We're not having an affair," Liza angrily corrected him, "so there is no reason to use that as a threat."

"You don't expect me to believe that," Wainright smoothly replied. "My brother-in-law's reputation would certainly turn any doubters into believers in a moment. Think about it, my dear," Wainright generously offered. "You can give me your final answer later."

Too furious to speak, Liza stomped out of Wainright's office. Nearly blind with rage she collided with a broad chest that cradled a paper bag in a strong arm.

"There went the sandwiches. They're squashed now," Scott commented good humoredly. "Do you think you'd like to eat them anyway?"

Liza paid no attention to what he had said. Instead she began to sputter out her fury. Her eyes were dangerously bright. Her cheeks glowed with her angry flush. Her breasts heaved up and down dramatically.

"That man," she began what was obviously to be a tirade, "that rotten, no good, lecherous jerk."

Scott grabbed her hand and pulled her after him. "Come on, let's get you out of here. Then you can tell me all about it."

She followed him without resistance as he led her across the broad green lawn. He found a long concrete bench nestled in the deep shade under a huge spreading oak tree. He sat her down and put a sandwich in her hand.

"Now tell me about it," he suggested.

Liza did. Hurrying to get all her feelings out, she spoke non-stop, completely disregarding the sandwich or the can of pop he had handed her.

As he listened Scott was furious at his brother-in-law, but not surprised. Carleton Wainright had acted about as he had expected.

But Scott was also enjoying Liza's fury. She looked beautiful when her rage set her on fire. Her whole being reacted, responded, to her intense emotions. There was nothing artificial or calculated about her. She was fresh and natural and intensely exciting.

"So, when he threatened to make our affair public, I didn't know what to do," she despaired. "I certainly don't want to put you in an awkward position with your new book coming out and all." Her eyes were pleading when she finished, pleading for an answer to her dilemma and his.

"You're the one in the bad position," Scott commiserated. "Wainright can't hurt me. In fact, maybe we can steal his thunder. How about it?" Scott's eyes twinkled devilishly.

Liza regarded him cautiously. "What do you mean?"

"Publicity pictures," he explained with satisfaction. "I'm supposed to have some taken tomorrow. I'm not exactly sure what fabulous female I'm supposed to be dating this time. But I think I'll tell them who the person is for a change. That person will be you," he reported with glee.

"Me?" she asked, incredulous.

He nodded, smiling broadly.

Liza regarded him out of the corner of her eye. "I'm not so sure it's a good idea," she uneasily replied. "Your reputation—"

"It's your reputation that's more at stake," Scott warned. "Everyone already assumes that I'm a philanderer. It's your name that hasn't been besmirched in the press yet."

"I don't know," Liza thoughtfully replied. She wasn't altogether sure why the prospect troubled her. It wasn't just the publicity, or the public linking of her name with Scott's. In fact that gave her a secret pleasure.

"It's up to you, of course. But I'd like it very much," he told her.

His last statement got her. She instinctively wanted to do things that made him happy. Liza agreed.

"Good. I'll send a car for you about six. We start at the Ritz-Carlton in Water Tower Place."

"Oh, you don't have to send a car. I can get there by myself. What time?"

"Six thirty," he replied.

"Anything particular you want me to wear for the pictures?" Liza asked.

"Something stunning, like that black crepe you wore to the ballet. Wear it just for me."

Liza got off the city bus at Chicago's historic Water Tower. The old carved limestone block building was a strange sight amidst the graceful, modern buildings which soared over Michigan Avenue. It was a low, square building, and it rested heavily on the earth. Rising from it at each corner were medieval-style turrets and in the center was a proud narrow tower. Once it had been the highest point in the city. Now it was dwarfed by skyscrapers.

Liza had always felt that the landmark was out of place on the busy street. It was a little bit of Camelot in the center of busy Chicago. And the noisy cars, the hurrying crowds, and the buses that belched diesel fumes rushed past the dignified survivor of the devastating 1871 Chicago fire.

But one of the newest, most elegant buildings on the fashionable street, a sleek, white, marble-clad giant took its name from the venerable old structure. The newcomer called itself Water Tower Place, and within its block-square confines were some of the city's most exclusive shops and restaurants. It also housed movie theaters, and the Ritz-Carlton Hotel with its luxurious rooms and condominium apartments.

Liza rode the mirror-paneled elevator up to the hotel lobby which was nestled high in the majestic building. The elevator doors smoothly glided open and she stepped into the lobby. Valerie had once described the hushed, almost cushioned atmosphere there as "the elegant quiet that only money can buy."

Liza walked through the vast, high ceilinged central area to the bar at the rear of the lobby. Polished marble, gleaming brass, richly grained woods, and a huge splashing fountain made a fitting background for the sumptuous, upholstered furniture. The bar looked like an enormous, comfortable, well appointed living room.

Scott had seen her almost from the first moment she entered the lobby. Something within him had alerted him to her presence, and he trained his eyes on her as she gracefully moved toward him.

As he had suggested, she wore the black crepe cocktail dress he remembered. He was somehow pleased that she hadn't been compelled to buy something new. The dress seductively draped her voluptuous curves and played havoc with his body chemistry.

As Liza walked toward him, her hips, sheathed in the crepe, swayed enticingly. Her breasts were full and high, and her carriage was proud. Yet there was a lack of artifice about her, a lack of self-consciousness and body-consciousness that was new to him in women he dated. Liza Manchester was one-of-a-kind.

He wondered again as she walked toward him how she would be in bed. He seemed to be thinking about it a lot lately. And he also wondered how she would react to the phony world of publicity that she was about to enter.

Scott didn't like the publicity pictures, or the whole idea of publicity itself, but he knew it sold books. So he left the details of it to Monica Grant, his publicist, and tried hard to be pleasant enough and to do as she said. Now he stood by his chair, waiting for Liza, wishing he could have her to himself instead of both of them going through this ridiculous charade. And while he watched her move toward him he wondered if she was sleeping with another man. Maybe Jeffrey Childers.

He was in a bad mood anyway, and the thought of Liza sleeping with Jeffrey filled Scott with unreasoning fury. As Liza neared where he stood all he could see was Jeffrey's hands on her welcoming body. Scott's rugged features molded into an angry scowl. He couldn't look at Liza's smile of greeting. It only made him wonder how she greeted other men.

He glanced down at his watch. "You're on time," he scolded, noticing that it was only six twenty-eight. His mood was as irritable as though she had kept him waiting for hours.

"Of course I'm on time, silly," she countered with a little laugh. "All I had to do was get on the right bus."

He blinked at her as though she had suddenly turned from a princess into a frog. His scowl deepened into a furious frown. His dark brows drew together menacingly. And his deep-blue eyes clouded as the sky before a storm.

Liza patiently waited for him to seat her as had been his custom. But he did not. He merely stood there staring at her with what seemed to be murderous intent. She shrugged gracefully and sat down in a tall, leather-covered wing chair.

He stared down at her, his anger abated, but his look now incredulous. "You came on the bus? Dressed like that?" he demanded. "In a cocktail dress?"

He was still standing, now towering over her. His strong, tanned hands were firmly planted on his slim hips. The jacket of his pin-striped suit gaped open across his chest.

"It's a warm evening," Liza coolly defended herself. "Now, why don't you sit down. The ice is melting in your drink."

She had never seen Scott angry before. Always his attitude had been calm, unruffled, distant and contained. But now his color was high, his eyes bored angrily into hers, and she could see a pulse beat rapidly in his throat.

"Nobody takes the bus. Not to come here. Not dressed like that," he caustically informed her as he sat down. "Not when there are going to be publicity pictures. Everyone uses a limo. At least." His hand automatically reached for his drink. He downed a large gulp.

"I take the bus," Liza returned brightly. "It only makes sense. The parking is expensive here. I assumed you drove and I couldn't see having two cars. Now stop making such a fuss about it." Liza sat waiting calmly for his hurricane to blow itself out.

The waitress appeared and took Liza's order. Scott ordered a second drink for himself. And as the waitress left, he gulped down the remainder of his first.

"Did you have a nice day in Evanston?" Liza questioned, wide-eyed. She was doing her best to stifle the amused grin that threatened to erupt on her face at any moment. She couldn't imagine what had happened to put Scott off, to make him so angry. But it was highly amusing to her.

After his initial period of irritablility gradually disappeared, Scott talked pleasantly about his day of meetings with professors at Northwestern University. And he told her about the new research project they were launching.

"Sounds fascinating," Liza enthusiastically concluded. She had been watching him with rapt attention while he sketched out the psychology experiment in great detail. And as she observed him, she noticed so many little things about him. She watched the way he ran his strong fingers through his thick dark brown hair when he was thinking. She studied every little nuance of expression that came to his ruggedly handsome face.

After Liza's comment about his work, he was silent for a long moment. He just stared at her. Then his eyes opened wide in a look of mock disbelief. "Liza," he asked quite pleasantly, "are you flirting with me?"

His brows were raised. His head tilted slightly to one side as he waited expectantly for her answer. Most of his dates had no interest in his work, and he could tell it, even though they asked all the right questions.

"What do you mean?" she indignantly responded. "I said what you were talking about sounded fascinating. Is that flirting? Only if you don't mean it, then it is flirting of the worst sort," Liza answered her own question. "Are you so unimpressed with your work that you think no one else would find it interesting either? If so, I suggest you find another project."

A long, hearty chuckle started deep in Scott's throat. It spilled over to spread happiness to his whole body. He had challenged Liza and she had come up the winner. He couldn't have been more delighted, though he wasn't even sure why.

"If something I talked about was boring to you, what would you say?" he questioned. "What would you tell me then? Would you stare up at me with your misty gray eyes and declare in sugary tones, 'Dullest thing I ever heard'?"

He was still smiling and his eyes were still lighted with mirth. But he realized the answer to that question was important to him. Very important.

Liza did not give him his answer quickly. Instead she had to think about it for a few moments.

"I hope I'd be polite enough to listen without commenting about how awfully boring your subject was," she answered finally. "But I certainly would not say anything was interesting if I didn't think it was."

"No, I'm certain you wouldn't," he replied, quite satisfied with her answer. His generous lips curved into a crooked half-smile. Lively lights of amusement danced in his eyes.

Liza smiled mischievously. "Why don't you try me. Why don't you tell me something incredibly boring," she suggested impishly. "Talk to me in a dull monotone. Go into excruciating detail about something I don't care about at all. See how I react. And then when whoever comes to take our picture, I won't be staring at you with rapt fascination. I'll be yawning a huge yawn instead."

"What a wonderful suggestion," Scott promptly replied. "I believe I'll tell you the story of my life. I'll go into excruciating detail. Then you can tell me if it was boring or not.''

It was not boring. Not to Liza. She listened to every detail and quickly committed it to memory. Instinctively she knew she would want to remember it all later when she was alone and could think about it all. She was interested in Scott. She wanted to know what he was like as a child. She was curious about his parents, his home life, the schools he attended. When did he first ride a bicycle? How did he look as a baby?

The photographer came too soon. Scott had only gotten through his grade school experiences.

With the photographer came Monica Grant.

"Darling," she gushed as she rushed to where Scott stood to greet her. The raven-haired woman rushed into his arms and kissed him soundly while the photographer clicked away. Liza counted eight-nine-ten flashes as the young, sandy-haired photographer caught their kiss from several different angles.

Liza unsuccessfully tried to hide her displeasure. She glared at the kissing couple with unconcealed disgust.

Monica's back was to Liza when she finally stopped kissing Scott and spoke to him. "I've lined up several eligible women, darling. They'll be along soon. And I've gotten reservations at the Pump Room and at Jacques, so we'll have a variety of backgrounds."

Monica's voice was husky, her manner authoritative. She still clung possessively to Scott's arm. Liza liked the woman less each time she saw her.

"I've only agreed to having my pictures taken with Liza," Scott easily informed her. "I'm sure you've gotten enough information on her to make it suitably interesting."

Monica turned slowly and regarded Liza as though she were a low form of life. "She's nobody," Monica curtly reported. "I can't make a story out of a nobody."

Scott stared daggers at Monica. He had given her a short biography of Liza. When his secretary had collected the information, Scott himself had been suitably impressed.

"You can and will," he ordered, "or there will be no pictures at all."

Chapter Eight

Liza was seated at her desk, but her thoughts were on Scott. Memories of last night's kisses were crowding everything else out of her mind. Even the totally new experience of being photographed for publicity purposes paled in relation to the later, heady experience of his kisses. And, again, she felt the tingling warmth of desire surge through her, and the intimate glow that only Scott could give her.

The phone rang, its insistent blare hardly registering through the pleasant fog of Liza's delight. Smiling she reached to answer it. Silently she prayed it was Scott.

"Hello." Her voice was pleasantly musical.

"Ms Manchester?" The caller was female. Liza frowned with disappointment.

"Yes," Liza confirmed, barely concealing her sigh. "Speaking."

It was a student, a reporter from the University's newspaper. And she wanted to make an appointment for an interview.

"What about?" Liza queried, perplexed.

"It's about the experiment you're working on. The experiment with Dr. Harburton."

Liza said nothing. It took her a moment to remember what the experiment was. It was about door opening and the like.

"The one I read about in the paper today," the caller explained.

"Oh," Liza dully replied, her heart sinking.

Mostly out of curiosity, Liza agreed to an interview. She had no idea what kind of publicity Monica had generated, but she guessed it wasn't good for her. When the student reporter got to Liza's office she introduced herself as Mary Lindahl. She could have been a pretty girl, with wholesome features and blond hair, but her hair hung long, straight, and untrimmed. Her face was without makeup, and she wore worn and faded jeans and a rumpled and shapeless navy blue T-shirt which proclaimed "Graham University" across her braless breasts.

"In an early copy of today's paper I caught a picture of you with Dr. Harburton."

The reporter showed her the page. There were Liza and Scott, heads together, talking intimately. The caption read: "The Chauvinist and the Feminist" and identified Scott as the author of a soon-to-be-released book on how to court women the old-fashioned way. Liza, it explained, was a staunch member of Graham University's women's rights group.

Monica Grant had certainly dreamed up a story. Warily Liza wondered how much Scott had to do with it.

After getting no reaction from Liza on the photograph, Mary Lindahl read from a nearby column by Burton Judson, a Chicago reporter, whose lively column sparkled with witty stories about the city's great and near-great.

Scott Harburton's new book as much as says that any man can get anything he wants from a woman, he has only to use the tried and true courting methods: flowers, music, small courtesies and thoughtful gifts. His new ladylove, Liza Manchester, takes a different view. She doesn't even want her doors opened for her.

Is it a classic case of opposites attracting? Or is Professor Harburton merely using Manchester as a proving ground for his newest theories? If so, how long will the lovely Liza stay in Scott's perennial parade of beautiful women?

Liza sat stunned. She said nothing for a long time. All she could do was wonder how close to the truth the allegations were. Was Scott only using her to prove his point?

Mary pulled a booklet from the backpack she had slung next to her chair. Liza dimly recognized it as the proceedings from one of a series of women's issues conferences Graham had held last spring. Liza had made some comments there. They had been recorded in the proceedings, but Liza had thought no more about it.

"In your comments last spring," Mary began, leafing through the book to find her marked page, "you took women to task for doing things that contributed to their own degradation."

The student located the marked page and began to read from it.

Every time a woman expects, allows, or encourages a man to open her car door, carry her packages, take her arm to help her cross the street, she is contributing to her own inferior status.

As for gifts of candy and flowers and the like, things which men send to women when they woo them, these are only subtly disguised payoffs for services rendered.

The next time you are out with a man, don't let him open your doors. Insist that he give you the dignity of ordering your own meal, instead of mouthing your words to the waiter. And, for heaven's sake, if he sends you flowers, send them back.

Mary looked over the booklet at Liza, choosing her next words carefully. "Now, Ms Manchester, you have a large bouquet of lovely yellow roses on your desk. Are they from Dr. Harburton? And would you care to comment on them?"

Liza felt as though she had been run over by a large truck. It took everything she had to pull her concentration back to the student reporter.

Had she said those words that Mary Lindahl had just read? Yes, she had. She remembered them. She had even believed them.

"Yes, I'd be happy to comment on the flowers," Liza replied smoothly. "They are from Dr. Harburton and they're very beautiful."

Mary Lindahl gazed at her in openmouthed horror. Had Liza stripped naked and displayed herself on campus as a walking, talking sex symbol, the student could not have been more upset.

"How can you say that?" she demanded. "These flowers symbolize everything that is wrong with man-woman relations today. They are a subtly disguised pay-off. You said so yourself."

Liza laughed. "Let's not blame the poor flowers for what people have turned them into," she admonished. "Frankly I'm just enjoying them for what they are."

The student reporter frowned in disgust. She found another passage from Liza's speech and quoted it to her.

Even women who have climbed the ladder to success, women who are established in a profession and secure within themselves, even these women wait for men to take the initiative in a relationship.

It is the men who, with rare exceptions, do the inviting out. It is the men who pay the bills. It is the men who most often initiate sexual relations.

And if marriage is in the picture, then the woman still routinely waits for the man to do the asking.

As long as they do, men and women cannot have a true relationship between equals. The men are still more equal than the women.

The reporter paused meaningfully and put down the booklet. She regarded Liza solemnly. "Ms Manchester, do you still believe those things you said?"

"Of course," Liza immediately returned. "They are truths that need to be told. And I haven't changed my views one whit since I said them, except maybe to gather more evidence that convinces me of their validity."

Mary Lindahl seemed satisfied. Her shoulders, which she had held stiff and tense, relaxed a bit. Her faith in Liza seemed restored.

"I take it you would have no compunction about asking Dr. Harburton out to dinner and paying the bill yourself? Or even asking him to marry you if it ever came to that?"

Liza couldn't imagine herself asking him out to dinner. But, even worse, she couldn't begin to think how he would react if she offered to pay the bill. And as for asking him to marry her? She couldn't even consider the possibility.

"Ms Manchester," the reporter prompted. Obviously she was waiting to have Liza answer the question exactly as she herself would answer it.

Well, why not, Liza thought daringly. After all, it was what she believed. Women were equal to men, weren't they? Then the answer had to be yes.

"Of course," Liza agreed wholeheartedly. "There is no reason why a woman shouldn't take the lead in a relationship. Even to asking a man to marry her."

"The article I write should be in Friday's paper," the reporter informed Liza. Then she picked up her backpack and slung it onto her shoulders. "Thanks for the interview," Mary Lindahl said as she headed toward the door. But she turned before she went out. "You're doing a lot for women here on campus," she commented with a grateful smile. "Thanks."

The backpack bobbed on sagging shoulders as the reporter walked away. As Liza watched her graceless walk, she wondered if Mary had ever had ballet lessons. Madame Aubert would have helped her a lot.

Liza had not counted on the fact that Mary Lindahl would interview Scott, too. In the article he was quoted.

Liza Manchester is a stunningly beautiful example of just how wrong a woman can be. The ideas she supports are biased by some of her own unfortunate experiences. It is certainly more scientifically accurate to support objective laboratory-tested data than the subjective opinion of any single woman.

The rest of the article was cleverly written to infer that Liza was having an affair with Scott, and that they were broad-minded enough not to let their personal differences of opinion affect their very satisfactory love life.

"Liza Manchester is one of the most completely satisfying women I have ever met," Scott was quoted in one of the last lines of the long, and to Liza, infuriating article.

"What a story," Valerie blurted out as soon as she hit the office. "What he says about you. Wow! You two must put Romeo and Juliet to shame. How romantic," she sighed loudly.

"Valerie, this is a lot of trumped-up nonsense," Liza angrily declared. "That reporter must be trying out for the scandal sheets. She's blown it all out of proportion. Why, she makes it sound like—like—"

"I know. It's fabulous," Valerie gushed happily. "He calls you completely satisfying. In quotes yet. And it sure doesn't sound like idle speculation. He means it. Wow! Oh, Liza, do you know how lucky you are?"

Liza glared angrily at her delighted friend. "Stop it, Valerie, just stop it. This is ridiculous. And it's not true," Liza staunchly maintained.

"Sure sounds like it to me," Valerie cheerfully insisted, oblivious of any protest from her friend.

Valerie had only been gone a few minutes when a messenger came. He brought a rose, one perfect red rose in a hobnail milk-glass bud vase. Attached to the vase with a red florist ribbon was a small envelope.

Liza's suspicions were confirmed when she fumbled with the envelope and pulled out the card.

Dinner at the Pump Room. Pick you up at seven.

S.

Her delicate mouth immediately formed into an angry frown. She guessed the rose was a peace offering of some sort. He had probably seen the paper, too, and guessed she was mad. She took a deep, angry breath and let it out slowly. She couldn't be bought so easily, she told herself. And she resented his thinking that she could.

Liza indignantly turned the card over and over in her tense fingers. For a moment she concentrated hard on what her next move would be. Then a light came to her eyes. A gleam of satisfaction lighted her face.

She went behind the desk and resolutely sat in the chair. She reached into the penholder to get a red marker. And she wrote. "No. L.M." on the back of Scott's card. Then she pulled out the razor-sharp stencil knife that she kept in her drawer. She lifted the rose from the vase and carefully, very carefully so as not to damage the stem, she trimmed off the thorns. With clear tape she attached them to the back of the card. Then she returned the card to its envelope.

"Oh, Jennie, will you come into the office," Liza sweetly called to the junior secretary. "I want you to run an errand."

She gave Jennie specific instructions. "Take the envelope to the Psychology Department, please. To Dr. Harburton. Be sure it's delivered directly into his hands," Liza cautioned. "Wait all day if you have to, but be sure to do exactly as I say."

"Yes, ma'am," Jennie obediently replied.

Scott Harburton sat in his book-lined office staring pensively out the window. He was thinking about Liza, worrying about her reaction to the campus newspaper article, and wishing that he had seen the article before he had sent her the rose. Maybe he would have handled the situation differently if he'd known how the article would sound. It did sound as though they were having a torrid affair. He wondered if, in fact, he had said anything to make the reporter believe they were lovers. He had certainly wanted to make it clear that he admired Liza.

His phone buzzed, interrupting his thoughts. "A message for you, Dr. Harburton. The person who is delivering it says it must be hand delivered."

Scott frowned. "All right," he agreed without enthusiasm.

Jennie was in his office in a moment. She timidly handed the note to him and watched his big, tanned hands open the tiny envelope. His blue eyes were startled momentarily when he saw his own card, its back taped with rose thorns and a bright red, "No. L.M." scrawled on the front.

His startled expression turned quickly to a smile. The broad grin transformed itself into a laugh. Scott Harburton threw back his head and laughed long and hard.

Liza's audacious gesture snapped the tension that had filled him when he began to worry about her reaction to the publicity. It broke his dam of reserve and let his feelings flow free. It also opened his heart just a little wider. For a moment he wondered what he had ever seen in any other woman.

Jennie reported back to Liza. "I don't know what you wrote," she timidly related, "but Dr. Harburton loved it. He just laughed and laughed."

Jennie was completely surprised to have Liza rudely send her away. Liza was furious again. Still, Scott was the most difficult man she had ever met, she told herself. Impossible, really.

Well, that was that. Experiment or not, Liza had had enough. She never wanted to see Scott again.

At five o'clock Scott appeared in Liza's office, closing the door behind him. There was a self-satisfied grin on his tanned face. He had the confidence of a conquering hero as he strode across the dull gray rug and came to the back of Liza's desk.

He lounged carelessly against the edge of the desk, looking down at Liza's astonished expression. Dancing lights of mirth and sensuality sparkled in his cobalt-blue eyes.

"What do you want?" Liza snapped.

She was disturbed by his closeness. It made it harder for her to breathe, harder for her to control her heartbeat, harder for her to keep herself from reacting to his potent maleness.

"I want you," he revealed in a husky whisper.

Liza thought she would strangle with the rush of emotion that followed his declaration. Her body almost betrayed her. She almost let herself get up and throw herself into his waiting arms. But she couldn't. She wouldn't. Especially after what he had said about her in the paper.

"Well, you can't have me," she answered testily as she pretended to concentrate on the work on her desk.

"Oh, but I will," he announced throatily as he took her hand and pulled her to her feet. She rose as though in a trance and listened to his hypnotizing voice. "I'll hold you in my arms," Scott promised. "I'll kiss you, caress you until you quiver with desire, until you cry out for me to take you."

"No," Liza protested weakly. Her eyes were glued to his face. She felt rooted to the spot.

"Oh, yes, Liza, my Liza," Scott softly crooned. "We'll learn each other's secret pleasures and marvel in the joy we can bring each other."

"No," Liza forced herself to cry.

"Oh, yes," Scott whispered.

He was about to kiss her. His lips lowered to hers, and Liza knew she would be lost, utterly lost, if she couldn't stop him, and stop him now.

"What will Monica Grant say?" Liza demanded, wondering where she got the strength to utter the words.

"Monica is in California," Scott explained, unperturbed. His arms encircled her now. His fingers caressed her back, sending shivers of delight through her.

But had he designed his words specifically to anger her, he could not have chosen them better. Liza went rigid in his arms.

"Oh, I see," Liza frostily said. "There's no conflict. Monica is in California and I'm here. Do you have someone else in New York? How about Florida? And for your jaunts to Europe? Is there someone else for those?"

He was unflustered. He was so sure of his own desire for her that he couldn't quite believe that she wasn't responding to him. After all, Scott had just that afternoon come to the conclusion that Liza was worth having at almost any cost. He now expected her to obligingly fall into his arms.

"You're being ridiculous," Scott replied with a light laugh. He was fully convinced that any resistance she might put up was only token.

"Me ridiculous?" she fumed. "Me ridiculous? I'm not ridiculous. You are. You and your huge collection of women from coast to coast. And your public inference that I've joined them."

"Liza," Scott good naturedly protested, "I don't—"

"I don't want to join your party," Liza interrupted. "I don't want to be part of Scott's Scientific Seduction System. Not now. Not ever. Now get out."

Scott shook his head lightly. He hoped Liza was calming down. He scheduled another few seconds to let her lower her anger level. Then he would appeal to her reason. He waited.

"How about dinner?" he finally asked. "We're set for the Pump Room."

It was too much. The flame that had burned in Liza turned to a conflagration, an angry, out-of-control burst of red-hot fury.

"I'm sick of those fancy places you're always taking me. The Pump Room, indeed. Nothing but a lot of rich sauces. Those menus are sickening after a while. And the restaurants. They're ridiculous. I'm a real person, not a varnished and veneered Kewpie doll of a society woman. Fancy restaurants are fun about twice a month. After that they're a bore. All glitter. Not that much substance. They're filled with all kinds of self-important people who smile phony smiles at each other with their capped teeth."

He studied the spewing Liza with an intensity that he used only when puzzling out the most difficult of his patients.

"You would love some of my parents' friends," Scott commented dryly.

"And yours, too, for that matter," Liza savagely returned. "Monica Grant of all people. The very pinnacle of empty-headed femininity. A symbol of all that is wrong with dependent womanhood. A simpering, slithery, clinging vine who measures success by running a tape measure around her bosom."

Liza stopped for a moment to catch her breath. But in that moment she lost her advantage. A devilish gleam lighted Scott's eyes. A wicked grin spread across his handsome face.

"Liza," he confidently suggested, "you're jealous."

Liza felt the blood rushing past her ears. Her heart thudded wildly in her bosom. She furiously clenched her fists at her sides until her knuckles were white.

"Doctor," she said slowly and distinctly, "you're crazy. Have one of your colleagues examine you. You have a pitiful grasp of reality. Now go away," she ordered through teeth that were nearly clenched. "I have work to do."

He didn't move. He only watched her, studied her with an amused smile on his face. And then he began to kiss her.

He kissed her firmly, thoroughly. His teasing but firm pressure parted her lips, and she felt her fury turn to a seething warmth that flamed through her body as his kiss deepened and her passion began to flare.

His caressing hands sensuously rubbed her back, then her waist, urging her closer to him. When they moved slowly over the curve of her hips, she felt that her body was full of millions of brief, exquisite explosions. The air left her lungs, and with it went her will.

The kiss ended and he whispered in her ear, his soft breath leaving a trail of fire along her cheek.

"I'll be back in an hour. And you can decide where we'll eat."

It was long minutes before she could again sit at her desk to work.

Scott came back. Liza had known he would. And just as surely she had known she would go out with him. She wanted to be with him, she wanted that very much, and she was ready to admit that the reporter might easily have slanted her story beyond even Scott's publicity-savvy, wildest dreams.

In the hour while Liza simmered down and waited for him to return, she thought about the basic differences between them, their different world views. She resolved that very evening to show him something of her world, or at least the world of her youth, and watch his reaction to it.

When Scott returned, it was Liza who asked him out to dinner that night. They went to White Castle.

They stood behind the wide white enamel and polished steel counter while uniformed attendants cooked tiny hamburgers on open grills.

"Ever been to a White Castle before?" Liza inquired as she watched Scott, who seemed fascinated by the assembly line process of cooking the small, square hamburgers. The speedy workers deftly shoved them into their neat white and blue paper boxes.

"Never," Scott revealed, his fascinated gaze still watching the food preparation.

"And you thought you had a privileged childhood," Liza teased.

He watched her nose wrinkle attractively and he felt his heart lurch. She was full of surprises, Liza was. But the biggest surprise for Scott was realizing how he felt about her.

When their order was taken, Liza paid for it. "Tonight is my treat," she informed him in a voice that left no room for argument.

Scott smiled good-naturedly and followed her to a small, white table. "I can't even help you with your chair," he dryly observed as they sat down on the low, stationary stools.

Liza giggled with the delightful abandon of a playful child. Scott reacted with an overwhelming desire to protect her childlike innocence, her lack of sophistication and artifice.

"Like it?" Liza asked as she watched Scott devour a hamburger in two big bites.

"It's good," he replied in amazement. "Small but good."

Liza smiled back at him, her eyes twinkling merrily.

"The trick is to eat lots," she told him. "Either that or wait until you get to Gertie's."

"Who is Gertie?" Scott asked as he reached for another hamburger.

"Just wait," Liza mysteriously replied. "Just wait."

After dinner they went to a movie. The theater was old and run down, but reasonably clean and the admission was cheap. Liza paid it. They saw a rollicking comedy that had them both laughing until they ached. And they came out of the theater into the warm summer evening still weak from laughter.

"Now for the mysterious Gertie," Scott declared, eyebrows raised in expectation. "Where do we find her?"

Liza pointed down the street. "There," she declared.

She pointed to an old-fashioned corner ice cream parlor, complete with white-uniformed attendants working behind a long, mirror-backed counter, filling tall dishes and glasses with huge scoops of ice cream. They flooded their creations with rich looking sauces, mounds of fluffy whipped cream, and topped them off with a glistening, red cherry.

There was a long wait before Liza and Scott could get one of the old wooden booths. They stood by the homemade candy counter and watched the immense ice cream dishes parade by on the waitresses' heavily laden trays.

After they were seated, Liza confided that she had

come to Gertie's often as a child. "We lived only a few blocks away," she revealed. "My grandfather often brought me here for a treat. After he died, I saved my allowance for a cone. I'd be up here nearly every Saturday, even in February, licking away blissfully. They make their own ice cream, you know."

"I didn't know," Scott replied, smiling at her with amusement, "but I might have guessed."

His gaze changed to one of burning intensity. "You must have been a cute little girl."

He wondered how it would have been to have the young, probably pigtailed, Liza on his lap. But all he could think of was Liza now, on his lap, curled up in his arms. The very thought stirred his senses. He could feel his desire rise.

Liza was flustered by his compliment and his intense scrutiny. His eyes were filled with desire as he gazed at her, finally taking her hand and holding it across the narrow table. His broad thumb traced erotic designs on her sensitive palm. He languorously slipped his index finger in and out between her fingers while his deep-blue eyes bored boldly into hers.

Her pulse raced dangerously. Her breathing almost stopped and she felt suspended in a cloud of wild sensation. The only reality for her was Scott.

The waitress had to ask for their order twice to break their spell. Scott ordered an old-fashioned banana split, Liza a raspberry sundae.

After the waitress disappeared, he huskily asked her, "What were you like as a child?"

Liza told him of her growing up in the nearby neighborhood. Playing hopscotch on the sidewalk, jumping rope in the schoolyard, going to Girl Scouts and playing paper dolls.

After they finished their ice cream, Scott insisted that they stroll through the neighborhood. He wanted to see the house where Liza had grown up.

He held her hand as they walked, and she delighted in how right it felt, how amazingly, perfectly right it felt to have her hand in his, to feel his lightly calloused palm pressed to hers, to have his strong fingers firmly laced into hers.

The soft glow from the streetlights shone on small but well kept lawns, tree lined streets, and rows of brick bungalows. An occasional low apartment building or two-flat was mixed in with the single family homes. Liza's was a modest, typical Chicago bungalow, red brick with a cement front porch and steps. A large urn of petunias stood on the porch rail, a riot of red and white spilling over the edges of the stone planter.

Liza was just thinking how comfortable and unpretentious the neighborhood was when Scott spoke.

"I like the house you lived in. And I like the neighborhood. A real solid, substantial place," he observed.

Even as he spoke she thought about Scott's wealthy suburban upbringing. Where he came from glitter was important. Status was everything. For Liza those things were low on her list of priorities.

"Nice neighborhood," he said genuinely.

She relaxed. She was glad he felt that way. So glad that her heart began to sing.

When Scott brought her home he took her in his arms. She yielded to the sweet, teasing torture of his lips on hers, opening her mouth to let him explore her sweet softness. Her body molded to his as though it were the most natural thing Liza could do. And, in fact, it was. Her breasts ached to be crushed against him. Her hips fitted against his, and she felt herself straining to be close, closer to him than to any other man ever before.

Her arms twined around his neck, and she clung to him as though her very life depended on keeping him close to her always. Her body yearned to surround, envelop, absorb his.

"Oh, Liza, we belong together," he whispered throatily as he held her fast against him, "really together. I want you. Oh, how I want you. Now."

It was a groan that came from deep in his soul. And it was a plea, too. A desperate plea that Liza say yes and end the frustration and misery that consumed them both. The knowledge that he wanted her sent a wild, electric thrill through Liza, a thrill that left her breathless and panting.

Hungrily he claimed her partly open mouth, kissing her deeply. His hands slid down her back and forced her hips harder against his. Liza felt the strength of his desire. It filled her with a thrilling weakness. She clung to him hungrily.

His kisses were claiming, insistent, demanding her surrender, and promising dizzying satisfaction for them both. But he had said nothing of love. And as that fact slowly registered in Liza's passion-fogged brain, she fought with herself to regain her sapped strength. Then gently, painfully, she pulled herself away from him.

"N-no," she whispered. The sound barely rose out of her aching throat.

"When?" he huskily demanded. He still kissed her and insinuated his hard body against hers. Liza trembled with longing. She was so absorbed in the heady sensations that claimed her body that she didn't, she couldn't, answer right away.

"When?" He whispered his impatience as he rained wild kisses down her neck, then on her earlobes and in the sensitive hollow beneath her ear.

She pushed against his chest with trembling hands to steady herself. Her voice was shaky.

"I—I don't know," she answered, feeling sad, deprived, and inadequate all at once. "Maybe never." Her solemn gray eyes gazed up at him silently, apologetically pleading for understanding.

He watched her critically for a long moment before

he spoke. At first she thought he might be angry. She knew he had a right to be angry. Every response of her body had been full of the promise of passion, every response until she finally said no.

When Scott spoke, it was as he was going out the door. He repeated his earlier statement.

"We belong together," he firmly told her. Then he left.

Despite his physical frustration, as Scott watched the elevator doors smoothly draw together, he was at first aware of an immense feeling of relief. Maybe it was better that he hadn't gone to bed with Liza. Something was happening between them, something that he was not sure he could control. It was good that he would get a break from her.

As for his last comment that they belonged together, he attributed it to the passionate heat of the moment. Sexual drives could do that to a man.

Scott hadn't felt quite so driven by passion, or as unable to control his emotions ever before in his life. He was beginning to resent it. Always he had been able to dictate his own reactions to women and manage his own life on a sound, reasonable basis. But his reaction to Liza defied reason. And it made him nervous.

The elevator stopped at the lobby. Scott practically bolted out. He quickly strode out the big front doors and down the walk to the parking lot.

His face was grim as he seated himself behind the wheel of his powerful sports car. He frowned in disgust as he inserted the key into the lock. The engine roared.

"Damn," he swore softly as he put the car in gear. The tires squealed in protest, and he raced away from the parking lot as though the devil himself were in pursuit.

He hadn't even told Liza the reason he had wanted

her more than ever that night. He hadn't even told her that he was going away, on a tour to promote his book. He wouldn't be back for weeks.

Chapter Nine

The first week Scott was gone, Liza was scheduled to be out of the office much of the time. She was coordinating a meeting of midwestern anthropologists which was held in the Palmer House, a fashionable old hotel in Chicago's downtown area, usually called the Loop by Chicagoans because of the way elevated trains circled the huge area.

Liza was glad to be out of the office. She had very little to do with Wainright while the meetings were in progress. And she was delighted that a new position seemed virtually certain for her, and she would never have to see the objectionable anthropologist again.

The busyness of the meetings helped her forget exactly how miserable she was. She refused to let herself think of Scott and the fact that he had not called since she stopped him from making love to her. She shrank back from any thought of him, the way she might pull back from a painfully searing flame.

Tuesday evening Liza dropped into her office at the University to leave some papers there on her way home. She stopped to check on her friend Valerie. She was still there, still working.

"You look awful," Valerie candidly told Liza. "Did you just learn that you are about to be marooned on a desert island or something?"

"Don't be funny, Valerie," Liza complained with a

frown. "I'm in no mood to take it. These meetings are a real drain."

"I can see that," Valerie returned easily, unruffled by Liza's harsh words. "I think what you need is some fun. Let's go cruise around the neighborhood and see if we can find some good looking men."

"We're in the wrong neighborhood for good looking men," Liza answered with a grim smile. "All the men around here are either scruffy students or married professors."

"Well, then we'll go someplace else," Valerie brightly suggested. "We'll just keep going until prince charming runs into my battered Volkswagen bug with his gorgeous old, completely restored Jaguar."

"You can't drive that far," Liza argued pessimistically. "Besides prince charming went out with the last century. He doesn't exist anymore."

"Oh, yes he does," Valerie cheerfully insisted. "And he's just waiting to find me, my dear. Oh, how I wish he'd hurry up," she sighed. "I'm getting tired of typing."

"You're incorrigible," Liza announced. "But fun. How about a hamburger and a movie instead of this continuous hunt for the man of your dreams."

"Oh, all right," Valerie reluctantly agreed, her lower lip sticking out slightly. She looked like a young child pouting. Then she brightened. "Maybe he'll be at the movies. Prince charming," she unnecessarily explained.

"Maybe he'll be the hamburger cook at the fast food restaurant," Liza added dryly, "although I've seldom seen one over nineteen and free from acne. Let's go."

The next night Jeffrey appeared at the Palmer House just as Liza was finishing up for the day. He suggested that they try to get last-minute tickets for the latest road show musical at the Shubert Theater.

Liza agreed, hoping the play would keep her mind off Scott. She had never been so depressed in all her life because she hadn't heard from a man. When she thought about the pain he was causing her, she began to hate him.

Between her night out with Valerie and the theater date with Jeffrey, Liza had had two late nights in a row. She was tired on Thursday morning and decidedly grumpy, even before there was a barrage of complaining calls.

A particularly arrogant and obnoxious graduate student planted himself in front of her desk and questioned Liza's interpretation of a ruling on transfer of credits. The student was one whom Wainright advised. Wainright was not available. Liza had to cope. And everything else had to wait while the student gave a long-winded explanation of his own view of things.

"See me later," Liza finally told him, trying hard to mask her irritation. Several times she had quoted him chapter and verse on why he couldn't do what he wanted to do. The facts hardly seemed to matter to him.

Liza didn't want the overbearing student to take up all of her time. He was obviously more impressed with his own self-importance than in what the rules said.

"Look, I have some errands to run," she finally said in exasperation, hoping to shake him.

He followed her around the administration building and back to her office, arguing with her all the way. By the time Liza reached her desk, she was exhausted and angry, yet the student just kept talking to her, kept trying to prove his point, despite her repeated, carefully worded, patiently voiced explanations.

The phone rang. Already irritated and annoyed she quickly grabbed the receiver.

"Hello," she snapped.

"Where have you been?"

The equally sharp voice on the other end belonged to Scott Harburton. He was scolding her already. She certainly wasn't up to any more arguments from anyone, least of all him. She hadn't heard from him in nearly a week. Usually he had dropped into the office several times a week at a minimum.

"What is that question supposed to mean?" she challenged. "Where have I been?"

Despite her powerful anger, Liza felt the gentle tingling, the soft, thrilling awareness she experienced whenever Scott was near. But the churning emotions turned to anger now and added fuel to her irritation.

The arrogant student was tapping his foot against the floor, waiting with unconcealed impatience for her undivided attention once again. She gazed at him and frowned, but the frown was for Scott, too. He had no right to snap at her the way he had.

"It means I want to know where you were. I tried calling you all last night. And the night before. You weren't home." His deeply masculine voice was edged with an almost savage impatience.

"How brilliant of you to deduce that, Professor," she sarcastically replied. "No wonder you are highly renowned in intellectual circles."

She heard a muffled oath on the other end of the phone.

"Where were you?" he persisted.

Liza was furious now. Scott had made no commitment to her. He had even seemed to forget about her all this week. Yet he was talking to her as though he owned her.

"It certainly is not any of your business," Liza informed him archly.

The student looked at her strangely, obviously questioning the conversation. She found herself wishing that he were gone, wishing that she could really tell Scott what she thought of him at this moment. He wanted control of her life, her time, even her body, without giving anything of himself. But she couldn't say all that. And especially not with an audience, not even one as objectionable as the student standing by her desk.

"I could ask you the same questions," Liza countered. "In fact I think I will."

"Now stop all that liberated female nonsense with me," Scott growled.

"Yes, sir," she crisply replied. "I'll remember my place."

He took a deep, exasperated breath. Liza could almost see his broad chest rise and fall heavily. He tried a different approach. "I called to ask you to have dinner with me Friday," he informed her. "I've been in New York. I'll be home by then," he revealed, only partially explaining his lack of contact.

He could have phoned, Liza told herself angrily. "Where would we eat?" she asked in an almost pettish tone.

"Is that so important?" he asked, now irritable again.

Liza sensed that he had wanted an immediate yes answer. Perversely she refused to give it to him. "Naturally it matters where we eat," she replied all too pleasantly. "I'll have to pick the proper clothes, at the very least."

"My place. Eight o'clock. Can you make it?" he asked curtly.

She allowed a meaningful pause to elapse before she answered. "You mean get there myself? I don't know where you live. Shall I take the bus?" she asked with mock innocence.

He groaned. I'll send a car for you. And you'd better ride in it," he threatened.

"How nice of you," she replied with exaggerated good manners. "Shall I plan to cook?" Liza pressed her advantage and thoroughly enjoyed the confusion and discomfort in Scott's voice.

"Of course you won't cook," he savagely replied.

"Then you will?" Liza asked innocently.

"No. Cora cooks," he flatly announced.

"I see," Liza archly responded, "you have a woman for that."

The student was watching her warily. He began to look uncomfortable. Good, Liza thought with satisfaction. His kind deserves to look uncomfortable once in a while. It might wipe the self-assured look off his face for at least a moment.

"The 'woman,' as you call her, is sixty and has white hair and wears sensible shoes."

"Of course. How nice for you," Liza smoothly replied. "And does she do the dishes?"

"Stop it," Scott ordered. "You know she would. I'm not the domestic type."

"Pity," Liza declared with saccharine tones.

"What the hell is happening out there?" Scott fiercely demanded. "What has gotten into you?"

Liza was about to make another cutting reply when there was a noise at the other end. A purring female voice sounded in the background.

"Come on, darling, we're late."

The voice was not only purring, but very sultry. Liza could identify it. Monica Grant.

"I've got to go now," Scott immediately said. "See you Friday."

Liza held the phone in her hand for a long moment before she carefully replaced it in its cradle.

Now angrier than ever, Liza turned back to her troublesome student. Her thoughts were murderous, both about him and about Scott. She listened to the student awhile longer, and then quietly, patiently, and thoroughly she explained to him why all his thinking was complete rubbish.

Friday did not go well at all for Liza. Before ten in the morning the coffeepot stopped heating. Liza had to go down to get a cup of coffee from the Finance Office pot. On the way there she ran her pantyhose on a giant staple from a discarded packing box that had been left near the elevators. After she got back to her own office, her fingernail ripped when it got caught in the workings of the typewriter as she tried unsuccessfully to fix the tab stops. She had to space everything out painstakingly all day after she learned that the typewriter repair service was shorthanded and couldn't possibly be there until next week.

One of the junior secretaries never showed up for work, so Liza had to type the urgent report she had left with her. And when Liza checked with Mrs. Johnson, as she did every half hour or so, she found she had a dozen calls to return. There were even three from Burton Judson, the columnist. She decided not to return any of the calls.

In the late afternoon Mary Lindahl called. As Mrs. Johnson was away from her desk, Liza answered the phone. When Liza heard the reporter's voice, she wondered if Mary was slouching in a chair somewhere, or if her posture had magically improved since their last encounter.

After exchanging a few pleasantries, Mary asked Liza how she liked the article in the morning paper.

"Sorry, I didn't see it," Liza admitted honestly. And she realized with astonishment that she had hardly given Scott's publicity a second thought since the first articles. She only knew that she didn't want any part of it.

"What did the article say?" Liza inquired, vaguely apprehensive about what she would learn.

"It was Burton Judson's column again" was the almost impatient reply.

A cold chill ran through Liza. She sensed that what he would say wouldn't be good.

"I'll read it to you," the reporter said.

Scott Harburton, the celebrated psychologist and professor at Graham University and author of the best seller, *Think You Can*, and the newly released book, *What Women Want*, is engaged in a modern-day battle of the sexes with a new twist. The popular bachelor has been dating Liza Manchester, a staunch member of Graham's radical feminist community.

The good Doctor Harburton's thesis is that all women really crave the little courtly attentions. But can he prove this to a radical, liberated woman like Manchester? Ms Manchester has publicly stated that she wants equality, not roses. But reports from Graham's campus are that the lovely Liza is falling into Harburton's arms.

Watch this column for further details of the affair of the professor and the feminist.

Mary finished reading the article, and Liza immediately began to sputter.

"Affair?" she demanded. "What does he mean by affair?"

"Probably he means it both in the narrow and the broad sense," the reporter suggested. But Liza barely heard the reporter's response. She was angry. Furious. The whole thing with Scott was getting out of hand. She didn't want her name in the papers, certainly not as though she had succumbed to Scott's irresistible charm.

"But I'm not—" she began to protest.

"Why not? Most women would," Mary immediately replied. "Dr. Harburton has tremendous sex appeal."

Liza disliked the reporter's whole attitude, which seemed to be that if a man has a lot of sex appeal, he is worth an affair, whatever else is happening.

"Would you care to comment on your relationship with Dr. Harburton?" Mary asked.

"No, I would not," Liza answered frostily. There was a moment's pause, an uncomfortable silence.

"I'll call you when you're not so upset," the reporter promised. "I didn't think you would be so uptight, embarrassed, to have a public affair."

Liza had barely put the phone down when Valerie dashed in, a folded newspaper waving from her excited hand.

"You made the papers again," Valerie announced, her voice a mixture of wonder and delight. Her whole body seemed to vibrate happily with what she saw as her friend's good fortune.

"I know," Liza glumly replied. She frowned at her cheerful friend.

"But it's wonderful," Valerie insisted. "You're a celebrity." Valerie's green eyes shone with the wonder of it all.

Liza grimaced and actually felt relieved when she heard the phone ring. At least there would be a change of subject.

It was Mrs. Johnson, who was now at her desk. "Burton Judson, the columnist, is on the phone," the woman announced.

"I won't talk to him," Liza curtly replied. "I don't want to talk to any reporters. I don't want to talk to anybody if it isn't about work," she snapped. She banged down the receiver and glared angrily from behind her work filled desk.

Valerie tiptoed out of her friend's office, her newspaper now clutched close to her bosom. She left Liza to stew in solitary silence.

It was a few minutes before five when Jeffrey importantly strode into Liza's office. "How's the celebrity?" he asked. "You're so popular that Mrs. J. wouldn't put my phone call through because I wasn't a strictly business call."

Liza scowled and turned back to her typing. "I have half a page to finish, then I'm done. I'll talk to you then," she replied crossly, continuing to type while Jeffrey parked himself in the office chair.

"Fame hasn't changed you much," he dryly commented.

"I don't want to be famous," she hotly replied, still typing, her eyes and fingers working together at lightning speed. "I want to be left alone."

"A Greta Garbo complex already, I see. Tsk, tsk," Jeffrey teased, but there was an unmistakable angry edge to his voice. "And imagine you falling for all that phony stuff. Flowers. Door opening. Chair holding. Traitor," he bitterly accused.

Liza kept typing, now glowering at the page that filled with words. At that moment she hated Jeffrey Childers. She hated her job. She hated the report she was typing. But most of all, she hated Scott Harburton. He was at the root of most of her anger.

Jeffrey had wanted to take Liza out. But she refused. It would have been easy to go with him and to not be available for Scott's dinner. But she had no wish to get Jeffrey's bitter lectures all night.

She went home and tried to rest, but instead found herself poised to answer the telephone or the doorbell, whichever would ring first. But both were totally silent.

Liza's heart was heavy that evening. At the time she should have been dressed for her dinner date with Scott she found herself in an emotional tug of war. She finally decided to stand him up, not even to show up for his dinner.

"Let him call his cutie from New York to come," she angrily decided. When she was to have been picked up, she cleverly arranged not to be home. She walked over to Valerie's, telling herself that she'd show Scott

that all women didn't fall at his feet each time he beckoned. No matter who was purring at him in New York,
Liza herself was above such things.

But another part of Liza cried as she walked. She admitted that she had missed Scott and couldn't wait to
see him. She missed his ready laugh, his tall, muscular
body, and the delightful way his lightest touch made
her tingle.

As though Scott expected Liza's fight with herself,
flowers had arrived at her apartment early that evening.
Two dozen exquisite long-stem red roses. The delicate,
velvety petals were just beginning to open out from the
firm, closed buds. With eager fingers she had torn open
the tiny envelope and read the card.

These roses grow more beautiful as they open. So
do you. Until tonight.

Scott

She had read the card twice, a bemused smile on her
face. Was she opening she wondered? And soon she
had the answer. She had opened her heart, made room
in it for Scott. And that was something very precious
and beautiful.

But he hadn't called all that week. And when he had,
it had been a summons, not a real request for her company. Besides she resolutely reminded herself that
Scott's interest wasn't confined to her. There was Monica Grant to think of, and heaven only knew how many
others.

When she reached Valerie's apartment she had
stopped arguing with herself. If there was no future
with Scott, and she was convinced that there wasn't,
there was no point in there being any present, either.

The car Scott had sent for Liza came back late and
empty. He phoned her, worried that somehow she had

missed connections. The phone rang twenty times. There was no answer. He slammed it down angrily.

He called himself all kinds of fool for flying in when he could only spend one night in Chicago. He had done it because he had wanted to see Liza. His eyes hungered for the sight of her as though he needed her to keep on living. His body ached for the touch of her, for the feel of her rounded suppleness against him. And the independent, perverse, maddening woman had stood him up.

In the sleek magnificence of his Lake Shore Drive apartment Scott poured himself a generous measure of Scotch and stared moodily out the huge glass wall window at the moon shining on the sparkling surface of the lake. He hated the serenity of the scene. It was so unlike his own, churning feelings.

He downed his Scotch in a few great gulps. He welcomed the burning sensation the alcohol produced in his throat and the comforting warmth that seeped through him. He poured himself another large drink, and mechanically his travel-weary body sought the comfort of the living room couch.

Liza certainly wasn't working out the way he had thought. After doing Madge's private detective work for her, his plan had been merely to confirm his opinion on liberated women, use Liza as a kind of walking, talking laboratory for his theories. Maybe he could even teach women like Liza a lesson. He was sure all women craved the little courtesies that were symbols of man's adoration, whatever the feminists might say. His own research had confirmed that often enough. But now, instead of proving his point, Scott was finding out that he needed Liza, that he wanted her, and that want was beginning to consume him. He desperately wanted her in his bed, lying beneath him, opening joyfully to him.

He had to talk with her. Really talk. He couldn't let this situation continue. Something had to be done. He dialed her number, letting the phone ring and ring. When there was no answer, fear gripped him. He knew it was late. He looked at his watch. Eleven. She should be home in bed, he decided.

What if something had happened to her. What if she were even now lying face down on a pavement somewhere, attacked, bleeding, hurt. Or what if she were in someone else's bed? That thought flew into his mind to torture him. What if she were sleeping with the cold-blooded snake Jeffrey Childers? He'd almost rather she was physically hurt, he thought, before he rationalized what that would mean.

Valerie. The cute redhead. She knew about Liza and had even openly volunteered to give Scott any help in winning her. The petite secretary had neither tact nor guile. She was as completely open and honest a person as Scott had ever met. She had told him how much Liza loved the ballet. And she had even given him her home phone number.

Scott fumbled through the pages of his pocket appointment book until he found the number. As he dialed it he was surprised to realize that he was praying, praying that Liza would be with Valerie and not Jeffrey, and praying that she would be safe.

"She left five minutes ago," Valerie pertly informed him. "She was headed home."

"Good, I'll call her there," Scott told her, relief evident in his voice.

"I wouldn't if I were you," Valerie warned. "I'm still not sure what it is you did to her, but she's mad as anything about it. She can't even mention your name without sputtering."

"What?" Scott demanded, incredulous. "How could she be mad at me? She's the one who stood me up."

Valerie decided to tell Scott what she knew. After all, what could it hurt? The relationship was in a shambles anyway.

"It's partly the newspaper article, partly the 'summons,' as she calls it, to dinner, and partly that she doesn't want to be your own private experiment any more. Right now you are about a minus ten on her list of favorite things."

"Thanks a lot," Scott sarcastically replied. Then he hung up. His hand gripped the receiver hard, squeezing tight. "The nerve of that woman," he stormed at the empty room, "the absolute nerve of her."

Nothing Scott Harburton had yet done had brought Liza to her knees. It was the last time, the very last time he would put himself out for her, he angrily told himself. And as he tossed and turned in his lonely bed that night he told himself that tomorrow night he would be in New Orleans. Monica would be there, taking care of his publicity at a southern booksellers association conference. He was their banquet speaker.

Scott hadn't slept with the sultry brunette in weeks, even though there had, as usual, been ample opportunity.

He'd rectify that tomorrow, he vowed. He'd whisk her off to his suite right after his banquet speech. Maybe he'd invite her beforehand, too. Monica was willing enough, and her technique was highly polished. Fantastic. She knew exactly how to satisfy a man in a variety of ways.

Scott finally fell into a fitful sleep. He told himself he was content with his plan. It was time he slept with Monica again, anyway. However when he awoke a few hours later, he had a very different idea. As he cheerfully set about implementing it, he found himself whistling again.

It was Saturday morning and Liza's bell buzzed insistently again. Liza knew it would be Valerie, as they had made arrangements only the night before. She crawled sleepily from her bed and pushed the button to admit her friend.

Her bleary vision revealed that her caller was dressed in a sport coat and wore a tie and was far too tall to be Valerie. It was Scott.

"What do you want?" Liza asked crossly.

"I'm going to take you out to breakfast," he informed her.

A smile tugged at the corners of his mouth. His eyes twinkled with a mischievous delight that made Liza decidedly uneasy. But it was too early for her to wrestle with any challenge he was preparing. She had no strength at all.

"Breakfast," she muttered, slowly shaking her head. "I'm not hungry. Go away."

He didn't move.

"I just want to go back to bed," she complained piteously.

"All right," he promptly agreed, "I'll take you to bed." He took her arm and propelled her toward the bedroom.

Startled into action Liza furiously shook herself free of him. Even in the fog of her sleep she reacted to him, and her chief reaction was fury. No man had ever made her as mad as Scott Harburton.

"Stop that," she demanded, stamping her foot like an angry child. "Leave me alone. Go away. I'm tired," she whined.

Dully she realized that last night she had missed him terribly after she got back from Valerie's. She had sobbed softly before falling into a fitful sleep. Now she was driving him away. It didn't make sense.

"Did anyone ever tell you that you are cute when you're mad?" Scott teased, completely unperturbed by Liza's protests.

She turned to confront him, her delicate features drawn into an angry scowl, her eyes still half-closed with sleep. "That's a rotten thing to say, a rotten patronizing thing," she accused.

"It's true," he confirmed with a smile as he pushed her toward the bedroom.

Liza's anger rose within her. Her pulse raced, her back stiffened, and she could hear the blood rushing past her ears.

"Stop this. Stop it now," she insisted.

"You have some apologizing to do to me. Here I flew in for the night just to see you and you stood me up. I figure you owe me something," he suggested, his eyes blatantly displaying his desire.

Liza blushed hot. Her response fanned her fury. "Get out. Get out. Get out," she commanded, now nearly hysterical with anger. He was arrogant, rude, and domineering. How had she ever thought he was as important to her as life itself?

Totally unaffected by Liza's furious protestations, Scott strode confidently to her closet. He left her by the bed, watching him with uncomprehending eyes. He threw open the door, and inspected the clothes hanging on the rod.

"What are you doing?" Liza angrily demanded. "Get out of there. Get out of here. Leave me alone. Get out of my life," she sputtered furiously.

"Ah, I think this will do nicely," he commented as he pulled out a soft navy-and-lime linen dress with short sleeves and a matching lime blazer. He lay the outfit across the bed. "Do you want help dressing, or shall I wait in the other room?" he pleasantly inquired.

"I'm not going to get dressed," she insisted. "You are going to leave and I am going to get some more sleep. That's what Saturday mornings are for. Sleep. They are not for getting all dressed up just to go out to breakfast." She was awake now, awake and angry, even though her body still ached to curl up in the softness of her own warm bed.

"Ah, I see you'll need help dressing," he responded, unruffled by anything Liza had said. He calmly walked across the room toward her, and moved his hands to the tiny ties at her shoulders.

The touch of his fingers on her bare skin sent an electric shock through her whole system and played havoc with her senses. He began to unfasten a tie.

She would not, could not, allow him to affect her so. "Get out, get out," she fiercely demanded, backing away from him. "I'll dress myself."

"Good. You've got ten minutes," he revealed, then he retreated out the bedroom door.

"You're the most insufferable man I've ever met," she called after him. "Selfish, mean, rude and overbearing. You couldn't make me do this if I weren't still half asleep. A real man would wait until after noon to fight with me. You're despicable, and what's more, you know it." And to emphasize her charges against him, she slammed the bedroom door.

A low chuckle broke from his throat as he settled comfortably on the sofa to wait. He could always depend on Liza for fireworks. But she could be serene, too.

He was thinking about how peaceful a time they had had just last week. She had been restful to be with, a marvelously undemanding companion. He looked for more of that same Liza now. But instead she had turned into a little spitfire. He smiled to himself when he admitted that he liked the volatile Liza, too.

She emerged from the bedroom and was not dressed in the outfit he had chosen for her. Because she resented being told what to wear, she had donned something equally attractive, a moss-green suit with a multicolored silk flower-print blouse.

Her hair and makeup were adequate, though she had barely been able to see in the mirror to check their arrangement. Compulsively she stuffed a few basic grooming items in her purse. She could redo her mascara and lipstick later.

"You look simply stunning," Scott commented approvingly, noticeably silent on her choice of clothes.

"It's the fanciest I've ever gotten dressed up for breakfast," she sulkily protested. "This better be good."

"I think you'll see it will be worth it," he confidently predicted.

"I'd rather go back to bed," she petulantly added.

"Always glad to oblige," he quickly returned, watching her instant blush with barely concealed mirth.

"Let's go," she angrily announced, stalking toward the door. She was defeated. Liza knew she was defeated. He was bigger than she was, and stronger. And he was the most stubborn man she had ever met. She would have to go with him to his absurd breakfast. But she didn't have to like it.

It was only when they got outside into the pale light of predawn Chicago that she suspiciously asked him what time it was.

Scott glanced at his wrist watch. "Seven minutes after five," he reported, propelling her down the sidewalk and toward the nearby parking lot.

Liza stopped stock still. She planted her feet firmly on the sidewalk, prepared to stand siege right there.

"What do you mean, it's seven minutes after five?" she demanded, incredulous. "What kind of crazy person are you dragging me out at an hour like this? And for breakfast? I don't even eat breakfast."

"Shush," he warned in a loud whisper, "You'll wake the neighbors." And he recaptured her elbow and used it to again head her down the sidewalk toward his waiting car.

"I don't care if I wake the neighbors," she loudly protested. "I don't care if I wake the whole city. This is a ridiculous thing to do and I don't want to go."

He was pushing her now, but she was putting up a mighty resistance. He used his considerable strength to propel her forward. She refused to lift her feet from the sidewalk until he forced her to move. Each step was a battle. They made jerky progress in the general direction of the parking lot.

"Shut up, you little hellcat," he warned, "or I'll have to take drastic measures. If you keep this up someone will call the police. They'll think I'm abducting you."

"Well, you are," she agreed instantly. "That's exactly what you are doing. And I hope somebody does call the police. It would serve you right."

He resolutely inched her forward. She fought him every step.

"Liza, please shut up. Trust me. I think you'll like this," he rationalized. His patience was wearing thin now. But he had almost gotten her to the car. Another hundred yards and they'd be there.

"Trust you," Liza repeated, incredulous. She stopped abruptly, immovable. "Trust you! A man who barges his way into my apartment in the middle of the night, orders me to dress and leave when I don't want to go, pushes me down the sidewalk when I resist, and insists on dominating my day with his harebrained scheme for going out to breakfast. Trust you? Hah!" Liza exclaimed triumphantly. She'd told him what she thought of his ideas, and it felt good. It felt better than good. It felt marvelous. Pride in her own oratory swelled her breast with a giddy joy.

"Can't you just keep it down until we get to the car? Then you can screech at me all you want," Scott promised with a grim frown.

"No," she insisted, "you can't shut me up. You can drag me around, you can outmuscle and outmaneuver me. But you can't shut me up. If I want—"

His lips covered hers, muffling the words that formed in her throat. She struggled to free herself. She pushed on his great chest with all her might. But he wouldn't budge. With clenched fists she pummeled his shoulders. Still he crushed her to him, imprisoning her in the circle of his powerful arms.

She tried to kick him. But as soon as he sensed her intent, one large hand immediately slipped to the small of her back, forcing her closer to him, making her intensely aware of his blatant sexuality, and at the same time leaving her no room to move her feet to kick. And all the time she struggled he kissed her savagely, assaulting her mouth with a punishing intensity. Liza couldn't move, she could barely breathe, and she couldn't possibly escape his kiss.

Her first reaction was panic. Never had she been so personally overwhelmed before. Never before had anyone so successfully inflicted his desires on her.

She wasn't sure when she stopped struggling and, drained of resistance, stood helpless in his arms, consumed by the dizzying force of his kiss. But as the first waves of pleasure rose from deep within her, she began to feel it wasn't all so bad. Her body slowly delighted in his caressing hands and demanding mouth. The kiss went on and on. She knew only that the world was wobbling precariously under her feet, and that her only security lay in holding on to Scott with all her might, holding on to him and never letting go.

Her lips were swollen with the force of his kiss, but they smiled sweetly up at him. Her eyes shone brightly, happily bemused. And her face glowed radiantly. Somewhere in the back of her brain Liza remembered Valerie's teasing voice telling her that she could change her mind faster than anyone else she knew.

With tremulous fingers she could feel Scott's heart thudding under the soft blue silk of his shirt. His great chest rose and fell convulsively. And he gazed down at her with a strange, intense expression on his flushed face.

They were still for a moment, then he took her arm and gently propelled her to his Mercedes. She walked beside him, glowing, her mouth turned up in a smile. At that moment she was content. She would follow him wherever he led.

When they were driving down the street, he took his eyes from the road for a moment and smiled at her.

"You can go to sleep now, if you like. We've got a distance to go."

Sleep. What a good idea, Liza thought. She nodded obediently, rolled her seat back into a reclining position, and contentedly settled herself for a nap.

She felt the car stop, and dazedly she peered out of half-opened eyes. Scott got out of the car at a dark parking lot. It looked vaguely familiar to Liza. He came around and opened her door, helping her out of the car.

"Where are we?" she sleepily asked, glad for the support of his arm as she stood.

"The airport," he answered, tucking her hand into the crook of his elbow in a protective manner.

Liza shook her head, hoping to clear the confusion. "Where?" she asked as he led her through the huge, car-lined, concrete structure. Glass doors silently slid open as they approached. Liza gazed at him, bewildered.

"We're at the airport," he assured her, patting her hand comfortingly.

"But why?" Liza persisted.

She was waking up now. The magic of Scott's kiss had worn off with her sleep, and she was convinced that the autocratic man at her side was doing something bordering on insanity.

"I'll explain in a minute," Scott replied reassuringly. Then he led her down the long, deserted, echoing corridor toward the main terminal.

"I don't want to know in a minute," Liza insisted as she breathlessly rushed to keep up with Scott's long, purposeful strides. "I want to know now."

But he kept walking without responding to her, even as she futilely protested.

He stopped only a few steps from the ticket counter and turned to face her. Immediately she read the irritation in his flashing eyes. Without his telling her in words, she knew he was tired of her incessant questions and her argumentative attitude.

He frowned deeply and said only one word. "Liza!" It was a warning. It was a comment on his earlier patience and a notice that he had now reached his limits.

She shut her mouth and stood silent, strangely obedient for the first time in her life. Liza was afraid to incur Scott's wrath again. She knew that at this hour of the morning he could out-think her or, worse, kiss her and render her utterly defenseless. And so she waited, feeling uncharacteristically meek while he strode to the counter and handed his tickets to the agent waiting there.

There were few people in the enormous O'Hare International Airport at this early hour on a Saturday. As Liza and Scott strolled down the corridor only a few passengers rushed past them.

There was only a whistling, uniformed janitor who leisurely mopped the counter area.

After deciding her angry protests would do no good, Liza was determined to try a less volatile approach to find out what was happening. She deliberately took a deep breath, calmed herself, and tried a reasonable, logical, and non-argumentative style.

"Would you please tell me where we are going?" she asked.

The tactic worked, surprising her completely.

"We're going to New Orleans," Scott immediately replied.

"New Orleans." She said the name thoughtfully. It brought pictures of lacy iron balconies, pirates, and the broad, lazy Mississippi River to her mind.

"New Orleans." She said it again as the realization grew on her. Any anger she had felt at Scott had evaporated somewhere between the kiss, the drive, and her own waked-up state. Liza mulled the destination over in her mind for long minutes. Then she smiled like a child who had just been told she could go to the circus.

Chapter Ten

"Oh, it's as pretty as the pictures," Liza eagerly remarked as their taxicab entered the French Quarter of New Orleans.

The sky was a perfect azure and cloudless. A light breeze stirred in the trees. And up and down the old streets men and women, boys and girls, leisurely strolled along.

Liza sat on the edge of the slick leather cab-seat, grasping the bottom of the open car window and gazing out at the passing scenes with unabashed delight. Just as she had pictured, delicate, intricate iron balconies ran the length of most of the old two or three story buildings that lined the streets. Tall windows, many with gracefully arched tops, were opened to let the still summery breezes into the apartments and offices beyond.

Scott instructed the cab driver to stop at the Royal Orleans Hotel. "I've got to make a speech here later," he revealed when Liza eyed him warily.

He took his leather grip from the car and delivered it into the hotel. He was only there a few minutes before he returned to her and gave the jovial cab driver further directions.

"We're here," Scott announced, paying the driver and then helping Liza out of the cab. "This is where we are going to have breakfast. Hungry?"

Her eyes roamed the large old building then traveled eagerly to see the other parts of the street. The warm sunshine and otherworld atmosphere made her feel euphoric and a little as though she were living in a dream.

"Liza?" Scott gently prodded. His delight in her happiness showed in the twinkling in his eyes.

"Oh, yes, sorry," Liza apologized. "Oh, yes, of course I'm hungry. In fact, I'm practically starved," she admitted honestly.

"Well, then, good," Scott happily told her, "We've come to the right place."

The decor and the richness of the furnishings in Brennan's restaurant were from an earlier, more elegant age. Dignified waiters, formally dressed in black, moved around the several rooms that made the intimate dining areas. The table linens were white, immaculate, and silver and crystal sparkled brightly at each place setting.

Liza and Scott were seated, and before they could study their menus, their waiter asked, "Would you like anything to drink before your meal?"

Liza blinked, surprised. Surely he couldn't mean liquor. It wasn't even noon yet. She glanced around the room. People were drinking out of glasses that looked as though they held cocktails.

"A Virgin Mary." At least she wouldn't look out of place.

"Sazerac," Scott ordered without hesitation.

Silently the waiter disappeared.

"What's Sazerac?" Liza asked in a loud whisper, hoping to sound ignorant only to Scott, but not to make a general announcement to the obviously sophisticated crowd in the elegant room.

"It's a southern specialty," Scott explained. "A mixture of bourbon with an anise flavor. Try it when it comes."

"Drinking liquor? In the morning? It's decadent," she loftily pronounced.

"Yes, it is rather." And without another comment, he picked up the menu and began to study it.

Liza couldn't believe her eyes. Never before had she seen such lavish breakfast dishes. And as she eyed the creations being carried to the tables around them, she was further impressed. At the next table, a waiter stood by a silver chafing dish stirring flaming bananas in a rich brown sugar sauce. He then spooned generous portions of the fruit and sauce over mounds of vanilla ice cream.

"Ooh, I want that," Liza gasped, her eyes sparkling just at the thought.

"Of course," Scott answered, enjoying the delight she did not try to hide. "But you'll have to eat something else first, something a bit more nourishing," he cautioned. "That's dessert."

Liza frowned and studied the menu again.

After they had both eaten eggs and gently-flavored garlic sausages, the waiter set up the chafing dish by their table. Liza watched with rapt fascination while he gently sautéed the bananas in butter, added brown sugar and rum, and then set the whole thing aflame.

"It's as though it is Christmas or something," Liza commented after her delicious looking portion was set before her. "I mean, this hardly happens every day," she explained as she picked up her spoon and enthusiastically scooped a silver spoonful of the extravagant dessert.

Scott smiled at her, pausing before he took up his own spoon. "I've never been out with a woman who has enjoyed her food quite as much as you do."

"Oh, dear," Liza replied, frowning between bites but not letting his opinion diminish her own pleasure one bit, "I guess I am a bit of a glutton."

A low chuckle rose from Scott's throat. "Liza," he

explained, amused, "I wasn't criticizing you. In fact I'm beginning to see what a sensual person you really are. You enjoy your pleasures immensely. The kiss of the wind on your face, the music at the ballet, the sights of New Orleans and the rolling of the waves when we were sailing. Obviously enjoying your food is part of that picture, too. And that pleasure makes you a gourmet, not a glutton," he gently chided. "It's the same sort of sensual attitude about life that must make you a marvelous lover."

Liza's spoon stopped in midair. Her mouth froze, partly open. Her eyes registered her shock, then they became wary.

She had never thought of herself as sensual before, even though she knew how very much she enjoyed things: sounds, colors, tastes, textures. But he was not only talking about sensual things. Scott was talking about sexual things. His boldness stunned her.

Mechanically she propelled the spoon into her mouth, hardly tasting the creamy dessert. She gulped the delectable mixture down in one swallow, and put down her spoon. It seemed to clatter with deafening noise against her plate.

The room around her froze like a bubble in time. Liza felt her own heart beating rapidly. Yet her mind seemed to be working slowly, very slowly. Her thoughts were strange and incredible. Scott talked about what kind of a lover she would be as though he had analyzed every part of her and processed the information. It was as though he were a human computer. And what he found was that she would make a marvelous lover. No doubt a grading on his scale.

"Is all this some sort of elaborate seduction scene?" Liza asked, waving her arm vaguely around the richly furnished room. "And you've got a hotel room reserved for us just around the corner?"

Liza was surprised by her own air of calm detachment. She was angry, disturbed at herself for being caught unawares in a situation so obviously leading to the bedroom. And she was angry because she was sure that the elaborate plane ride and breakfast were merely Scott's extravagant prelude to sex.

"You're very astute," Scott agreed with a congratulatory nod that made Liza's heart sink. "The hotel isn't far away. And I do have a reservation, as you surely guessed when I left my things there."

"And the plane tickets home? They're for tomorrow?" she calmly asked, even though she was seething inside.

He nodded, silent.

"That's very smooth work, Professor," Liza praised him as their waiter brought their coffee. "A real masterpiece of planning."

"Thank you," he responded, nodding his head deferentially in response to her praise. As she watched him, she wished her fingers didn't ache so for the feel of his skin, the springy vitality of his hair. And she wished that her heart didn't catch in her throat as he looked at her with his sensual blue eyes.

Liza had no idea what she would say next. The adrenaline pumped through her system and she was in a near panic before she had her answer. "There's only one problem," she reported with an air of logic and detachment that she did not feel. "I fully intend to spend the night at home," she said firmly. "Alone."

Whatever else was going on, whatever else she felt, this conversation alone convinced Liza that Scott was not in love with her. Indeed his basic orientation toward women seemed to be regarding them as a convenience, a living tool to avoid sexual frustration.

"If you remember the terms of the experiment that you said you wanted to conduct on and with me," Liza efficiently reminded him, "you are to treat me with the utmost degree of adulation and respect. You are to do lovely things for me, kind and thoughtful things. Truly chivalrous things.''

Liza was thankful that her quick thinking had come up with a plausible excuse. She was congratulating herself on her own success as she talked.

''I don't see how—'' Scott put in. But Liza kept right on with her explanation.

''Now, if we were to become lovers, and truly enjoyed each other in that capacity,'' Liza theorized, ''how would you ever get a real answer to your intellectual question. Our relationship would be on too complex a level for you to know if your cherishing or your skills in bed had proved your theory.''

He frowned thoughtfully and Liza, heartened by his response, continued. ''And if you were an indifferent or poor lover, and I found you very unsatisfying,'' she related without blinking an eye, ''I would probably come to the conclusion that you couldn't do much else right either, even if I absolutely adored all the little attentions you had given me. And the experiment's results would be prejudiced that way, too. You see, sex is out. Absolutely out,'' she firmly concluded.

He scowled deeply, his blue eyes clouded like the sky before a storm. His great chest rose and fell with a sigh of disgust.

Liza felt triumphant, and fought the urge to smile broadly in the face of her overwhelming success.

''Liza, we passed that silly experiment thing long ago. It's just you and me now. Two people who are actually attracted to each other. Or at least I am to you. I take it then that you find me resistible,'' Scott stated dryly.

He took a sip of his coffee as he waited for her answer. As he waited he realized he was steeling himself against possible hurt. What would he feel if Liza really did not want him the way he wanted her?

''Is that so disappointing?'' she parried, her expression vaguely apologetic.

"It's always a blow to a man's ego when a lady says no, for whatever reason," he returned grimly.

"Oh, but, Professor, you yourself told me that it isn't your ego that is involved in this experiment you started with me, it's your intellect," Liza sweetly reminded him.

She quickly raised her coffee cup to her already curling lips and conscientiously cast her eyes downward. Her nose told her something was different about the coffee but by that time she was committed. The deep brown liquid slipped between her lips and shocked her barely prepared taste buds. It was very hot and very strong and quite different in flavor. She gulped it down quickly, then replaced the steaming cup in its lustrous saucer.

"What kind of coffee is this?" Liza demanded in surprise.

Scott laughed at her shocked expression. And while he laughed, he was again struck by what a woman of contrasts Liza was. She was an intelligent woman, an outstanding secretary who would no doubt work her way up to editorial positions despite her recent setback. She was a good conversationalist. And yet there was much of the naive and delightful little girl about her, too.

"The coffee is blended specially with chicory," he told her with a smile. "You'll get it all over this area. I think they brew it specially to starch your innards," he teased.

"They certainly must," Liza agreed.

She sipped it again, experimentally this time. Thoughtfully she considered its robust taste. "I think I like it," she tentatively decided. Then she took another sip. "Yes, I do," she agreed cheerfully. "It's good. Different, but good."

Liza and Scott wandered leisurely around the narrow streets of the Vieux Carré, the old section of New Orleans. The buildings were in pastel hues, and they displayed a graciousness and artistry that Liza had seldom seen before.

"What is it about an old building," she mused, "that is ever so much more interesting than something brand new? The years seem to give them a softness and a glow and an air of mystery all at once."

They were in an antique store, and the clerk proudly related to them stories about the secret passage in the building, one that led to the old waterfront. The notorious pirate, Jean Lafitte, used to bring his booty covertly right into the heart of town through a long tunnel and into the shop.

"Bright colored silks, precious damasks, glittering jewels, gold and silver," the balding little man cheerfully revealed, "all stolen, of course. His treasures came right here."

Looking around the elegant shop, Liza could imagine that some of the colorful pirate's goods were still there, available to buy even today. Sumptuous velvet-covered chairs, huge oil paintings in intricate, gilt frames, highly polished tables and dressers, and sparkling multifaceted cut crystal were crowded into the shop. In the show case, antique gold jewelry shone with a deeply glowing luster. Liza examined it closely.

"Beautiful," she commented as she looked through the glass case at the intricately worked old chains.

"Let's see that locket," Scott asked the salesman, pointing into the case.

The salesman removed it, gently laying it on a dark blue velvet-covered tray to display it for them. The chain was delicate links of pure gold with the dark tone that only antique gold possessed. The locket itself was of the same color. It was round, with a lacy filigree of gold surrounding it like a halo. The smooth surface was set with tiny diamonds in the shape of a shimmering rescent moon, and a random group of tiny diamonds ormed glittering stars. On the back the initial "L" was ntricately carved in Old English script.

"This locket is old enough to have been pirate booty," the salesman reported agreeably.

"I wish it were," Liza wistfully replied. "But I think t is out of my league, price-wise."

The locket wasn't marked with a price, but Liza was convinced, just by its appearance, that it was a trinket oo rich for her carefully controlled pocketbook.

"Does a man who cherishes a woman let her pay for her own lockets?" Scott queried reproachfully.

"But you can't, you mustn't," Liza protested.

"Oh, but I must," Scott corrected her, and he smoothly fastened the delicate locket around Liza's neck. "You can't deny me every sort of pleasure," he whispered meaningfully, as his fingers lightly caressed the nape of her neck.

It was then that the salesman revealed the price. It was more than Liza made in a month of work. Her mouth dropped open in horror. Her hands flew to the back of her neck to undo the clasp. But while she was fumbling with it, Scott pointedly turned his back on her, thus denying any further discussion of the matter. Then he pulled out his American Express card and handed it to the salesman.

Liza blinked in surprise. She hardly knew what to do, now to react. Should she pull the chain off her neck and give it back to the salesman? The grandiose gesture might make her feel good. But she was beginning to realize that there were times when it was senseless to argue with Scott. He had a way of firmly planting his feet, and Liza didn't know enough about him to know now to make him move again.

She reluctantly admitted temporary defeat, and when Scott finished the transaction and gave her his arm, she resignedly accepted it and walked with him to the street. She lightly fingered the precious locket with her free hand. She knew she would treasure it forever.

The sunshine was bright, the sky a clear, clear blue. The leaves on the trees were dark and rich after a full growing season. The street itself had a festive atmosphere, as well dressed men and women strolled along, stopping to look in the windows of the many intriguing antique and specialty stores.

Despite the relaxed, even joyful, atmosphere on the sun-drenched street, Liza's uneasy thoughts blocked her enjoyment of it. Scott seemed to be ruling her life, denying her her own right to make decisions on what she would or would not do, what she would or would not have.

She had spent her life making her own decisions. She had always been firmly in control of her own destiny. But when she was with Scott, much of that control seemed to slip out of her hands and into his. And her expressed opinions often had little to do with his plans.

"Is the locket a string?" she perversely demanded as they walked along.

"A string?" he returned, furrowing his tanned brow. He was thoughtful for a moment, then the light of understanding dawned on his face. "Oh, a 'string,' you mean. As in 'no strings attached'?"

She nodded.

"No, it isn't a string," he assured her. "It's only a locket. And it looks perfectly lovely on you."

He admired her with unabashed interest, focusing on where the locket fitted into the open V neck of her blouse, nestled near the shadow between her breasts. And he smiled at her, an intimate and disarming smile that at any other time might have turned her bones to jelly. Instead it made her furious. Everything Scott had done that day seemed to be a more or less subtle way to manipulate her into bed. And she was sick of it.

"This isn't only a locket," she protested, reaching up with nearly trembling fingers. "You paid the earth for this piece of jewelry. You certainly must expect something in return."

"I expect you to enjoy it."

"And exactly how am I supposed to show my enjoyment? My appreciation? By jumping into bed with you at the next possible moment?"

"That would be delightful," he immediately responded.

"Absolutely delightful, I'm sure."

His eyes twinkled with amusement as he watched her clench her jaws and purse her mouth angrily.

"Well, I won't," she told him. "I won't do anything of the kind."

She stopped in the middle of the sidewalk and turned to face him. Her chin was raised defiantly, and her eyes shot daggers at him.

He tried to head off the storm of protest that he knew was coming. "Look, let's go someplace and discuss this calmly," he suggested, taking her arm and leading her down the street. She went along reluctantly, dragging a few steps behind him.

"Where are we going?" she demanded as he propelled her down St. Louis Street, past the front of the world-famous Antoine's restaurant.

"The Royal Orleans is nearby. I've got a reservation there."

Liza stopped stark still on the sidewalk. She felt as though this were a repeat of Scott's attempt to get her to the car much earlier that same day. He had successfully managed that. But she certainly didn't want to be alone in a hotel room with him. He had a physical power over her that had nothing to do with strength. And she feared that capability in him. She vowed to resist with every fiber of her being.

"I'm not going to any hotel room with you for some

shoddy little rendezvous. And furthermore I'm sick of—"

"It wouldn't be a 'rendezvous,' as you call it," he irritably reported. "It would be a chance to talk."

"Hah," Liza protested, "I'll bet you'd talk. Talk me right into bed, whether I wanted to go with you or not."

"Liza," Scott said with exaggerated patience, "rape is not my style. Now let's get off this street and get inside where we can discuss this without making a scene."

"I'd rather make a scene," Liza loudly protested. "I think a scene is a far better idea than anything you might have in mind."

Passersby watched Liza's furious protestations with unabashed interest. A few men even smiled, and one turned his head so that his laugh wasn't obvious as he hurried by.

"You are without a doubt the most difficult woman I have ever met," Scott accused Liza.

"I consider that high praise," she retorted, her eyes flashing dangerously.

He heaved a great, exasperated sigh. His broad mouth curved down in a frown. His eyes were dark and menacing. But his words offered Liza an out.

"Look, I promise not to touch you if you don't want me to," he conceded, "though I must say it will be mighty difficult to keep from wringing your neck. Right at this moment you're a sexual zero, so you hardly have to fear that I'll take you to bed."

The last comment struck Liza like a body blow. She felt as though the breath were knocked from her body. It took a moment to regain her poise and dignity.

"I won't want you to touch me," she finally, haughtily warned. "So I suppose it will be safe enough to go with you. Besides, while we're there, you will have a chance to change the plane reservations. At least for me. I'm going home tonight, whatever you might plan," she flatly informed him.

He stopped briefly at the registration counter, then led her through the luxurious, marble-clad lobby to the elevator.

"We have a two bedroom suite," he reported grimly. "The sitting room will be neutral territory."

She blinked in surprise and wondered if he had been able to change reservations at the last moment. She was willing to bet that that was not the way his original reservation had been made.

The elevator smoothly carried them upstairs, and within minutes they were in their suite. Surely the sumptuous lobby should have prepared her for the elegant suite. The sitting room was furnished in soft earthtones. Intricately patterned damask drapes hung at the window. Two beige roll-arm sofas faced each other at one end of the large room. There was a small dining table and chairs at the other. Two occasional chairs, covered in ivory satin, completed the casually tasteful setting.

Liza however spent little time taking in the decor. She stood in the middle of the room, defiantly put her hands on her hips, and faced Scott.

"Now change the plane reservations," she demanded. "Call the airport."

He ignored her command, turned his back on her, and leisurely strolled to one of the sofas. He sank into its comfortable cushions. Immediately his hands went to his neck. He loosened his tie and deftly unbuttoned the top button of his shirt. Then he lifted his long legs onto the small coffee table directly in front of him.

"Sit down, Liza," he said. It was a quiet order, but it was an order nonetheless, and she resented it.

"I don't want to sit down. I want you to change the plane reservations."

It was after noon now, and Scott had been up since

nearly four o'clock after going to bed around one. He hadn't slept at all well. He had been through some exhausting battles with Liza. And he had to give a speech tonight.

All he wanted now was a nap. No. He changed his thoughts. What he really wanted was for Liza, in her peaceful mood, to soothe his ragged nerves. But the peaceful, agreeable woman with whom he had enjoyably spent a weekend sailing had disappeared. She had been replaced by an irritable spitfire. And her peaceful side seemed determined to hide itself forever.

As a psychologist he should have been able to predict or explain or even understand her behavior. Instead he was stupefied. He was giving her a dream weekend, one most women would envy. And instead of falling all over him with gratitude, she was fighting him every inch of the way.

Now she wanted to go home. Well, if she had asked him nicely, if she were only more reasonable, he might consider calling the airline and changing her flight. Instead her demands just made him more determined not to do what she wanted.

"Didn't anyone ever tell you that you could catch more flies with honey than with vinegar?" he irritably asked.

"I don't want to catch flies," Liza retorted immediately. "I want to go home. Now."

Scott knew he couldn't take much more of her insistence. He stood up and stretched. He was scowling, and telltale lines around his eyes revealed his exhaustion.

"Look, I'm tired," he informed her in curt tones. "I'm going to go into that bedroom and take a nap," he said, waving at the door on his right. "If you've a mind to join me, fine. Otherwise you can do what you like. There's another room for you," he flatly said, indicating the other door. "There's a phone. You can call for room service. You can call the airport and get a reservation out. You can call a taxi and leave. It really doesn't matter to me."

He pulled his wallet out of his pocket and opened it. He took out a large number of bills and shoved them carelessly onto the tabletop. "This should pay for your trip home. I guess I owe you that much. If you're gone when I wake up, I'll assume you've left." He paused, shook his dark head regretfully and smiled a sad smile. "Funny, when I planned all this, I thought you'd love it."

And with that he left her, left her standing alone in the middle of the elegant sitting room. She was dumbfounded by his admission that he wanted to please her. And, ironically, that knowledge left Liza feeling as though it were she who had done something wrong, not he.

After Scott left, the big sitting room seemed incredibly empty. The beautiful chairs and tables, the sparkling lamps and tasteful pictures, seemed senseless. A waste. She focused on the closed door to his bedroom and frowned thoughtfully. She missed him already.

What was it about Scott that caused such emotionally charged sparks to go off between them? Most times when she had disagreements with her friends, she had no trouble coming to a compromise that suited them both. But then most of her friends were not as forceful as Scott Harburton, she admitted.

He didn't seem to be in the habit of compromising, at least where women were concerned. But he had seemed intent on pleasing her, truly giving her a good time. And that was something that most of the men she dated didn't really do. They made plans for what they wanted to do and merely asked Liza if she wanted to come along.

Was it because of the idiotic experiment that Scott had gone all out? She could question that. But she also knew there was something more. She was sure that he liked her. Or at least he had liked her until her willful shows of temper today, she admitted regretfully.

She walked over to the marble-topped coffee table where the money lay. She picked it up, carefully fingering it. There were several hundred-dollar bills, and many of smaller denomination. There was more than enough to get her home, first class, too.

Needing time to think, she decided to order a soothing cup of tea. She dialed room service, ordering a pot of English tea and some finger sandwiches. She was hardly hungry, but it seemed to be such a delightful and extravagant thing to do that she couldn't resist. Just before she hung up she thought of Scott. Whether she was there or not when he woke up, she thought he might like a drink.

"Send up a bottle of Scotch, too, please. Chivas," she specified, ordering what she thought to be his favorite brand. "And a bottle of Bristol Cream," she added impulsively, reasoning that she could always take it home with her if she left. "And ice."

"Yes, madam," the efficient sounding voice agreed.

When the order came, she settled down with a cup of tea and nibbled absently on the sandwiches as she pondered her situation.

Now that Scott had given her an option, she wanted to stay in New Orleans, stay with him. She knew they could have fun together, and she was convinced he wouldn't demand payment with sexual favors. He had said as much, and she believed him.

Was she such a flighty creature that she changed her mind at the least little whim? She asked herself that question several times before she had an answer. No, she was sure it wasn't that she was so flighty. It wasn't that at all. She simply didn't like to be ordered around. She was a woman who wanted an option, wanted a choice. If Scott would accept that facet of her, they might get along very nicely together.

Liza looked at the coffee table where the bottle of Scotch rested. She knew now why she had ordered it. It was a peace offering.

She cleared away the tea things and set the tray on the floor in the hallway. It would be cleared away by the efficient housekeeping staff. On the coffee table she neatly arranged the bottles of Scotch and sherry, the ice bucket and two glasses. Next to it she put the money. She wanted him to see it first thing when he got up. Then she went off to the second bedroom for her nap, kicking off her shoes and shrugging off her jacket. Wearily she fell into bed and was immediately asleep.

She felt the kiss first, right through the fog of her sleep. It was whisper-soft and tantalizingly light, and it sent a delicious thrill through her sleepy body.

"You're beautiful when you're asleep."

It was Scott's husky voice, a low, caressing sound. Liza's eyes fluttered open and she smiled a lazy, contented smile. She snuggled her body more deeply into the comfort of the bed, closed her eyes, and drifted back to sleep. The smile still lighted her face.

"You do have trouble waking up, don't you?"

Liza didn't respond. She had heard his voice, but felt no power to move. She just lay there enjoying his nearness, the warm sensation she got just from his presence.

As she again opened her eyes to look at him, she saw his mouth descending to hers, his lips parted slightly, his eyes dusky with emotion. She made a small gasp of surprise. It gave Scott the opening he ached for, and at the moment their lips touched, he thrust his searching tongue deep into the waiting warmth of her mouth. He explored its soft recesses with a lingering thoroughness that fanned the flames of Liza's passion until they all but consumed her.

His hand gently cupped her breast. Breathlessly he deftly undid the buttons on her blouse and pushed aside her bra. Sure, sensual fingers leisurely explored her contours. They circled the nipple in ever narrowing sweeps until he teased it to an exquisite hardness. Liza felt the shuddering wave of ecstasy engulf her. An electric joy rushed from her now throbbing breast through her pliant body to the recesses of her deepest being. And all the while his hand worked its mesmerizing magic.

His eyes closed for a moment as he briefly pulled away. Liza could see his rapid pulse beating at the base of his throat. She stared up at him, utterly bemused. Her body was a floating mass of glorious sensation. Every inch of her felt alive, new and gloriously longing for more and more deeply sensual responses. She knew her body was waiting to experience them, longing to know them, share them with Scott.

"We could spend the afternoon in bed," Scott suggested, his voice a deep whisper, "or we could go out. It's completely up to you."

Liza's pulse raced.

Scott's lightly calloused index finger traced the curve of her ear, then gently teased the lobe before he smoothly inserted his fingertip into the opening and lightly moved it back and forth.

Liza's breathing stopped. She hung suspended in a swirling cloud of dizzying desire that brought her trembling to the brink of surrender. Every atom of her being clamored for what only Scott could give her. Every nerve, every sense blocked out all of the world but him. She said nothing, but when he looked at her, he knew. He could see it in her eyes. She was ready. She was his.

"Oh, God, Liza," he groaned just before his lips claimed hers in a sealing kiss, a kiss that went on and on while he crushed her to him.

He was still kissing her when she felt his body lying next to her on the big bed. Impatiently he pushed the covers back and she pressed her body to his, arching sensuously against him as she felt the strength of his desire. It was a measure of how much he wanted her, and Liza was intoxicated with her own power over his body.

Her hands explored his broad back as they caressed the hard muscles through the thin cover of his shirt. Wildly she knew she must touch his skin, must feel his firmly muscled back with no barrier to hamper her. Pulling frantically at the back of his shirt, she worked it loose from his pants and slipped her seeking hand beneath it to glory in the warmth of his skin.

An electric charge went through her as he began to moan and kiss her neck, as he struggled to remove her blouse. Her lacy bra was no barrier and was thrust quickly aside while he buried his face in her swelling breasts, kissing them wildly, hungrily rubbing the hard nipples with his quick, rough tongue. Liza felt a tingling weakness claim her body. There was no strength in her except for holding him, clutching him to her. There was no awareness of the world of time. At that moment he was her universe, her all.

"Oh, Liza," he whispered into the soft skin of her neck, "this is what I've wanted to do since the first moment I saw you," he softly crooned. His caressing hands worked their magic on the curve of her waist, moving lower, rubbing the round of her hip, and slipping down to her thigh.

It took Liza a few moments to understand what he had said, moments when Scott was kissing her and finally with an air of possession, exploring her most intimate parts.

When she realized the deepest meaning of Scott's words, an alarm went off in Liza's brain. What he had wanted from the first day could only have been her physical self, her full breasts, her rounded hips, and the curve of her thigh. He had wanted the sexy facade that chance and destiny had given her.

Now strangely detached from her body, and even from the sensations that still filled it with a blood-pounding and dizzying desire, she knew she could not let him make love to her. She wanted not his physical adoration but, oh, so much more. She wanted the kind of love from him that she felt for him. And it didn't seem to be something Scott was ready to give.

She felt him slowly slide his hand up from her knee, up the soft flesh of her inner thigh. She groaned her own sadness at having to say it, but she cried out an anguished "No."

His hand froze. He lay still next to her and she could feel the thudding of his heart.

"No," she repeated, more loudly now. "No." It was a tortured cry.

"Liza, what's going on?" he demanded in disbelief.

"I said no," she repeated with forced patience.

His response was savage. "Do you do this with all your men? Or am I just special?" he bitterly inquired as he glared down at her, furious. Do you get some kind of perverse pleasure in torturing men into a frenzy?" he demanded.

"You said if I didn't want you to touch me, you wouldn't," she said in her defense. "I don't want you to touch me."

"Like hell you don't," he spit out. "You were as ready as I was."

Liza couldn't deny that, so she said nothing.

Scott pulled himself up and stood next to the bed, not bothering to tuck in his shirt. He scowled down at her, silently demanding an explanation.

"You once said that I was the most difficult woman you had ever met," Liza told him, her voice shaking. "This ought to convince you that you were right."

She watched him clench his jaws, then force them to relax. His shoulders rose and fell as he heaved a great sigh. Then he turned on his heel and stalked out the loor. A few seconds later she could hear ice clinking in glass, then the tap of glass on glass. He was pouring himself a drink.

Liza sank back on the pillows to recover her composure. She was shaken to the core. It was nearly fifteen minutes before she felt sufficient confidence to go out o the other room, to go out and face Scott. He stood, drink in hand, staring moodily out the window. With ome trepidation Liza walked across the velvety thick arpet to the polished, marble-top coffee table where he had left the money. The money was still there. And Liza suspected it would be there for her to take at any time.

She reached for a glass, but her eyes were on Scott. He still stood at the window, motionless. Without seeing his face Liza could tell Scott was in distress. Was it because of the set of his shoulders, or the tilt of his now dearly familiar head? Or was it because she loved him and because of that had a sixth sense where he was concerned?

She glanced down at the ice bucket. Picking up the cubes she paused a moment, chilling her hand while she thoughtfully looked at him. She dashed the cubes into the crystal tumbler, then reached for the sherry. But, instead, she found herself wanting the Scotch, wanting its dusky taste and its powerful strength.

Gracefully she sat down on the sofa, though after she was seated she felt awkward and ridiculously out of place. She took a drink of the Scotch. The rich amber liquid burned her throat and left her breathless.

Scott turned around and regarded her with a deep frown. "Liza, you are a challenge to my ego as well as to my professional competence. I can't get you off my mind. I can't get you into my bed. And I can't even begin to understand you." He slowly shook his head as he frowned thoughtfully. He threw back his head and grimly downed some more Scotch.

Suddenly Liza knew something wonderful. Her intuition gave her a sure, secret knowledge that he was more affected by her than just physically. The knowledge made her happily lightheaded. "So, I'm a challenge, am I?" she returned. "If there was ever a man who could overcome any challenge he put his mind to, it's you."

He stared at her a moment, uncomprehending. He rolled his tumbler back and forth between his hands, focusing on the swirly movements of the ice cubes in the liquid, and the cool, smooth feeling of the glass against his palms. Then he looked at her again, his eyes deadly serious.

"Does that mean if I try again later, you will let me make love to you?"

Liza squirmed uncomfortably. "I think I can promise you that I will not let you make love to me. At least not here, not now. Not this weekend," she said most specifically. "You could make it very unpleasant for both of us if you demand that I do. Now if that means you would like me to hop a plane and go home, I will. I'm sure you would be able to find some willing woman down here who will be more than eager to get intimate knowledge of your—ah—charms. She might more properly appreciate you."

She thought it was a generous offer on her part. An understanding one, too. She was just congratulating herself on her own good sense when he scowled at her fiercely.

"That about does it, you idiot woman," he seethed with barely concealed rage. "Here I go and spend a good deal of time and energy planning what I thought would be a delightful weekend for us. And what do I get from you? First you fight me, then you tease me, then you tell me to get someone else. Someone who will appreciate me, meaning of course that you don't. Damn it, haven't you ever learned anything about

en?" he fumed. "All you crazy feminists think men
nd women are alike. That they think alike. Well, they
on't. And no amount of legal or ethical mumbo
umbo will change that basic fact. Now just because I
idn't 'score' with you right now, as some men so
rudely put it, does not mean my weekend is ruined. Or
iy life. I came here to give a speech and have some
ublicity pictures taken. Usually Monica is my nominal
ate, and she sets up women to be photographed with
ie. But tonight I plan to have you with me," he
rdered, his voice just one decibel short of an angry
hout. "But before that we are going to go shopping."

"Shopping?" Liza queried. She was still processing
ie information that Scott wanted her to be with him.
he felt herself glowing inside.

This storm-along Scott would be frightening if he
asn't so amusing. And she realized that she could be
mused because even at his full fury, Liza knew she
as safe with him. Safe and cherished. If he didn't care
or her he couldn't possibly be so angry at her and yet
ot want her to leave.

She drank no more Scotch, yet she began to feel in-
oxicated. Ripples of pleasure and joy swirled through
er as he continued his furious tirade.

"Yes, we're going shopping," he barked, "You don't
xpect to go out to a fancy banquet and probably a
ight on the town in that sedate and sensible little suit
ou are wearing, do you? You'll need something else,
nd so will I. So we're going shopping."

His voice was insistent. He stood up and strode
cross the room to grab his sport jacket from the back
f a chair. Then he waited impatiently for Liza to join
im at the door.

She did not. She stayed sitting on the sofa. She was
irrounded by an air of contentment and calm.

"Well," he challenged, his hands now firmly planted
n his slim hips, his stance clearly impatient.

Liza sighed, then smiled at him sweetly. "You are a good, kind, generous man," Liza complimented him. "Also intelligent."

He eyed her suspiciously, bracing himself for what would come next.

"And beyond that, you are very, very sexy," she continued, taking her time between words. "You would no doubt be a fantastic lover."

His eyebrow rose at the last comment, and he waited expectantly for more.

"But one of the bases of our difficulties is that you constantly tell me what to do. I know you are sure that everything you dream up will be for my delight and pleasure. But, Scott, I like to be asked, not told about things."

She said the last gently and with a warm smile on her face. It was not a condemnation, but rather a comment. Further, if he could but look at her closely he would see that it was a comment from someone who loved him. Loved him very much.

But he didn't look at her. Instead he frowned. His hand reached up to scratch the back of his neck. He paced from the door to the window and then back to the door again. Midway back to the window he paused and faced Liza.

"You're telling me I'm a bossy male," he challenged.

Liza didn't say anything. She only waited. She knew he was still thinking, still absorbing the meaning of her words.

Finally he chuckled, then he laughed out loud. With an abashed grin on his face he slowly shook his head from side to side. "Most women love it," he said by way of apology. "It's very macho, you know."

Scott was laughing at himself, enjoying the joke. He wasn't hurt or crushed or devastated by her revelation. Instead it had helped him to understand her. And he was glad.

At that moment Liza knew that the man she loved was the most macho man she had ever known. He was strong enough to dominate her—he had shown that. But he was also secure enough to look at himself hard when somebody else's feelings were involved. And he was caring enough to reassess something he had already decided.

In the next moment he was sitting next to her on the small sofa, holding her hand in his and looking into her eyes. The scene would have been poignant if there hadn't been the devilish sparkles of delight dancing in his eyes.

"Liza, my Liza," he said with an infectious smile, "would you like to come shopping with me? I'd like to buy a lovely dress for your beautiful body. A dress that you can wear when we go out tonight. And, furthermore, it will be a dress with no strings attached, except possibly to hold it together." He said the last with a wicked grin.

And when he asked, she knew she could not refuse. She knew she could truly refuse him nothing. She loved him and wanted to please him always.

"I'm a typical woman," Liza answered by way of explanation. "I adore shopping. I'd love to go," she added, smiling.

He took her hand and led her to the door. They walked across the rich carpeting with light hearts and happy smiles on their faces. They had just had a fight. And, miraculously, they both had won.

As Scott put his hand on the knob to open the door, Liza stopped him. He eyed her quizzically.

"Do you think you could kiss me before we go?" he asked.

He didn't answer. He just pulled her to him and kissed her soundly. Then, smiling, he tucked her hand into the crook of his arm and led her out the door.

Chapter Eleven

Liza felt that the afternoon was like Christmas and her birthday all wrapped up in one. Never had she had such attention lavished on her. Never had she gotten so many freely given gifts.

First there was the dress. It was a teal-blue silk jersey with a close fitting halter top and bare back. The full-length slim skirt hugged her body like a second skin. They had been to three stores before Scott was satisfied with what any of the sales persons had shown them. When Liza stepped out of the dressing room wearing the blue silk, he nodded approvingly and said, "That's it," with a firmness that convinced her that even if she had not liked the dress, it was at least immensely flattering. As it was, the dress was her choice too.

After the dress was settled, Scott insisted on a bathing suit for her. "There's a pool on the roof," he explained. "Surely you'll want to take a swim tomorrow morning."

"But I can buy my own suit," Liza had protested. "I can afford it."

"Would you have bought one today if I hadn't brought you here?" he questioned.

"No," Liza answered honestly, "I have a perfectly good one at home. But—"

"But nothing," Scott silenced her. "I'm responsible

or this expense because I'm responsible for having
ou down here." That was that.

Shoes were next. Delicate strap-sandals of black kid.
"Why, these cost a small fortune," Liza complained.
fter learning the price from the salesman.

"Hardly," Scott commented dryly. And before Liza
ould say anything further, he informed the salesman,
We'll take them."

They were laden with packages as they trudged down
ne narrow sunlit streets. It seemed to Liza that they
ad more packages than items bought, but then maybe
ne hadn't kept track, she told herself. There were all
er clothes and her shoes and even a suitcase.

"How else could we get all this back home?" Scott
ad reasoned as he bought the expensive leather
immed bag.

"Would you like something to eat now? Or to
rink?" he asked Liza as they rode back to the hotel.
We won't dine until eight."

The cab traveled the picturesque streets, and Liza
aught glimpses of St. Louis Cathedral, the beautiful
ld building that was completed in the late 1700's, and
ext to it Pirate's Alley, peopled with painters and tour-
ts who inspected their work.

"I'd love some tea," Liza answered him. "But I'm
ot terribly hungry."

She neglected to tell him that she had already nib-
led her way through most of a tray of finger sand-
iches, while Scott had had nothing since Brennan's
mple breakfast many hours earlier.

"Shall we eat in the suite? Or would you prefer a
afé?" he pleasantly inquired.

"Oh, the room would be lovely," she responded
rithout hesitation. And as she did she realized some-
ning wonderful had happened. He had asked her what
ne wanted, not told her.

"Hey, you're a quick learner," Liza complimented

him. "All that asking me what I'd like." She was grinning at him broadly, her appreciation glowing from her eyes.

"I've got a good reason to learn," Scott answered cryptically. But there was no chance for him to say more, or for her to question him as their cab pulled up at the front of the hotel.

The elegant ballroom was crowded with dozens of round tables, all filled to capacity. Liza sat at the speaker's table between Scott and the affable, talkative association president.

"We expect Scott's new book to outsell the last one," the distinguished, sixtyish man revealed. "After all, he can give scientific answers to the questions that have plagued men from the beginning of time. Even the best and brightest of us have never been able to figure out what women want. Now we can buy a book and find out."

Liza wasn't at all sure how to reply. She was relieved to discover that the man was more interested in the sound of his own voice than in anything Liza might say. She settled back comfortably to be a good listener.

Scott's speech was as good as Liza had expected it to be. She found herself agreeing fully that women liked to be shown courtesy and appreciation.

"Somebody very close to me has informally retitled the book, *Scott's Scientific Seduction System*," he revealed to the audience. "Of course these things I advise can be used in that way, to carelessly seduce. I might add that sort of behavior has been going on since the beginning of time. The men who practice it hardly need my book to tell them what women want. They seem to have a sixth sense about it. It's the average guy, the man who looks at his wife with complete, unabashed amazement because he doesn't know what she wants. That's the person I've written this book for. I

ope it will help men properly understand and cherish
ιe women they love.''

The applause after he finished was long and enthusias-
c. People crowded around him afterwards. Holding her
and in a tight grip, Scott kept Liza firmly at his side the
hole time. It was the green-eyed, tight-lipped Monica
ho was the only sad note in the otherwise beautiful eve-
ing. Her angry voice rose distinctly above the others as
ιe boldly questioned Liza.

"Miss Manchester, has Dr. Harburton been able to
ιange your mind about feminist issues? You've al-
ays been quite clear that women's equality depends
n women's independence. You have publicly spoken
ξainst the very things Dr. Harburton promotes in his
ooks. Has the good doctor used his charms to con-
ince you you are wrong?"

Liza could feel Scott stiffen a bit while he waited for
ετ to answer.

"Dr. Harburton has convinced me that when a
oman becomes president of the United States, as
meday one must, she will still be delighted when the
ιan in her life sends her roses for the Oval Office
εsk,'' she replied with dignity. She turned her head
actionally and felt a warm rush of pleasure at Scott's
pproving smile.

Monica opened her mouth to speak again but was
ιterrupted by other questioners. She frowned sulkily,
ared murderously at Liza, and furiously walked away.

After the banquet Scott and Liza went for a walk.
hey drifted through the French Quarter in a pleasant
aze. Liza was lightheaded from the wine or from
:ott's nearness. She wasn't sure which.

"Are you trying to ply me with liquor to get me in
ur bed?" she lightly teased.

"Would it work?" he bantered back. "I'll order a
ιse of your favorite—anything—right now." His tone
as light, but his underlying meaning was serious.

"No, silly," Liza easily assured him. "That won work."

"Humph," he grumbled. But that was all.

Funny how she could joke about something so im portant to her, something so basic, something so crit cal. Liza didn't quite understand the change in herse from the melancholy thoughts she had had only th afternoon. But Scott shared her carefree mood, and a they walked along the streets of the French Quarte they held hands like lovers.

The crescent moon overhead shone brightly, and th stars sparkled like diamonds in the deep velvet of the sk Liza's hand went to her neck and she fingered the lock Scott had given her just that afternoon.

"The night sky is like the locket," she dreamily sai "The crescent moon and shining stars sparkle like jev els. You bought me a lot of things today," Liza wer on. "Very nice things. Thank you."

"You're welcome, of course," Scott replied with courtly nod of his head.

"Where are we going now?"

"We're heading that way," Scott revealed. He pointe up the street.

They got completely caught up in the carnival atme sphere of Bourbon Street. Liza delighted in watchir people who walked down the street, and then crane her neck to see inside each night spot they passed.

They walked with arms entwined, their hands locke together. "This has been like magic," Liza said with sigh. "I'm having a wonderful time."

"It isn't over yet," Scott huskily replied. And b brought his free hand under her chin and turned he head toward him.

His light touch sent a flurry of sensation throug Liza's body as they stopped, mid sidewalk, to kis Flames that had smoldered all evening long flared int full fire. Every look he had given her, every touch the had shared had prepared her body for his kiss and the exquisite mingling of bodies and senses she knew when he caressed her.

Scott dragged his mouth away from hers to whisper in her ear, "There's more magic to come, Liza."

She felt all strength flow out of her. It was replaced instead by a flood of breathless sensation. Her heart throbbed wildly in her breast. A wave of longing, of wanting, of drugging desire, overwhelmed her. She could feel and see only him.

Scott's eyes smoldered with the light of desire. His lips were full and tantalizing and demanding. And his powerful arms crushed her against his broad chest until she felt lost in the heady mystery of his body. She closed her eyes slowly, languidly. Instinctively she rose on tiptoe and fitted her body to his. It felt so right, the two of them molded to each other. She moaned low as he kissed her mouth, her cheeks, her neck. Her soft breasts were crushed against the hard wall of his chest as he slid his arms down her back, over her hips and gently but firmly forced her hard against him. Immediately she felt the strength of his growing desire. The knowledge washed through her like an intoxicating wave.

A small group of reveling passersby laughed heartily, enjoying the sight of Liza in Scott's arms. Their bawdy comments sobered Liza. She pulled away, feeling flustered and apologetic.

Scott's face was flushed, his breathing deep, almost labored. "Let's go," he whispered, taking her by the arm and propelling her in the direction of the hotel.

When they arrived at their suite, he bolted the door behind them. Then he reached for Liza. As one hand caressed her bare shoulder, the other traveled up her other shoulder to her neck. His thumb slid slowly, sensuously up her chin while his fingers played havoc with the sensitive skin beneath her ear.

"You're beautiful," he whispered, and she could

feel his breath on her cheek, a sweet, intoxicating ca
ress, before his lips claimed hers.

The kiss was his possession, his mark, his declaratic
that she was his to do with as he would. Liza was pov
erless to deny him anything as she felt herself meltin
melding with him. They trembled on the brink of
union so incredibly beautiful that Liza wondered wher
she found the strength to utter the word to end it a
But she did.

"Stop," she cried from deep in her throat. The wor
was pulled from her with a force that seemed to cor
from outside her body, outside her own desperat
yearnings. "Stop," she sobbed it now.

He froze, stiff, while his arms still enfolded her, sti
held her close.

If only he had talked to her of love. Even if it were
lie, at this moment she might have believed it. It mig
have been enough to let her know the heady sensatio
of being his in every way. But Liza had to know mor
than his body. She had to know his heart. She had to b
a part of his life. If she couldn't have that, the physic
union would be nothing but a sham.

"Stop," she hoarsely whispered.

It was a desperate plea, a plea for him to let her go.
he had held any other woman in his arms he woul
have been furious, walked away, and never come back
If any other woman had promised such passion in he
kisses, then refused to make good the promise, h
would have labeled her a cold hearted tease an
shunned her forevermore. But Liza had an edge on a
other women. She stood out from the parade o
beauties that had shared his bed. He didn't know wha
was going on inside her proud head. But Scott knew h
wanted to possess Liza's heart and soul as well as he
body. And to do that, he knew he'd have to wai
though he was thoroughly confused as to why.

"Right now I'd give anything I have just to know

vhat it is you want," he grimly confessed as he eased
ter out of his arms. He strode to the window, impa-
iently shoved the luxurious drapery aside, and stared
moodily out into the black night.

Liza's heart thudded in her breast as she watched
him from across the room. He seemed miles away instead of only a few yards. Her limbs trembled for his
touch. Yet she couldn't utter the word to explain herself to him. She wouldn't, couldn't tell him that all she
wanted was his love. Liza was silent. She only stared at
him with huge, sad, apologetic eyes.

Her look pierced his heart as though a steel saber had
been thrust in deep and hard. His breath caught in his
throat and he knew with complete certainty that Liza
had come perilously close to being vital to him, an in-
dispensable part of his life. And it was as though he had
no control in the matter, no control at all. An alien
panic gripped him. He had the overwhelming urge to
flee.

"I'm going out," he curtly announced, and disappeared out the door and into the seductive New Orleans night.

He was going to find a woman, Liza immediately decided. A willing woman, maybe even Monica Grant.
Aching with her own physical frustration and disappointment and fighting off the misery that came when
she thought of Scott with another woman, Liza wearily
trudged to her bedroom. Without even turning on the
light, she stripped for bed. By the dim light that seeped
in through the sheer curtains, she carelessly hung up
her elegant dress. It brought her no joy now. All her
finery seemed such a waste, such an empty, sad, and
senseless thing to be joyful about. It all meant nothing
without him. All the silks, all the laces, all the jewelry,
could not comfort her now.

She fell naked into bed, unwilling to put on any of
the expensive things Scott had bought her. She wanted

only one thing from him. A thing he did not seem prepared to give. She wanted love.

And he wanted two things from her, she decided.
Neither of them were love. First, he wanted to have a
successful experiment. He wanted to prove his point.
And second, he wanted to get her into his bed.

Liza was sure that since she wouldn't let him make
love to her, Scott would soon find a woman who would.
The women were out there, ripe for the taking. She had
watched them watch him with covetous eyes. And she
was sure that one of them would lay beneath him yet
tonight. Monica was no doubt willing.

It was her last, tortured thought, before she drifted
into a restless sleep.

Scott wandered the streets of the sleeping city cursing
his frustrated state, cursing Liza for her ridiculous de-
nial of the intimacy they both craved, and most of all
he cursed himself for not being able to get her out of
his mind.

What the hell did Liza want anyway? he savagely
asked himself as he paced the dark sidewalk in front of
Antoine's. The things he had given her, the places he
had taken her, the way he had wined and dined her
didn't have their usual effect.

She certainly wasn't frigid. He'd be willing to bet on
that. Her responses to him were immediate and passionate. He remembered her lips yielding beneath his.
Her mouth opened hungrily for him. Her breasts
swelled at his lightest touch. And when, tonight, she
had fitted herself so closely to him and sinuously
arched against him, he thought he would go mad with
desire. If they hadn't been out on the street at the time,
he would have had a devil of a time stopping himself,
whatever she might have said, and whatever he might
have promised. Whatever was going on in Liza's pretty
head was intolerably frustrating to him.

Briefly he toyed with the idea of getting another woman. He knew Monica was back at the hotel, but she had no appeal for him now. He walked past Jackson Square. In the shadow of the statue of Andrew Jackson on his horse there was a lone woman leaning provocatively against the high iron fence. In her too-tight red dress and elaborate hairdo and makeup, she was completely repulsive to Scott. Whatever she represented, that night it wasn't anything he sought.

He forced himself to think of other women, women he knew, women he had dated and slept with. He grimly admitted that none of them even appealed to him now. It was only Liza, Liza the forbidden. Liza, the one he couldn't have. It was only Liza he wanted now.

"Damn," he swore softly. And he wished he had never met her.

A light rain began to fall. A drizzle shrouded the old city in misty mystery. But Scott kept walking, up and down the now empty streets. He walked beneath elaborate iron balconies and past closed and shuttered shops. He walked until the gray light of dawn broke through the dismal rain and sent its own eerie light through the sky.

When he got back to the hotel in the early morning, he was exhausted, chilled from the rain, and his feet ached from the miles he had walked through the streets. Yet he hadn't been in his room two minutes before he was thinking of Liza, wanting her in a way he had wanted no other woman before. He wanted now, in his tiredness, only to hold her, to feel her in his arms, warm, soft, and caring. He wanted only to feel her comfort and concern.

Scott sighed deeply as he shrugged out of his wet suit coat. He hung it carelessly over a chair in his bedroom and pulled off his tie. His shirt was plastered to his back. He pulled the shirttail from his trousers, impatiently unbuttoned the shirt, and cast it into a heap on the floor. He slipped out of his sopping shoes and fell heavily onto the end of his bed to pull off his wet socks.

He still wanted her. Angrily he walked to the bathroom and briskly towel-dried his dripping hair. He rubbed and rubbed, hoping to not only rub away the drops of rain, but his frustration as well. It didn't work. Instead the activity seemed only to increase his desire to be with her. He threw down the towel in disgust and paced back and forth across his bedroom, searching his tired and befuddled brain for a way out of his misery.

Maybe at least he could talk to her, he thought. Maybe he could just see her. That would be something. Maybe she was as awake as he was.

Hopefully he strode across the sitting room to her bedroom. The door was closed. He knocked softly, telling himself he didn't want to disturb her if she was sleeping. There was no answer.

He called her name. "Liza." It was little more than a whisper. There was no response. "Liza, are you awake?" he called more loudly. Still no response.

His powerfully muscled shoulders sagged as his exhausted body absorbed the surprisingly powerful disappointment he felt. He frowned in disgust. He just wanted to see her. He wanted to be near her. He didn't want her—not in the physical sense. He was too tired for that. His body ached for rest. But it also ached for her presence and closeness. He just wanted to be with Liza.

He stood by her door, wondering why he should feel that way about her, somebody who had fought him, defied him, and resisted his advances. Had she been any other woman he would have written her off long ago. But she was Liza, and he was beginning to learn that she was special.

All his years of psychology couldn't tell his weary brain why he felt the way he did. There were times when he felt like strangling her. But he knew there was

n instinct, a drive deep inside him that kept him want-
ng her and needing her as he had no other woman
efore.

The closed door was suddenly a hated object. It was a
eparation that kept her even from his sight. He had a
vild moment when he had to stop himself from smash-
ng it with his fist. His anger and frustration grew to a
evered pitch. He had to be with her. He had to be with
er now. And the despised door stood between them.

A stab of cold fear gripped him. He felt the anger
rain out of his body with a rush, replaced instead with
surge of panic. What if she wasn't there? The ques-
on flashed through his mind once, then it returned to
aunt him. It came back over and over. What if she
asn't there?

What if she had left while he was gone? What if she
asn't in her bed at all? If she was angry enough, she
ould have left. Gone. That would have been it.

He shook his head to clear his senses. Of course she
as there. Where would she be? It was dawn. She had to
e in her room. He glanced at his watch. He groaned. He
ad been up for more than twenty-four hours, except for
ie brief nap he took in the afternoon. No wonder his
iind was muddled, he told himself. No wonder his brain
nd body both ached. Yet the question came back again.

What if Liza wasn't in her room? What if she had
ed in the night, wanting only to get away from him?
he thought gave him pain so intense he could barely
and the possibility. He couldn't wait until later to see
she came out of her room. He had to know now.

Slowly his hand went to the doorknob. He grasped it
rmly, resolutely. It was cold against his moist palm.
tealthily, like a thief in the night, he turned the knob.
ilently, inch by inch, he eased the door open. His
eart beat loudly in his chest. His mouth was dry. All
ie while he was afraid of what he would find. He was
raid he would see an empty bed.

The faint light of dawn filtered through the shee
curtains at the window. It lighted the room with
gentle, gray light. He blinked, giving his bleary eye
time to adjust to the dimness. Then he stood still an
stared for a long time before he would let himself be
lieve it was really Liza in the bed, Liza whose hai
spilled gloriously across the pillow, its deep honey
blond highlights gleaming like burnished gold.

Her face was turned toward him. Noiselessly h
walked across the velvety carpet in his bare feet unt
he got to the bedside. In sleep she looked beautifull
serene and vulnerable. Could she be the same woma
who fought like a wildcat when he ordered her about?

She stirred, lifting an arm above her head and throw
ing back the covers to expose a breast. It was beauti
fully round, full, and rosy-tipped. There was perfectio
about it, about Liza that held his eye. Even in his ex
haustion he knew that she wasn't perfect. But some
how she was perfection to him, and he never wanted t
stop looking at her.

Sleepily he stumbled to the easy chair that sat be
tween Liza's bed and the windows. He could look a
her all he wanted to now, look at her and she woul
never know. He could be with her silently and secretl
and she'd never be the wiser. His weary eyes roved he
sleeping form for only a few moments before hi
leaden lids closed and his exhausted body no longe
fought its aching, insistent demands for sleep.

Liza waked slowly. At first her only consciousnes
was the sensuous slipping of the cool and satiny
smooth sheets across her bare body. She felt deligh
fully wicked as she made her first, tentative, still sleep
motions.

She always wore a gown to bed. When she was a littl
girl her mother told her that young ladies wear wha
she called "proper nightgowns" to bed. Well, Liza ha
graduated to what she was sure her mother would ca

'improper" nightgowns, but they were nightgowns
onetheless. Nude sleeping was definitely different.
Liza liked it.

She smiled her secret delight as she blinked her eyes
pen to the morning light. She stretched with the grace
f a cat. The light filtering through the filmy window
urtains now carried with it a golden glow that held the
romise of a beautiful day. A sharp memory of un-
leasantness on the night before clouded her thoughts
riefly. Then she glimpsed Scott, clad only in his
ousers, his bare feet thrust straight before him. He
as asleep in her chair.

The agony of the night came rushing back. The pain
he had felt as he left her, left her alone, abandoned
er because she would not let him make love to her.
Ie had abandoned her, she had thought, for another
oman.

Her brow furrowed as she considered the reality of
is presence here in her room. Why? Liza was sure of
ne thing. It wasn't the sort of thing a man would do if
e had spent the night with another woman. And it
asn't the sort of thing a man would do if he never
anted to see her again.

He mustn't hate her, she decided. She had turned
im down last night, and he didn't hate her. And
hough she wouldn't allow herself to speculate further
n exactly what Scott did feel for her, she again knew
he giddy joy she had felt before. She knew the intoxi-
ating delight that came from the very thought that he
hight care for her just a little the way she cared for
im.

Contentedly she lounged back against the soft pil-
ows and studied him in luxurious leisure. At first she
ad a satisfied smile on her face as she traced the lean,
uscular lines of his body with her eyes. His broad
hest had a light sprinkling of dark hairs that arrowed
xcitingly down below his belt. His arms revealed pow-

erful muscles, even in repose. And his powerful thighs strained the elegant fabric of his trousers.

But Liza's smile slowly faded as she studied his face. His head flopped against the chair-back at an uncomfortable angle. There was a worry line between his brows. And his jaws seemed clenched. Even in sleep he did not look relaxed.

Liza's immediate desire was to comfort him, remove his worries, his cares. She had an overwhelming wish to take care of him. She wanted to soothe away the unhappiness she saw reflected on his face.

As though he sensed that she watched him, he sleepily opened his eyes and frowned. It took a moment of concentration for him to remember where he was and why his neck ached the way it did. His back, too, was stiff and sore. His eyes barely focused at first. And when they did, they instinctively sought out her face.

She was smiling an indulgent, understanding smile. "You look awful," she gently commented as soon as she was sure he was awake enough to hear her. Her eyes were lighted with the glow of love.

"Thanks," he replied dryly, through a haze of sleep. As he moved to straighten himself in the chair, every muscle seemed to have an ache all its own. He grimaced uncomfortably. His eyes shut wearily again and he sank deeper into the chair.

"You need to stretch out," she advised as she reached for the blue silk gown that lay across the bed. She deftly pulled it on over her head and fumbled beneath the sheets to straighten out its long skirt. At least it covered her nakedness.

His eyes were still closed. She slipped out of bed, throwing the covers back. For an instant she glimpsed herself in the big mirror that hung above the dressing table. The gown was delicately beautiful and provocative all at once. Its deeply plunging neck exposed her

cleavage daringly even while its exquisite lace and re-
strained construction seemed to say, "A lady wears this
gown, a refined, sexy lady."

Liza spared only a moment for studying her reflec-
tion. She was too concerned about Scott. He was obviously exhausted and needed his rest. She walked to the
chair and grasped his hand, tugging at him gently.

"Come on, get up. I'm going to get you to bed."

He opened one eye cautiously, and then the other.
She stood before him, a barely clad vision in blue. He
could not do other than she commanded.

He rose and followed her to the bed that was still
warm from the heat of her body. She urged him into it,
lifting his bare feet to stretch them out on the smooth
sheets. Then she covered him up, bringing the blankets
up to his chin. Briefly she sat beside him on the bed,
smiling down at him as though he were a precious but
ill-behaved child.

"What time is the plane out?" Liza asked softly.

He stirred and moaned, but said nothing. He only
settled his sleepy head deeper into the downy pillows as
his body relaxed in the comforting warmth of her bed.

"The plane out," she repeated, more insistently
now. "What time does it take off?"

Reluctantly he opened his eyes and blinked. She was
here. He smiled briefly, then closed his eyes again.

She sighed and smiled at the same time. Then she
tried again. "What time do we leave? When does the
plane take off?" she asked in loud, distinct, no-
nonsense tones.

He grimaced uncomfortably and forced his eyes
open. "Four thirty," he mumbled. "You're beautiful."

A great silly smile spread across Scott's tired face.
The lines of exhaustion were still there, but the pained,
drawn look was gone. He lay in the great bed, a tired
but supremely happy man.

"Sleep," she ordered. "I'll take care of things now."

And she realized she really wanted to do just that. She wanted to take care of things. She wanted most of all to take care of him. It was part of her loving him, part of her caring.

He closed his eyes. His smile was still there. Liza leaned over and lightly kissed his brow. Her lips lingered on his firm flesh. She wanted to memorize the feel of his skin as she kissed it.

His hand moved up to gently caress her scantily clad breast. The easy familiarity of his action both shocked and delighted Liza as a glow of pleasure suffused her body.

"Sleep," she ordered sternly, and his hand reluctantly dropped away. He was still smiling when she left the bedside and left the room.

Chapter Twelve

Liza felt a pleasant intimacy with the sleeping Scott while she moved around the suite getting things ready for their departure.

She dressed in the suit she had worn on the plane, and quickly did her hair and makeup. She packed both their suitcases, then she left the suite briefly to pick up a few magazines for herself and a paperback novel. For Scott she bought one of the latest mysteries. And then, thinking that he might already have read it, she picked up a spy thriller too.

At about one o'clock she checked on Scott. He still slept soundly, barely stirring. With the door to the bedroom open she could hear his every move, and she listened for him while she read her magazines.

She waited until after two to waken him. And then only after she had called room service to order a hardy southern breakfast of ham, eggs, grits with gravy, and freshly baked biscuits.

He was awake when she went into the bedroom. Awake and smiling a crooked smile that spoke of his contentment. The bedsheets were bunched around his waist and his trousers were in a heap on the floor at the side of the bed.

Liza's eyes went from Scott's well muscled chest to the trousers on the floor, and she blushed. She felt as silly as a schoolgirl as she felt the hot, embarrassed flush spread over her face.

He laughed softly, his eyes twinkling with wicked delight. "Man was not made to wear trousers in bed," he teased, while Liza struggled to regain her composure.

"I—I ordered your breakfast," she explained, turning away from him as she talked. "It should come anytime now."

She was overwhelmingly aware of his state of undress, and it did funny things to her blood pressure and heartbeat, both of which were rapidly getting out of control.

"I heard you order it," he told her, the tinge of amusement still in his voice. And he watched her with wonder. There she was, Liza-full-of-surprises, naively shy once again. He wondered if he would ever plumb all the depths of her nature.

She was slowly moving toward the bedroom door, retreating to the safety of the sitting room.

"We were supposed to go to Commander's Palace for their jazz brunch today," he revealed as he called after her.

"Oh, some other time," Liza airily replied. And she closed the bedroom door behind her, dropping her shoulders in relief as she did.

"To be sure," Scott answered, chuckling softly.

He came out of the bedroom just moments after room service had delivered his breakfast. He had only a towel wrapped around his waist, and droplets of moisture from his shower still clung to his dark brown hair.

He looked so tall and rugged and strong that Liza found herself staring at him, at his broad shoulders and muscular arms, at his flat stomach and powerful thighs.

"Like it? There's more," he teased, grasping the towel with both hands as though to pull it off.

Liza reddened, but this time the flush brought out her anger too. Must he always get the better of her?

Must he always embarrass her? "Go get dressed," she
scolded. "Your breakfast is getting cold."

"Yes, ma'am," he assented with a mock salute. And
to Liza's great relief, his nearly nude body disappeared
behind his own bedroom door.

The flight home was over too soon, and Liza was back
at her own apartment, unpacking her things from
Scott's elegant, leather trimmed bag. She handed him
the suitcase when she finished. And as she did, she
realized it meant he would be going. He wouldn't be
with her anymore. And after two days of being together
practically every minute, they wouldn't be together at
all. Liza felt desolate. "Coffee?" she suggested as he
stood by the door waiting to go. She knew it was a last,
desperate attempt to keep him there a moment longer.

"No."

He shook his head, and an unruly lock of hair broke
loose and fell onto his forehead. Her hand ached to reach
up and smooth it back. But she didn't move. Instead she
stood still and listened to him as he calmly began to say
good-bye. However the words were hardly out of his
mouth when he frowned, ran his hand through his thick
hair, and then rubbed the back of his neck.

"Could you tell me what's wrong with my approach?" he demanded, realizing with a completely uncharacteristic panic that the problem between them
might truly be that she did not want him to make love
to her, that there was something wrong with him and
with his approach to her.

"Are you used to a more or less hurried lover?" he
questioned, both curious and hurt. "Do you like the
'slam, bang, thank you ma'am' sort? Or are you happier with the man who takes hours to arouse you? Because if that is the case, I've misguessed you badly," he
admitted. His face was oddly contorted, displaying his
own pain.

When she sensed his agony, Liza was consumed with sympathetic anguish. She couldn't tell what he wanted from her, or what she really meant to him. In her bewilderment her innate honesty came to the fore.

"I don't sell myself cheap," she defensively informed him, her chin held proudly high.

"Cheap?" Scott thundered angrily. "You think what we feel between us is cheap?" The fury of his response was as much a surprise to him as it was to Liza. She stared at him mutely as he calmed down. Moments later he offered his explanation and his defense. "You want me as much as I want you." His eyes pleaded for understanding. His voice was husky with emotion.

"No," Liza confessed miserably, "it's worse than that." She bit her lip, precariously close to tears. "I want you more. Heaven help me, but I love you," she admitted through a painfully tight throat. Then she raised her head and spoke clearly, refusing to be ashamed of her own feelings, whatever his reaction might be. "I want to spend the rest of my life with you," she revealed. "I want to marry you in the 'forsaking all others, until death do us part,' sense of the word. I want to sleep in your bed every night and never worry about whether you will go to another woman or get tired of me. And I won't settle for anything less than that."

Scott felt as though he had been rammed by a battleship. He sank into a chair. His eyes focused on the floor, for he knew he could not look at Liza. Marriage. It was something he hadn't even considered she might want. It was something that had never really seemed like a viable option for him.

"That about lays it on the line, I guess," he said, still refusing to meet Liza's gaze. "Am I to take it you just proposed?" he asked, glancing at her for a brief moment before he again focused on the floor. His face was a frowning study in misery.

"Yes, I guess I did," Liza admitted bleakly.

He said nothing. He didn't move. He didn't look at er. He didn't do anything to show her what his reponse was to her outspoken declaration.

Liza grimly admitted her own defeat. A second later he was wondering how she would ever live the rest of er life without Scott. Yet she loved him enough to let im go gracefully, without tears or recriminations.

"You'd better go now," she told him in a voice arely above a whisper. She was anxious to have him ave. She wanted to have him go before she lost her st shred of composure and broke down completely.

cott was stunned when he left Liza's apartment. Marving Liza certainly didn't fit into his plans. His parents' lamorous and glittering, fast-paced lifestyle had given im no role models of fidelity. Instead he knew his 1other and father remained together because it was onvenient for them to do so. But he was aware all 1rough his growing up years that both his parents had 1eir casual, physical alliances with others.

What Liza wanted was simply not in his repertoire. ut she would settle for nothing less. It was no marage, no Liza. It was that simple. But what he felt for er wasn't that simple. It wasn't that simple at all.

took all of Liza's strength just to go through the basic 1otions of life after Scott left her. She could count on er fingers the number of weeks she had known him. It idn't seem logical that someone she had known for 1at short a time could be so important to her. But she :luctantly admitted to herself that what she felt for cott defied logic.

Even starting her new job didn't give Liza a lift. She ad gotten the editorial assistant's position on a prestiious history journal, and her new salary was far better 1an Angela would be getting. But even as she buried erself in work she got no joy from it.

Valerie kept her advised of what the press was saying about Scott, and clipped several pictures in which Liza herself appeared. Liza regularly refused all interviews.

The new class of students came to Graham. The fall semester was usually a busy, happy time. But none of its enthusiasm transmitted itself to Liza. Instead she walked zombielike through the days and weeks, cut off from all her feelings, lest she be overcome with pain.

Each night she dreaded sleep. Her dreams were tortured. In them she kept reaching for Scott, but her hands grasped only air. Her eyes lost sight of him each time she tried to get closer to him. He said nothing in the dreams. He merely regarded her with impassive eyes, as though she were not important to him at all. Liza tossed and turned and wailed and whimpered all through the night. Even the irrepressible Valerie could not cheer her up for long.

"Let's watch the Mark Allen show," Valerie suggested late one evening. She went to the television set and switched it on before Liza could say no. A popular TV star was talking with the show's host. The picture faded to a commercial.

"You don't have to stay to keep me company," Liza protested. "It's way past your usual abominably early bedtime. Go on home. I'll see you tomorrow."

Valerie shook her head. "There's someone scheduled that I want to see," she told her. "Humor me."

"Oh, all right," Liza conceded, "You watch. I'm going to make some popcorn." She got up from her chair and started for the kitchen when Valerie caught her arm.

"Not yet," Valerie insisted. "I want you to see this too."

Liza gazed at the screen in disgust. "A commercial for fabric softener?" she demanded, incredulous. "That's what I'm supposed to watch?"

"No, silly, not that. Sit down. Wait," Valerie ordered.

Liza grumpily settled down on the couch, warning, 'This better be good."

"It will be," Valerie promised, her eyes glowing like a child trying to hide a Christmas surprise.

Soon Liza listened to the show's host introduce Scott. Seconds later Scott appeared on the screen. Liza stared at him in rapt fascination while her body reacted to his image with a quickened pulse and warm thrill of joy. She gazed at him, hungrily remembering the springy feel of his hair beneath her fingers, his firmly muscled back, and the heady sensation that spread through her when her body pressed against his.

After some general discussion of Scott's new book, the host raised the question of feminist reaction to it.

"As a rule the feminists who have really read it think it is fine," Scott revealed. "I'm not advocating some new form of slavery. Quite the opposite. I'm all for women's lib," he confessed. "For the most part it makes perfect sense."

Liza smiled, knowing he always spoke what he believed to be the truth.

"Doctor, how do you feel about the role reversals of today? Do your dates ever ask you out? And do they pay for your dinner?"

"That has happened," Scott replied with a grin.

"And do you like it?" the interviewer persisted.

Liza's breath stopped as she waited expectantly for his answer.

"It depends on who does the asking," Scott quickly replied. "As a matter of fact, a perfectly wonderful woman has not only asked me out and paid for my dinner, but has asked me to marry her as well. I'm going to take her up on it too."

His announcement left the show's host momentarily speechless. A soft ripple of conversation spread through

the television studio audience. Liza stared at the televi
sion set openmouthed in disbelief. Valerie jumped up
and went to the door.

The conversation continued on the glowing screen
but Liza could scarcely make out what was being said
She heard Scott say, "She just figured out a long time
before I did that we should be married. She's a very
intelligent woman."

Then, as if by some incredible miracle, Scott stood
before her. Out of the corner of her eye she saw Valerie
leave, firmly closing the door behind her.

Liza stared from Scott to the television picture of
him, then back to Scott himself. She watched him as
though she were in a trance.

"It was taped hours ago," he explained to answer
Liza's amazement at seeing him both on the screen and
live, in her living room.

"You said—you said you're going to be mar—mar
ried," Liza stammered as he neared her chair.

He confidently took her hand in his and gently pulled
her to her feet."I said *we* are going to be married,"
Scott corrected her.

He was his smooth, unruffled, confident self. And
Liza was flustered and upset and wondering whether i
was a dream or whether it all was indeed a precious
reality.

"We are?" she asked weakly. She gazed up at him in
an unbelieving wonder.

"Yes, we are," he confirmed, smiling, then kissing
her lightly on the tip of her nose. "Thanks to you and
your ultimatum."

"Ultimatum?" Liza parroted dully.

Her heart was pounding wildly and her limbs felt
leaden. She was rooted to the spot where she stood
Her eyes were glued to Scott's ruggedly handsome face

"Yes, ultimatum," Scott huskily whispered. "No
wedding, no Liza. Those were your terms."

"But why didn't you call or anything all this time?"
Liza demanded. "You didn't even have the kindness to
nd a postcard. I was miserable thinking that you
dn't care."

"I was thinking," he patiently pointed out. "I can't
st change my entire lifestyle in an instant of passion.
ou wanted a commitment, nothing less. I had to think
over."

"It took you long enough," Liza complained. "That's
rdly flattering."

"Will you shut up, woman?" He frowned his dis-
easure.

"But—" she began. Her protest was abruptly si-
nced by his mouth covering hers. His body began its
rilling magic over hers as he held her against him
hile his mouth hungrily plundered hers.

She was weak and breathless when he finally, gently,
it insistently pushed her away.

"We have some things to settle first," he firmly told
er.

"Yes, sir," Liza responded, her eyes now dancing
ith joy.

"That's better," he affirmed. "Now this is it. No
hite dress, no long aisle, no audience, no wait. We get
arried tomorrow. I've got everything arranged."

"If I agree," Liza pointed out, her brows raised
eaningfully. She had never really wanted a big wed-
ng with all the trimmings, but she wanted to be con-
lted, not told, how things would be.

Scott sighed, chiding her with an impatient glance.
f you agree," he replied guardedly, bracing himself
arily for her objections.

His obvious concern about her reaction was enough
 prove to Liza that he wasn't just a thoughtless dicta-
r. "I agree," Liza eagerly cried, just before she joy-
lly threw her arms around his neck and kissed him
undly.

When the kiss was over, he was smiling. "For th
rest of our lives, dear Liza, you will sleep in my arms,
he whispered with satisfaciton.

Liza's eyes fluttered innocently, then opened wid
"Sleep in your arms?" she probed, her gray eyes hug
with disbelief. "Only sleep?"

Scott's smile grew to a broad grin. The dimple aj
peared on his cheek for only a moment before he thre
back his head and laughed. "Do you mean to tell m
that my chock-full-of-excuses ladylove is going to tur
into a shameless hussy just because of some legal hocu
pocus?" he asked when his laughter subsided.

Liza grinned wickedly. "Oh, I do hope so," sł
crooned. "I really do hope so."

Then slowly, with an exquisite, intoxicating motio
Liza stood on tiptoe and again pressed her hips again
his. She snuggled her breasts against his broad che
and invitingly parted her lips for his kiss. Silently, sc
emnly, her enticingly sensual body promised Scott th
exquisite fulfillment of their shared passion.

Despite her overwhelming love for him and her body
insistent clamoring for fulfillment, Liza felt shy onc
they were alone in the elegant bedroom of their suit
They were back in New Orleans, back in the same lux
rious hotel they had stayed in earlier. But, at Scott
insistence, their suite had only one bedroom.

"Don't even consider the possibility that we won
sleep together," he had grimly warned.

His determined frown made Liza giggle. She was ei
phoric, delighted as a happy schoolgirl to know his lov
was fierce and that he wanted her. Now she wante
only to please him with her body, to be all the woma
he would ever need. Her own high hopes brought
flurry of butterflies to her stomach and a hard lump
her throat.

"I'm going to kiss every inch of your delectab

ody," he had huskily promised just before she disap-
eared into the elegant white and gold bathroom. The
memory of the vow brought a flush of warm pleasure
ooding through her body as she slid into the per-
amed waters of the huge sunken tub.

She lay in the silken water, breathing fast, all her
enses alert to every sound, every movement Scott
aade in the next room. The heady aroma of My Sin
afted around her as the door opened and he strode,
aked, like a pagan god, into the bathroom.

"I couldn't wait," he throatily admitted as he pulled
er from the scented waters, and grabbing a huge, thick
wel, impatiently dried her sleek body, caressing her
ith eager hands while his eyes devoured her breasts,
er hips, her smooth stomach and the soft, warm, area
etween her legs.

She was still damp and fragrant as he pulled her into
is powerful arms for a fiery kiss. Her bare breasts
arobbed with excitement as they were crushed against
ae hard, lightly-haired wall of his chest.

In one smooth, effortless motion he lifted her into
is arms, cradling her head against the drumbeat of his
eart as he strode to the huge satin-covered bed.

He laid her down gently, almost reverently, as
aough she were a precious, irreplaceable jewel. "I love
au," he whispered from deep in his throat, "I need
au to be mine."

A wave of sensation washed through her, a quiver-
g, trembling ecstasy that was an intoxicating mix of
ensual pleasure and spiritual joy. "I've been yours
nce the moment I was born," she confessed, knowing
to be a certain truth.

His eyes were the deep-blue of the turbulent sea and
ghted with the glow of desire. His sensual lips slowly
rned up into a seductive smile.

He caressed her gently, molding his lightly calloused
ands to the silken softness of her face, her throat, her

shoulders. Then he lightly traced the rounded contour of her full breasts, gently circling their rosy peaks a they tensed, and strained under his adoring fingers.

One large hand enticingly slid down her side, caress ing her waist briefly, then sensuously stroked her hi while his warm, moist, devouring mouth slowly de scended to her throbbing breast.

A vibrant, electric thrill surged through her body. triggered a wild, yearning, aching need deep in he core.

"Oh, Scott, I love you. I love you," Liza moaned th admission as her fingers raked through his dark hair.

He rained brief, butterfly kisses up her throat an over her face until he claimed her lips with a deep drugging, erotic kiss.

"My woman," he breathed into her silky hair as h gently separated her legs with his own. He slid betwee her smooth thighs and buried himself in the sweetne inside.

Her welcoming body embraced every inch of his. H was part of her now, his body, his dreams, his hope his fears. It was more than a union of two halves. It wa the completion of one whole.

Every movement he made, every thrust he drov deep within her, increased her incredible frenzy. H skin tasted salty-sweet to her as her wanton mout roamed his face and chest, caressing him with her lip and her tongue. His groans of pleasure brought a re sponsive reflex within her, and she arched against hir boldly, provocatively, until together they shared a sha tering explosion of heart, soul, body and will.

Liza felt as though she were floating far above th surface of the bed. Her body wasn't substance, on glorious feeling.

Sweet tears filled her eyes, tears of incredible joy. was as though she was too full of happiness, satiate with satisfaciton, and her body simply overflowed wi

e wonder of it all. Smiling down at her with a tender
armth, Scott had lovingly kissed the tears away.

After her breathing neared normal she whispered
fty, "Oh, how I love you."

He took her hand and brought it to his lips. "You're
l the woman I'll ever need," he promised her throat-
. They dozed briefly, drifting into a contented sleep,
en waking and caressing each other with unhurried
light.

Liza smiled lazily with the languorous contentment
fulfillment. "You once told me that I was beautiful,
d you wanted to be around when I discovered that
ct. I learned it just now," she revealed. "I never felt
beautiful before in my life."

"Ravishing," he confirmed, studying her glowing
ce with satisfaction, "absolutely ravishing." He cov-
ed her mouth with his while his fingers lightly ex-
ored her body with tantalizing movements.

"I think you're beautiful, too," she told him, her
es shining with sincerity.

He threw back his head and laughed heartily while
e gazed up at him, her face mirroring her hurt.

"You are beautiful to me," she explained defen-
vely. "You're the most beautiful thing in my life."

He smiled down at her, his cobalt-blue eyes now
owing with the love he felt for her, only her, of all the
omen in the world. "Oh, my Liza, just keep thinking
at. Think that now and when we are both old and
rinkled and hunched over. Think that forever, and
ve me. I need you so much," he confessed.

"We need each other," she whispered just before
e gently wrapped her leg around his, urging their
dies into intimate contact.

Teasing lights danced in her soft gray eyes as he
zed down at her with adoration. "I think I'm going to
el like the most beautiful woman in the world before
ng," she said with a gentle laugh.

"That, indeed, is the plan, my dear Liza," he happi
assured her just before his body again joined hers ar
transported them both into a whirlwind of ecstasy ar
delight.

BARBARA DELINSKY
Fingerprints

...rly Quinn is a
...man with a past.
...n Robyn Hart, she
...s forced to don a new
...ntity when her intensive
...estigation of an arson-ring
...ulted in a photographer's death
...d threats against her life.

...n Cornell's entrance into her life
...s a gradual one. The handsome
...yer's interest was piqued, and then
...otivated, by the mysterious Carly—a
...man of soaring passions and a
...ret past.

Harlequin Stationery Offer

Personalized Rainbow Memo Pads for you or a friend

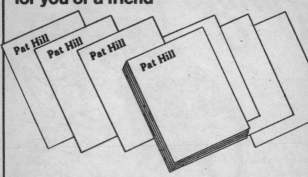

Picture your name in bold type at the top of these attractive rainbow memo pads. Each 4¼" x 5½" pad contains 150 rainbow sheets—yellow, pink, gold, blue, buff and white—enough to last you through months of memos. Handy to have at home or office.

Just clip out three proofs of purchase (coupon below) from an August or September release of Harlequin Romance, Harlequin Presents, Harlequin Superromance, Harlequin American Romance, Harlequin Temptation or Harlequin Intrigue and add $4.95 (includes shipping and handling), and we'll send you *two* of these attractive memo pads imprinted with your name.
